SECRETS AT THE OLD TICKET OFFICE DARLING ISLAND

POLLY BABBINGTON

POLLY B

PollyBabbington.com

Want more from Polly's world?

For sneak peeks into new settings, early chapters, downloadable Pretty Beach and Darling Island freebies and bits and bobs from Polly's writing days sign up for Babbington Letters.

W ith a picnic basket over her arm, a sun hat on her head, and a beach chair balanced over her shoulder, Emmy Bardot stood leaning over the barrier at the waiting area for the Darling Island Pride of Darling ferry. She absent-mindedly stared at the blue and white livery of the ferry on the other side. The water glinted sparkles here and there, a blue sky faded away as far as the eye could see, and the famous Darling Island fog was conspicuous by its absence. It had to be said Darling was looking rather nice.

Emmy took a massive deep breath of the Darling Island smell and let it zoom around her lungs: salt, brine, and fresh sea air that cleansed as it went through her body. Divine. The gentle hum of Darling life surrounded her, and she drank it all in. She glanced around, her eyes flicking from the far side of the water to the landing area for the ferry, where she stood with other passengers waiting to embark. A few young boys played down on a strip of sand to her right, their laughter floating on the breeze, a radio from a car in the queue for the vehicles crossing played a summer tune, and the hum of the ferry's engine from the other side floated across the water.

Emmy slipped her sunglasses from her nose to the top of her head, lifted her head upwards, and felt the warmth of the sun on her skin. It was one of those perfect English days – a warm cerulean blue sky punctuated with a breeze every now and then and the sun toasting the skin. A flock of gulls soared overhead, waves lapped against the wharf underneath her, and to her right, a group of elderly locals waiting for the ferry chatted, their conversation peppered with chuckles. She gazed to her left along the estuary at the line of white houses looking out to sea, the silhouette of the sailing club stood out against the sky, and the boats bobbed happily around on the water. All of it like a coastal postcard on a picture-perfect day.

As she watched the Pride of Darling leave from the other side on its journey back to the island, her mind drifted to Tom. Her relationship with him had slotted into her life as if it had always been meant to be. She liked that very much indeed. Since the time he'd told her he loved her, what they had going on between them had just got better and better. Despite thinking that she might mess things up, as had been the norm in her life, she had done nothing of the sort and things were trotting along quite nicely in the Emmy and Tom department. Long may it last.

Watching the ferry getting closer and closer, she happily pondered her new life on Darling Island and how it had veered from her initial carefully curated plan to something that was panning out to be quite different indeed. When she'd schemed and mapped out her move to The Old Ticket Office, it had involved opening the shop as soon as she could, getting her head down, and ploughing on with creating a future for her and Callum. She'd planned to sort the shop, renovate the flat, work at the port, and take her life by the scruff of its neck with not a lot of room for not a lot else. Emmy Bardot had been like a woman possessed. What had actually happened, and what she hadn't factored in, was going headfirst down a helter-skelter and falling smack bang in love. Falling in love hadn't been in any area of her plan. Falling in love had definitely not been part of her future. Falling in love had been so far from the spectrum of her life, she had trouble contemplating its occurrence at all. She closed one eye as she percolated what had happened with her and Tom around her head. It might not have been planned, but she did know that it was very, very nice. Absolutely fabulous, in fact. Ahhmayzinng. *It's so a yes from me.*

She thought about what had happened since the initial few dates with Tom. Since then, there had been many, and they had been all over the place on dates and outings. Tom had wined her and dined her, they'd been to Paris for a weekend, he'd met her mum and dad properly, Callum and Tom got on like a house on fire, and Amy was just as smitten as she was. Tom, it seemed, not only turned *her* nuclear, but everyone else in her life had fallen for him, too. Ding blimming dong. Most of all, though, Emmy just simply loved having Tom in her life. After years of Emmy being not much more than her job and mum to Callum, to be with and have Tom was like a breath of fresh air. Not that Tom made her whole, no, no. It was just that Emmy Bardot, by way of Tom, had actually realised that, yes, she was pretty damn special. She was so going to run with that.

Emmy shook her head at it all as she mulled it over. When she'd moved out of the rental cottage and bought The Old Ticket Office, the main purpose of the whole thing had been to get her out of the rental trap she'd been swirling around in for years. There had been no room in those years for Emmy. Emmy had been lost in survival mode, bobbing her head around in the murky waters of life, keeping her chin up, and paddling away like crazy under the surface. In that incessant lifesaving paddling, she'd kept everything on the straight and narrow – Callum, finance, divorce, rent, food, bills, and life. Now it appeared that Emmy, the person, was back. Emmy wasn't paddling quite as hard anymore. The muscles in the back of her neck that had kept her chin up to survive were more relaxed. It was all kinds of deliciously nice.

As the ferry bobbed closer and closer, she spied her sister Amy on the left-hand side. She raised her hand, waved, and smiled as Amy – dressed in denim shorts, a white shirt with the sleeves rolled up, and an enormous sun hat – waved back. Five or so minutes later, Amy – clutching the sun hat to her head, and together with a long line of foot passengers – disembarked the ferry. When Amy got to Emmy, she kissed her on the cheek.

'Hey! How are you?'

'Good. Really good. Lovely day for it!' Emmy replied.

Amy looked Emmy up and down. 'Ooh, look at you looking all Darling.'

Emmy frowned. 'What does that mean?'

Amy pointed to Emmy's pretty white sundress, tan espadrilles, round wicker basket with leather straps, and gigantic floppy sun hat. 'You just look very… What's the word? I don't know. Just relaxed and chic. Yeah, you have the Darling look about you. I like it, Ems. I really like it. A lot. It suits you.'

'Too funny. Do I?'

Amy frowned. 'You do. Come to think of it, it's more your aura that has Darling about it.'

'My what?'

'Something is surrounding you,' Amy noted, and mussed her hand around Emmy's head and then nodded. 'Yes, that's it. You're almost fuzzy. Soft is the word. Emmy Bardot, my beautiful sister, has softened.'

'Have you been drinking this morning for breakfast?'

'Mum said it too,' Amy said.

'What's that? I'm fuzzy and soft?'

'No, that you're different since you've moved.'

Emmy swept her hand around at the estuary. 'Living here helps. Just look at it. I mean, it's not exactly a tough place to live.'

'Or being in a love story,' Amy joked. 'That must help too, right?'

'Is that what I'm in?' Emmy clarified with a giggle. 'Am I a walking-talking romcom character?'

'I should say so. It's going to be a Netflix series next. You and Tom P Carter as the stars.'

'Ahh.'

'Yes, Ems, you look amazing. Radiant. Love it. Love you.'

'Thank you. To be quite honest, I sort of feel it too. Unbelievable, but true. I was just thinking about it as the ferry crossed.'

'I'm so happy for you,' Amy beamed. 'I love seeing you happy.'

'Thank you. Now let's get on with our day. I'm so pleased you're here.'

'I know! I can't believe we've actually managed to get away with this. A whole day just you and me on the beach. Mum and Dad looking after the children, Callum with Kev...' Amy trailed off and looked up at the sky. 'Even the weather worked out for us.'

'It's been a long time since it was just the two of us for the day,' Emmy noted, following Amy's gaze up to the sky.

'I cannot wait,' Amy said, tapping the basket on her shoulder. 'A picnic, a chilled bottle of bubbles, and a beautiful English day. What more could we ask for, Ems?'

Emmy put her arm through Amy's. 'Nothing much else I need.'

'Same here.'

They continued along the coastal path beside the estuary towards one of the beaches down past the sailing club. A mix of salty sea, and the wildflowers growing along the edge of the path wafted around in the breeze.

Amy inhaled and shook her head in little movements from left to right. 'What is it about Darling? There's something about this place. I don't know, it's just like it captures you almost. Or am I being weird?'

Emmy chuckled. 'You're always weird, but yep, I know what you mean.' She gestured towards the glittering water and then up at the sky. 'This helps with making you feel good.'

'True, if the sky was grey and it was raining, it wouldn't be quite as charming.'

'Nope.'

'I can see why you loved it that first day when you came to collect the cake. It really is lovely.'

'Yeah, that was a beautiful day too.'

'Look where you are now.' Amy sighed.

'I know.'

'A man who is smitten with you and doing all the things.' Amy nudged Emmy playfully.

'Oh, stop. We're still in the early days.'

'It feels like you've been together for ages already.' Amy shook her head and blinked rapidly. 'Strange that. Isn't it? Funny how things work out.'

'I know.'

'Next up, getting the shop done and dusted. That's the plan, isn't it?' Amy asked.

'That, and more. I finally feel as if I have good stuff in the pipeline. Getting out of that rented cottage was the best thing that's happened to me. It was like a noose around my neck. I thought it at the time and now I know it for certain.'

Amy squeezed Emmy's arm reassuringly. 'Life is good, and Love Emmy x is going places. I feel good about the future. I really do. It was a long time coming.'

Emmy laughed. 'I hope so.'

'A future with Tom P Carter in it.' Amy tilted her head. 'I knew there was more to it when you were first talking about him. Remember the not-a-date date? I told you then, but did you listen?'

'That seems ages ago now.'

'What about when he rescued you with the sunstroke and carried you indoors? Loved that.'

'Yeah. Same. Seems funny now.'

'And Mum and Dad like him,' Amy noted. 'Which is always a bonus. Especially Mum. We all cop it if she doesn't approve of someone.'

'I think that's pushing it. He's not quite been fully under the family microscope yet.'

'God help him.'

'Well, just remember, if he ever steps out of line, he has me to deal with. Or we just blame Kevin,' Amy joked.

'You're terrifying.'

'I aim to be,' Amy shot back, winking. 'No one messes with one of my sisters.'

Emmy frowned at Amy for mentioning their estranged sister. 'Anything on that? Have you heard from her?'

'No. Why would we hear from her now? It's been years. We don't even know where she lives. You?'

'No.'

'Why would she suddenly contact us? For all we know, she could be on the other side of the world. Would you even know if she had our numbers still?'

'True.'

The subject remained there, and the two of them continued their way down to the beach. Once they'd arrived on the sand, they looked around for the perfect spot. They went towards the shore, decided there were too many children, and ended up further up the beach tucked up near the beach huts. Emmy spread out a tartan picnic blanket, and Amy began unpacking bits and bobs. She pulled a chilled bottle of bubbly from the cool bag, took out two plastic champagne flutes, popped a few strawberries in each, poured in the bubbles, and handed one to Emmy.

'To new beginnings and sunny days on Darling Island,' Amy toasted and laughed, raising her glass. 'What a stunner of a day.'

Emmy clinked her glass against Amy's. 'And to a day to ourselves with no interruptions. Absolute bliss.'

They both leaned back on the blanket, letting the sun warm their faces, and just stared for a bit. Amy broke the silence as she continued to stare up at the clear sky. 'You've really found something special here, Ems.'

'Thanks to all your help I have.'

'Long may it last, eh?'

'I hope so. Let's drink to many more summers right here on this beach.'

'Yes, you, me, and loads of good things in the future.'

'Oh, yes. I hope so. I really do.'

2

The next day, Emmy had another day off from Love Emmy x, her actual job at the port, and renovating The Old Ticket Office building. She felt guilty and a bit weird at having another day of doing nothing, but with the weather forecast for a blue sky day and lots of sunshine, she was going to make the most of it. Emerging from the shower, she put a thick inverted plait into her hair, smoothed a blob of tinted moisturiser over her face, and swiped on some clear lip gloss. She then pulled on her comfy faded denim shorts, a blue linen shirt and tied a necklace with tiny little drop pearls around her neck.

Walking across her bedroom, she pushed up the huge old sash windows at the front, did the same at the back, and felt the sea air whisk through. At the back window, she observed as Tom got out of his car in the lane. He popped the boot, grabbed his bag, and headed towards her gate. As he walked along the path, she took in his polo shirt and shorts, the sunglasses tucked into his hair, and his tanned legs. It reminded her somehow of the first day she'd ever laid eyes on him, when he'd bumped into her on Darling Street, nearly knocking her and the cake that she had been carrying flying. She was now so pleased their paths had crossed.

She met him at the top of the stairs. 'Hi.'

'Hey! How are you?' Tom asked happily.

'Great,' Emmy replied as she hugged him, kissed him on the cheek, and inhaled. Tom, as ever, smelt amazing. 'Really good, actually.'

'How was your day off with your sister? Fun?' Tom asked. 'Did you spend the whole day on the beach? Surprised you're not sunburnt. You like a bit of sun-baking,' Tom joked, referring to the day when Emmy had got sunstroke and he'd ended up carrying her up to the flat. She'd liked that—a lot.

'Most of it.' Emmy laughed. 'We made the most of the sunshine, that's for sure. It was a beautiful day by the water. Oh, for more days like that before winter arrives.'

'Shame some of us have to work for a living,' Tom said as he followed her into the kitchen.

'Tea?' Emmy asked as she took the kettle off its base and looked at him inquiringly.

'Yep. Love one. So, what's the plan for today? Anything on? You said you might have another day off. Are you sticking with that plan?'

Emmy pointed to her phone. 'I've just heard from Cal. He's going to my mum and dad's and deciding whether or not he's going to stay there later. Seeing as the weather is like this again, I think, yes, I'm going to take another day off. I had planned to clean the windows at the front, but that's not looking too attractive now. Why'd you ask?'

'Just wondering.'

'Are you going to suggest something more agreeable than cleaning the shop windows?'

Tom screwed up his lips. 'I may have something much more interesting than that, yes.'

'What?' Emmy said, laughing. 'What could be more interesting than that?'

'I may have something for you, Ms Bardot. I think you are going to like it. I think, in fact, you may love it.'

'Like what?'

'Like something you might find very useful in your life.'

'What are you going on about?' Emmy replied. 'Why would I need anything useful in my life? Oh no. Not a power tool! We were talking about that the other night with Dad, weren't we?'

'Useful is probably not the right word,' Tom mused. 'I've bought you something I think you're going to love. Amy agreed you'd love it. So did your mum and dad.'

'You've been discussing this with Amy? Now I'm intrigued. What? It's not my birthday or anything.'

'I'm well aware of that. Does it have to be your birthday for me to buy you a gift?' Tom questioned.

Emmy poured the tea into mugs and passed one over. 'No, I suppose not. Exciting.'

'Follow me,' Tom instructed.

Emmy followed Tom as strange feelings swirled around her insides. It had been a very long time since anyone had treated her. Her mind flicked in an instant to Kevin, her ex-husband, when she'd been disabled by the shock of finding his gambling secret. That had been the only thing *he'd* surprised her with. Not one of life's best surprises. Plus, Kevin had thrown in a few more surprises along the way since, mostly around finances, mental health and the ups and downs of addiction. None of them were nice ones. Now here she was with a, quite frankly, gorgeous hunk of a man who was buying her things and surprising her. Actually being nice. Mostly, she was flabbergasted at how her life was turning out. Mostly, she loved the bones of him. Mostly, she wasn't going to tell him that too much.

She screwed up her nose as Tom turned right towards the

shop instead of left towards the store room and back entrance. 'What have you got for me here?' She frowned as she stepped in and saw a large rectangular cardboard box standing by the window. She shook her head. 'How did you get that in here without me knowing? What is it? Weird shape. I have no idea.'

Tom laughed. 'I have my ways. Err, that's the whole point of a gift. It's a surprise, so I wouldn't expect you to know what it is.'

Emmy smiled. 'Yeah, no, you're right.' She then just stood in front of the box, looking at the gigantic red bow on the front. 'I don't have a clue what this is.' She squinted. 'None.'

There was silence for a moment. 'Umm, are you going to open it?'

Emmy felt quite overwhelmed. 'What is it?'

Tom gestured to the corner of the box and then the ribbon. 'Pull that and you'll see.'

Emmy took a deep breath, did as instructed, and pulled at the ribbon. The flap of the cardboard box came open with surprising ease. She peeled the flaps back, revealing the gleaming frame of a classic English design bicycle. She turned to Tom and looked at him with questioning eyes. She seemed to have somehow lost control of her eyelashes.

'For travelling around Darling,' Tom said by way of explanation.

'Oh, wow…' Emmy's voice trailed off, not really knowing what to say. She was now definitely feeling overwhelmed. Her eyes darted over the frame, the brown leather seat, and the handlebars. A little matte copper-looking bell was fixed to the handlebars, and a deep wicker basket was affixed to the front. This was not a crappy, made-in-China mass-produced bike that would fall apart after a couple of uses. This was da-bomb.

Tom stepped forward, took the handlebars, and tilted the bike out of the box for Emmy to see better. 'It's an e-bike.' He pursed his lips. 'I thought you'd like the classic design, but it's electric, so it's the best of both worlds. What do you think?'

Emmy traced her fingers over the leather seat, her emotions roiling inside. She didn't say anything and just stood and stared for a good while.

Tom butted into her thoughts. 'Are you okay? Do you like it? I take it by your reaction that you don't. We can change it. I thought it would be good. You can ride to Darlings on it.'

'Sorry, yes, it's beautiful, Tom. I can't believe you did this,' Emmy replied and blinked back tears that threatened to spill over her lids. She turned so Tom wouldn't see. The gift of the bike had pushed a button for her. The button carried with it emotional weight, lots of implications, and somehow her feelings all wrapped up in one. It had been so long since someone had been so nice.

Tom hadn't quite realised that Emmy was emotional, though, and breezed right on. 'Yeah, I thought we could pop here and there on our bikes, only you get a bit of a helping hand on yours. Remember the other week you said you loved your bike when you were a girl?'

Emmy sniffled back her tears and pretended she was staring at the basket on the front of the bike. 'It's been ages since I last rode a bike. I can't believe you remembered me mentioning it that one time.'

Tom winked and joked, 'Every detail about you is worth remembering. Also, I'm collecting brownie points, so there's that.'

Emmy was on the verge of a full-blown emotional meltdown, but she giggled at Tom's words. 'So there's an ulterior motive to this gift, is there? What do I have to pay you in?'

'Nah, joking. It all started when an ad came up on my phone. I'm positive my phone is listening to me now. I mean, really, we were talking about bikes and then bam, every single advert on my phone was an e-bike. Anyway, it worked because I clicked, and before I knew it, I'd ordered it and it was on its way. The delivery was super quick too.'

Emmy eyed the bicycle apprehensively. 'I hope I can still remember how to ride a bike.'

'I'll catch you if you fall,' Tom promised, his tone half-joking, half-serious.

Tom started to wheel the bike towards the door. 'We'll try it out on the lane.'

E mmy was slightly wobbly at first when she kicked in the electric motor, but as she cycled over the bumps on the lane, she laughed and held one of her hands out. It was pure, unadulterated joy. 'Freedom! I love it. Wahoo! Thank you so much.'

After Tom had had a go, he parked the bike next to the gate, and they both stood there looking at it. 'I should have bought one for me too. How good is that motor?'

'I know. I can't thank you enough,' Emmy said again, feeling a little quiver in her voice.

'No thanks needed.'

Emmy hugged Tom. 'I mean it. Thank you so much. You, like, turn up with a random gift. I can't believe it.'

'I'm a super boyfriend. Make sure you note that down,' Tom joked.

'Ha.'

'Seriously. I thought you could now ride your parcels to the post office,' Tom said with a smile. 'I reckon Callum might have a go too. He was right into it when I was showing him.'

Emmy nodded. 'How did you do all this without me knowing?'

'I'm a master of deception.'

'Funny.'

I don't know about the post office. I could spend my life riding down to the beach and park it outside Darlings, like a proper local.'

'Can't be bad.' Tom laughed.

'Indeed. Sounds very good to me.'

Tom put his hand around Emmy's waist. 'Yep. I'm so pleased you like it.'

Emmy smiled to herself. It wasn't just the bike she liked in her life. Tom P Carter was up there with the best things that had ever happened to her. She couldn't argue with that.

3

E mmy and Tom wheeled their bikes off the Darling punt –
trailing single file behind a long line of foot passengers,
most of whom, by the looks of their bags and general paraphernalia, had spent the day at the beach. Although it was warm, the
afternoon had turned hazy, and the Darling blue covered everything around them in its famous hue.

Emmy, in navy blue linen shorts, a white top, and a blazer
neatly folded in front of her, was experiencing a first in life – a
bike ride to a supper date. She wasn't going to complain. As she
climbed onto her bike and flicked on the button, she felt the
motor kick in and glided along behind Tom. As she looked at
his back, she felt the nuclear heat that always seemed to envelop
her when she was around him creeping through her body. As
had happened many times since she'd started going out with
Tom, Emmy tried to suppress the thought that, at any given
moment, she was going to mess things up. She tried not to think
about it and just focused on the fact that she was going out on a
beautiful summer evening for supper to a little coastal village
with a very handsome man. There weren't a lot of things better
in life.

Tom looked behind. 'How is it?'

Emmy caught up and rode beside him. 'Really good. So easy.'

'Good. I'm now kicking myself that I didn't get two.'

Emmy looked down at the bike. 'I absolutely love it. Like, I really love it.'

'I'm glad. I thought you would. I must say, I didn't think it was going to be put to as much use as it has already.'

'Going out for supper on a bike was something I didn't know I wanted to do,' Emmy joked and flicked the bell on the handlebars as they whizzed along. 'This is fab. I feel about ten years old again! I loooooooove it.'

'I hope you say the same thing on the way back.' Tom laughed. 'When we're going up a few hills.'

'Good point.'

About fifteen minutes or so later, they were at the edge of a village green. Emmy had both her feet on the ground, holding onto the handlebars and looked across at a row of shops lining the far side of the green. A church spire poked up into the sky, colourful bunting was haphazardly slung across the front of the shops, and a bronze statue with its hand held aloft was cradled by two benches.

Emmy read the village sign, which informed her that they were in a hamlet. She let out a huge sigh at the lush expanse of velvety grass in front of her, the pretty Georgian houses lining the green's far side, and the tiny little windows peeking out through higgledy-piggledy roofs. Around the far side of the green, quaint, independent shops sat shoulder to shoulder with a couple of cosy pubs, pigeons flitted about an oak tree, and a few locals were sitting on picnic blankets with drinks on the section of the green outside the pub. Flowers in pots, window boxes, and hanging baskets were at every turn, and a little tearoom stood squat in the corner. Quintessential English village life was playing out right in front of Emmy as she looked around.

She squinted and turned to Tom. 'Where is the restaurant again?'

'Just over there at that strip of shops. The one with the bow-fronted window.'

'Ooh, nice. Yes.'

'I could eat a horse,' Tom said. 'That bike ride when you are not assisted by a battery works up an appetite. It was longer than I thought.'

'I wouldn't know,' Emmy joked. She peered towards the restaurant. 'It looks the part.'

A few minutes later, after wedging their bikes in the bike rack on the village green, they were hand in hand, looking into the restaurant window. 'Looks nice,' Emmy said as she peered at a huge chalkboard propped up against the wall. As Tom opened the door, Emmy was surprised to see most of the tables were full. Little gatherings of people were dotted all around the room, a further room's back wall was completely made up of windows and doors, and chatter, music, and clinking of china floated across the air.

A young woman with a huge smile and floral apron looked up from a small desk table tucked in behind the door. 'Hello. Table for Tom, is it?'

'Yes. How did you guess?' Tom asked with a smile.

The woman laughed. 'We've got precisely two tables left, and you're not Polly Bennett and Sarah Louman by the looks of you.'

Tom laughed. 'Nope.'

The woman pointed through to the back room. 'If you like, there's one tiny table in the courtyard. Do you fancy sitting out there? Such a beautiful evening for it. I don't think it will get chilly later, but there are heaters if it does. Up to you.'

Tom turned to Emmy, who followed the woman's gaze. She could see a courtyard with dark green cast iron bistro chairs and tables packed into an open courtyard. 'I think it looks nice out there. That would be lovely.'

Once they'd followed the woman through to the courtyard, Emmy was pleased with her decision. Masses of criss-crossed bunting layered back and forth across the courtyard, thousands of fairy lights twinkled, and large mismatched jugs of flowers sat on the tables. Pompom-edged place mats matched the cushions on the chairs, and ivy completely covered an old stone wall on the far side. Emmy whispered across the table as she sat down, 'I hope the food is as good as this place looks.'

'It's lovely.'

Emmy's mouth was watering as she read down the menu. 'Mmm. This all sounds delicious. I'm famished, too.'

Tom laughed. 'You sound like your son.'

'I know, right? He's always hungry. You've made that observation correctly.'

Under the illumination of the fairy lights, Emmy settled right into the courtyard. The atmosphere wrapped her in a mix of low laughter, clinking glasses, and music wafting from inside. She picked up the specials menu, her eyes scanning down.

Tom leaned over and pointed to the third item down. 'Considering you're famished, you should try the lamb shank,' Tom suggested. 'Sounds nice.'

Emmy nodded. 'I was just looking at that. Or the mussels, but I don't know if they'll be enough.'

After deciding on the lamb shank, Emmy was thoroughly enjoying a glass of wine and some olives. The night was warm, and the atmosphere lovely. The conversation flowed easily, and they chatted about the shop, Emmy's plans, and Darling Island.

'Life on Darling Island has really done me good,' Emmy noted.

'I thought that was me,' Tom joked.

'That too. There's been such a lot going on lately,' Emmy admitted.

'There has. You've certainly been busy.'

'I didn't realise how much I needed a change until I got here. Do you know what I mean?'

Tom nodded. 'What is that saying about a change?'

'Hmm. Not sure.'

'A change is as good as a rest. Something like that.'

'Yeah, not much rest going on for me. I really have to get the shop ready now.'

Tom took a sip of his drink. 'Well, at least we know the long-awaited council approval for the flower installation is in.'

Emmy fizzed inside at Tom, referring to them as 'we'. 'Yep. At long last. I dread to think what it would have been like without being a member of the Chamber of Commerce.'

'That was a funny evening,' Tom said, referring to the evening when Emmy had attended a Chamber of Commerce dinner.

'Not from my end,' Emmy said with raised eyebrows. 'I didn't think it was funny at all.'

'No?'

'I thought you were with that Cara,' Emmy said bluntly.

Tom grimaced. 'God, no! I can't even believe for a second that you thought that.'

Emmy shook her head. 'Why do you say it like that? She's nice and super pretty. What's not to like?'

Tom wrinkled up his nose and made a strange shape with his lips. 'Really?'

'Come on. She's gorgeous. Don't pretend.'

'Yeah, not my type.'

'What's your type then?' Emmy quizzed and giggled.

'Sitting right in front of me.'

'No, seriously. What's wrong with her?'

'Too, I dunno, done.'

'Done?'

'Yeah, like…' Tom swore. 'Makeup, clothes, fussing, and so OTT.'

'Wow. Right.'

'Each to their own, but not for me.'

'Yep,' Emmy agreed.

'There's someone for everyone out there. It's just a matter of time in finding that person.'

'I suppose so. Yes. Look at you sounding all prophetic.'

'Yeah, I don't suit it. Anyway, back to the flower installation. When is that happening?'

Emmy giggled at Tom's words. 'My dad is helping next week.'

'Right, I can help if you like.'

'I thought you would be too busy.'

'I'm a bit flexible this coming few weeks.'

'Okay, great. Deal. You will be surrounded by imitation flowers and the intricacies of trying to get them to go around the top of the shop window.'

'I do like a challenge.'

'I hope you do. Fair warning, it's a lot more complicated than it sounds. You have to navigate wires, hoops, the ladder and, of course, my dad.'

Tom grinned. 'I've faced more challenging projects. A few artificial flowers can't be that bad.'

Emmy raised an eyebrow. 'You say that now. Wait until you're balancing on a ladder, trying to keep the entire installation from toppling over.'

Tom chuckled. 'I'm more agile than I look. Your dad has a plan anyway, doesn't he?'

Emmy nodded. 'Oh yes, he's been working on the design for months. When I was first looking into it, we got some quotes, and they were way out of my budget. Dad has been watching videos on YouTube ever since.'

'Sounds impressive.'

Emmy's eyes sparkled. 'I can't wait for the flowers to be in situ. I tried to run before I could walk, but now, hopefully, everything is going to start falling into place.'

Emmy smiled as she discussed the installation with Tom – the arrangement of flowers, the layout, and how it would all come together. It was so nice to have someone in her corner she could talk to and just mull things over with. Nice to share something with someone.

Tom nodded. 'It's amazing when all the pieces start to fall into place after so much planning and hard work.'

Emmy leaned back in her chair. 'Exactly. It's taken a long time for me to get here.'

'It's exciting being at the start of something like this.'

Emmy couldn't have put it better herself. It wasn't just the flowers and the shop that were exciting, though. She loved sitting with Tom over supper in the courtyard, and she adored that he was genuinely interested in her and wanted to be involved in her world. As the evening began to wind down, Emmy felt very pleased with how her life had finally turned a corner. Although she couldn't quite swallow the idea that something might come along to mess it up, she told herself just to sit back, enjoy the ride, and make the most of it. Hopefully, messing things up now belonged in a life that was no longer hers. Little did she know what was around the corner.

4

Emmy looked around at the flat, feeling more than grateful. The walls were now clean and fresh, the old fireplace looked lovely, and the huge windows out onto Darling Street were sparkling, their architraves clean and bright. It was a far cry from the grotty little sitting room she'd taken possession of back when she'd first bought The Old Ticket Office. Raising her eyebrows, she smiled to herself as she remembered her first night in the flat when she'd heard a scuffling and realised that she and Callum weren't the only occupants. Those days were now long gone; she now had a huge double aspect bedroom with views to the sea and her own bathroom, and Callum had his own space. It all felt a far cry from the rental cottage she'd been in for years when she'd meticulously put aside money for the dream. Now the dream had arrived. She was actually living in it. Fab. You. Lous.

She opened the message from Jane, the woman who was selling the sofa she'd seen on Marketplace. There'd been quite a bit of toing and froing because Jane had been poorly, but now there was a time lined up for Emmy, with Tom's help, to go and collect Jane's sofa. Emmy had seen it on Marketplace and had felt her heart skip a beat it was that nice. Emmy looked at the pictures of the sofa again and squeezed her eyes together. Talk about a bargain. Jane had told her that she loved the sofa so much she'd upgraded to a bigger one, meaning Emmy had been lucky enough to bag the one for sale. Lucky wasn't a good enough word to describe it.

About ten minutes later, Tom arrived. 'Right. Ready?'

'Yep. Do you really think it's going to fit in the back of your car?'

'Are you doubting me and my measurement skills?' Tom bantered.

'I don't know. I just can't see it myself.'

'Trust me.'

'I put all of my trust in you,' Emmy joked. 'You're sure we don't need Callum to help?' Emmy asked, inclining her chin towards Callum's bedroom.

Tom shook his head. 'We'll be fine.'

When they arrived at Jane's house, Emmy swooned. She also felt a teeny bit deflated inside. Not that she was complaining, of course, but the part of Darling Jane lived on was gorgeous. The road was like something from a film made by Hollywood show-casing what they thought England was like – gorgeous and then some. Jane contributed to the film handsomely as if she'd just stepped out of a hair and makeup trailer. Emmy found herself self-consciously tapping the back of her hair to make sure it was neat and smoothing her jumper down as Jane smiled. 'You must be Emmy.'

Emmy smiled. 'I am.'

'The Old Ticket Office. I've heard so much about you. I meant to bring a basket over ages ago, but I never made it; sorry about that. As you know I've been quite unwell. I know what it feels like to move to Darling.'

Emmy was no longer surprised that people knew stuff about her. It was a Darling thing she'd begun to get used to. At first, she'd thought it was creepy and weird and not liked it at all. Now she was oddly sort of proud that she was part of the Darling community. 'Ahh, no worries.'

'How are you getting on?' Jane asked.

'Yes, good. It's slow, which I hadn't reckoned for, but I've decided to go with that.'

'Oh, I hear you. Things always take longer than you think.'

'Yep.'

Jane showed them in and continued to chat. Emmy nearly died and went to heaven as she looked around at the house, and they walked into the sitting room where three sofas were squashed into the space. Jane pointed to the pale blue sofa Emmy had seen in the photos. 'So, yes, this is it. Do you want to inspect it?'

Emmy chuckled inside, *that would be a no.* She couldn't quite believe her luck. 'No, no.'

'As I said in my message, I absolutely love it, but I realised I should have got the bigger one. It's a funny space.' She pointed to the corner of the room. 'See what I mean?'

Emmy didn't really, but she nodded anyway. As far as she was concerned, the room looked as if it had just stepped out of a Pinterest board. A very nice one. 'I see.'

'So yes, there we go.'

'Wow, your place is beautiful,' Emmy breathed as she looked around.

Jane chuckled. 'Let me assure you it wasn't. This room was complete with taxidermy, a lot of yellow, hmm, let me see, what else? Oh yes, the ceiling was bright pink, and the place smelt to high heaven. Yeah, not good. It's getting there. Baby steps and all that.'

'You never would have believed that,' Emmy said and looked out the window to the garden. 'The garden is so pretty too. You're into gardening, are you?'

'I dabble.' Jane laughed. 'The garden was a disaster. The soil was terrible, and the whole place was chock-full of gnomes. I went to sleep with gnomes in my head at one point. I had nightmares about the things.'

'Well, I think it looks absolutely lovely now,' Emmy said, admiring just about everything in the room.

'Thank you. So kind of you to say. Right, let's tackle getting this sofa out to your car.'

Tom smiled and looked at the door. 'Shouldn't be too hard. I've got a blanket in the boot and straps to put it on the roof if it's a problem.'

For a second, Emmy looked outside again to the garden. Flower beds bursting with shrubs and blooms sat by a weathered stone birdbath. Emmy thought about the yard behind the shop, knowing her work was cut out for her. Another job to put on her list.

'Right, if you head out the front door, I'll guide it through from this end once Tom's got it lifted,' Jane instructed.

Emmy took one end of the sofa, and Tom took the other. Jane's voice directed them down the hall, and Emmy had to stifle a laugh, picturing Tom at the other end, gingerly manoeuvring the sofa out the front door.

'You've got it!' Jane said. 'Nearly there now.'

Emmy and Tom carried the sofa down the front steps, and with a few grunts and wobbles from Emmy's end, they managed to get it loaded into the back of the car safely.

'I'd say that went remarkably smoothly,' Tom joked.

Jane beamed, clapping her hands together. 'Good job. I hope you're going to love it.'

Emmy knew she already did. She also couldn't quite get enough of Jane and her house. She was, in fact, having a life crush on Jane.

'Fancy a quick cup of tea before heading off?' Jane offered.

Emmy nearly bit her hand off before Tom could beg off. 'That would be lovely!'

Back inside, Jane bustled to put the kettle on while Emmy admired the sitting room.

'Told you that sofa would fit,' Tom said. 'It's going to look great.'

'I suppose I should know better than to doubt your spatial reasoning.'

'You totally should.'

Jane returned, balancing an assortment of mugs. 'There you go.'

'This really is such a lovely house,' Emmy commented. 'You really have an eye for it.'

'Ahh, it's not too hard when you live here. I swear it makes everything feel nicer when you're on Darling.'

Emmy nodded. 'It certainly does. I can't imagine living anywhere else now.'

'No better place. I haven't looked back, to be honest.'

Emmy knew precisely what she meant. Darling had been her fresh start and allowed her to dream big. She wasn't going to look back, either.

E mmy gazed out the window as they drove back to The Old Ticket Office.

'Quite a find,' Tom remarked.

'I feel lucky to have bagged that. How nice was the house? Gives me hope. Can you believe it used to have a pink ceiling and taxidermy?'

Tom grimaced. 'That would have been an adjustment. She seems to have worked magic on the place now, though.'

'Mmm, she really has. Both with the house and that garden. I'd love to get the yard sorted.'

'Yeah, it needs some love.'

'Imagine that amount of gnomes. Too funny.'

About twenty minutes later, the pale blue sofa was in the flat where the old sofa looked almost comically shabby next to it. They both stood back to admire it.

'Really nice. I'm well pleased with that,' Emmy noted.

'Yeah.'

'It's the little touches that are slowly making it all come together,' she joked and plonked herself onto the sofa, throwing her arms up. Tom laughed and did the same and then draped an arm around her shoulders.

'I reckon you could have a good few power naps here.'

'Yes, it will enable my sofa napping habit exceedingly well.'

'Your mum will love it.'

'She'll claim it as her new lounging spot.'

'Too right. We'll have to start rationing out sofa time slots.'

Emmy felt so happy about the sofa, as if it sealed a few things.

As if reading her thoughts, Tom joked, 'We make a pretty good team, you and I.'

'The best.' Emmy sent a silent thank you to the powers that be for intertwining her story with Tom, The Old Ticket Office, Jane, and Darling Island. All was looking very good in Emmy Bardot's life. She crossed her fingers that it would last.

5

Emmy pushed the button on the vacuum with her foot, straightened the rug under her bed, and gave her bedside tables an extra spray with the fancy geranium multi-surface cleaner that had been in one of the gift baskets that had been on her doorstep when she'd first moved to Darling. After plumping her bed cushions, she stood back with a smile on her face. Her bedroom looked fabulous, but nowhere near as fabulous as the view out the window. Waking up to the Darling view was something she hadn't quite factored in when she was planning her move. She definitely hadn't thought it would be as good as it was. She'd not even really thought about it properly. Now, she embraced it wholeheartedly and thanked her lucky stars every single night. She slept with the old sash windows at each end of the room slightly ajar, a sea breeze running through while she slept. In the morning, pulling back the curtains to the view was nothing short of gorgeous.

As she flicked the diffuser on the top of her chest of drawers to turn it on and moved around her room, tidying as she went, she relished in the pure joy of having her own space. She still couldn't quite believe it and felt as if it was a dream come true.

For years, she'd lived in the tiny cottage paying an extortionate amount in rent, wondering if she would ever own a home to call her own. Now she not only had her own flat, but she was the very proud owner of a bedroom with a distant view of the sea. Not only that, but there was also the ambience – the sound of the coast, the comforting trundle of the trams every now and then, and the hazy Darling blue to wake up to. Life had been worse.

She smiled at all the little bits and bobs all around the room courtesy of her mum, Cherry's, interior shopping habit. Cherry had, as usual, not had a budget in mind when planning Emmy's bedroom makeover. The lovely lamps on either side of Emmy's bed, the huge seagrass rug under it, and the gigantic jug of flowers on the side were a testament to Cherry's spending habits. Emmy finished polishing a framed photograph of her mum, her grandma, Amy, herself, and their estranged sister, Katy, and tucked it beside the lamp on the left-hand side of the bed. She then dusted a set of four framed watercolour paintings she'd found in the charity shop on Darling Street and wiped the top of her grandma Emily's jewellery box.

As Emmy tidied and cleaned each little detail around the room, it felt like parts of a puzzle were falling into place all around her. As if her whole life had been a jumble of jigsaw pieces suspended in the air until she'd moved into The Old Ticket Office. Once there, the pieces had stayed up in the air for a bit, and then one by one, they'd all sequentially landed into the correct slots. Emmy had landed right in the middle of the puzzle and felt as if it had always been where she was meant to be.

The scent of lavender and geranium filled the air from the diffuser and mingled with the fresh sea air coming in from the coast. As she sprayed and wiped the oversized mirror above her drawers, she barely recognised the woman staring back. The same Emmy smile she'd first seen when she'd been so excited to be going out with Tom had not only reappeared many times since, it had actually settled in and taken residence on her face. She was very glad to have it back in her life.

She felt a rush of gratitude to her grandma Emily and her mum, dad and Amy for helping her to get to Darling Island. She'd moved to a new life where opportunity and hope sat alongside simple things. Things like the ferry ride, the water, the trams, the community, and of course, the view. As she dusted and sprayed along the windowsill, the view took her breath away – the blue of the water, the bobbing pastel sail-boats, the horizon meeting the sky, seagulls overhead. All of it part of the new Emmy puzzle. All of it divine.

Emmy thought about her old life as, one by one, she took her perfumes off their tray, dusted them carefully, and arranged them back on the tray in perfectly straight lines. She mulled over the years she was in the cottage, where she'd thought she was relatively happy. She'd had a safe place to live, she'd gone to work, looked after Callum, seen her sister every weekend, and enjoyed what she'd thought was a fairly okay, if not mostly humdrum, life. She'd lived in a bubble of commuting to work, school runs and after-school activities, cleaning the house, keeping her car going, and generally spent most of her time keeping all the balls in the air.

Now life was different somehow. It was as if on Darling Island, though the balls still needed to be kept in the air, they'd also taken on a bit of a life of their own. The balls were no longer just going around and around the same old monotonous circle every day, every week, every year. The balls now had opportunity, a bit of hope, and, dare she say it, excitement. Actual life. She was liking these new balls very much.

After seeing the time was ticking on, and her dad and Tom were about to arrive after picking up something for the shop, she dragged the vacuum cleaner down the stairs, wedged it into the cupboard in the hallway, and then went into the kitchen to make a cup of tea. Picking up her mug, she pottered down the steep stairs to the shop, turned right, stood by the old counter, and looked around. The shop had taken a lot longer to get going than she'd thought, but there was a little part of her that was perhaps pleased with how that had turned out. There was also a part of her aware of the fact that she was now purposely going slow. As if somehow she was scared to actually open the doors to the shop. Frightened of what that would mean. Scared indeed to fail. Fearful of again messing things up.

She stood for ages by the counter and analysed what she had and how far she'd come. The floors, once covered with a horrid nylon carpet, were now stripped back and sported a dark stain. The walls, once a nicotine yellow cream, were now under-coated, primed, and wearing a beautiful fresh coat of brilliant white. The old windows sparkled, their turquoise inserts catching the light. Everything was clean, bright, and raring to go.

Just as she was finishing her tea, she got a text from her dad.

Bob: *We're just pulling into the lane. Pop the kettle on.*

Emmy: *Will do. How is it?*

Bob: *Good. I think you're going to love it.*

Emmy: *I'll put the tea on and see you outside.*

About ten minutes or so later, Emmy stood in the lane watching Tom manoeuvre a hired open-back van up onto the verge outside her back gate. She squinted into the back of the van at the shop display case she'd ordered before she'd moved to Darling Island. Alongside it were four antique doors, and tucked into the side, covered in moving blankets, were what she assumed were two sets of mirrored drawers. Wondering if the drawers had survived what must have been a precarious ride on the floating bridge, she smiled as her dad climbed out of the van.

'Hey! How was it?'

'Fine,' Bob said. 'Just hope the mirrored ones survived.'

Emmy took a step forward to get a better look. 'Do you think everything is okay?'

Tom patted the van reassuringly. 'Everything seems intact by the looks of it. Your dad's packing was good.'

'What a relief!'

Bob stretched his arms, rubbing the small of his back. 'That was some ride over the floating bridge, though. Thought we might lose a drawer or two. It was wobbling around there a bit.'

Tom chuckled. 'I think your strapping kept everything in order.'

Bob smirked back. 'I think it might have done.'

Emmy, amused at the banter, smiled. Tom, it seemed, was getting on well with her dad. It warmed the cockles of her heart. 'Well, I'm just glad everything made it.'

She stepped closer to the van, reached in, and pulled back the moving blanket that covered the mirrored drawers. The top caught the sun. 'Looks like they've survived,' she said, her voice filled with relief.

Tom nodded. 'Thank heavens for that.'

As the men began to unload the van, Emmy watched on and sighed. The flat, the shop, Darling Island, Tom, the lovely people, and the breathtaking views – everything was lovelier than she'd thought it ever would be. Squinting at the width of the back door as Tom and Bob heaved the display case off the truck, Emmy felt butterflies in her stomach, and her heart fluttered with excitement as the first piece went up the path. She stepped back, surveying the scene, her mind already arranging and rearranging the set-up and imagining what the finished place would look like. The vision had been in her head for years and years; now it appeared it was actually starting to come to life. Exhilarating and scary at the same time.

'What do you think?' Tom asked once the display unit and the old doors were finally in the front of the shop.

Emmy smiled. 'Getting there.' She peered at the beautiful

character of the doors. Their weathered surfaces, chipped paint, tarnished knobs, and fittings were just what she'd been looking for for the ambience of her shop. She could already imagine them displaying Love Emmy x things. 'They're lovely,' she admitted, running a hand over the worn surface of one of the doors. 'I think they're going to look great once they're all set up.'

As Emmy took a step back, she stood with her head to the side and peered at how the doors looked against the perfectly whitewashed walls of the shop. Just as she'd hoped they would, they contrasted with their surroundings perfectly.

'Good call on those, Ems,' Bob said, jerking his thumb towards the old doors. 'I thought you were barking up the wrong tree there, but I was wrong. Really good.'

'Yes, they're going to be perfect.' Emmy could almost see Love Emmy x bits and bobs sparkling against the vintage backdrops.

The doors, their off-white hues – from eggshell to ivory and from parchment to seashell – showed knocks and marks and a patina of time, which was what she'd envisaged as a backdrop for the store. All of it now ready to become part of Emmy's dream. Looking at the doors against the stained floor, Emmy smiled. She loved it – the aged floorboards, the high ceilings, the picture railings, the old chandelier, the fireplace on the far wall, and the ticket counter. She sighed at what was taking shape. The dull, forgotten shell of a room was now brimming with potential. Best of all, every single little bit of it was *hers*. It was that she loved most of all.

Tom grinned. 'So, what do you think? Worth hiring a van for?'

'Definitely. Thank you. I can already see it filled with all my stuff.'

'This place is going to be a hit.'

Emmy hid a gulp. It all felt *so* real now. She was scared. Petrified in fact.

When the men had lifted in the two sets of mirrored drawers, Emmy couldn't stop smiling. She'd found them on Facebook Marketplace going for a great price and had snapped them up without a second thought. There was a small hairline crack on the back of one of the sets, and one of the drawers was stuck, but for her needs, neither mattered at all. The drawers and surfaces were dusty and marked, and it didn't seem as if they had seen a clean for a long time. Tom touched one of the drawers. 'Yeah, these are going to need a bit of cleaning.'

Bob chuckled. 'I think we might need to get your mum on those. She's a master at stuff like that.'

Emmy laughed. 'I might make it Amy's job when she comes over.' She ran her fingers along one of the drawers. The surface was coated with dust and grime. 'They'll clean up nicely, I'm sure.'

'A bit of elbow grease, and they'll be good as new.'

Emmy smiled. Both her shop and her vision were slowly coming together. It was yet another reminder of how her luck had changed the day she'd bumped into Tom in the street. She stood there, letting reality sink in. The shop that had once existed in her head was now tangible and sitting right in front of her. Emmy felt a rush of gratitude for Tom and Bob at the same time as a shot of fear.

She picked up a duster and began to clean the mirrored drawers as Bob and Tom pushed the display unit further into place. She swallowed as she thought about finally opening the shop, another part of her ticket to a fresh start and a life she'd dreamt about for a long time. There was no turning back now, and quite frankly, she wouldn't have it any other way. She just hoped that she didn't mess anything up. Or that nothing else did. She could but wait and see.

6

A few days later, Emmy cursed Callum for forgetting his cricket stuff. She'd had to drop it off at Kevin's on her way to work. She'd got up at the crack of dawn, and the added detour to Kevin's had meant that she was a bit later than she usually was, which also meant that the staff car park had filled up fast. Her usual spot, the same one she'd parked in for years, was gone, as was her second backup space. She circled the aisles, settled on a space at the end, and pulled down her visor. There had been an email from HR reiterating the importance of personal appearance for customer-facing staff. As there was no doubt that she was customer-facing, she checked that her hair was neat. Long gone were the days when they were told what colour of lipstick to wear, but being presentable was still important. So considering she'd risen in the dark and slipped into her uniform, barely awake, and her hair or makeup weren't done, she'd thought it was good to check what she looked like before she walked into work.

Following her much-practised routine whereby she could nail a perfectly coiffed French pleat and acceptable face in about ninety seconds, Emmy scooped her toiletries bag up from under the front seat, whipped out her smoothing brush, pulled it through her hair, and twisted her hair into a pleat. Next, she dabbed on foundation with a brush covering up her late night, put on a few coats of mascara, fluffed on blusher, and dabbed on a nude layer of twenty-four-hour matte lipstick that did exactly what it said on the side of the tube. She squirted a spray of perfume behind each ear, added one to each wrist, and put her grandma Emily's earrings with the sapphires in her ears.

Feeling satisfied that, as the email had instructed, she was neat and tidy and also looking alive thanks to the blusher, Emmy adjusted the navy patterned scarf around her neck, wedged the toiletries bag back under the seat, and picked up her bag. She stepped out of the car, clicked the remote, and inhaled the crisp early morning air as she made her way towards the staff entrance. As she walked, the morning sunshine painted an orange glow against the glass façade of the terminal building. The port was already busy, and she could see from the far side the comings and goings of early passengers. From the other side, ground staff milled around, and just ahead of her, cleaning crews were pushing trolleys. It all hummed around her, creating a rhythm that Emmy knew well.

Arriving at the door, she pulled her pass from her lanyard, tapped it on the pad on the right, and waited for the doors to click. They automatically slid open, welcoming her into the staff entrance of the bustling terminal. She passed through the security check smoothly, checked her port ID was in place, and smiled at the security officers, many of whom had been working at the port as long as she had.

Emerging from the security lobby, the sounds of the terminal flooded over her – travellers, tannoy announcements, the hum of rolling suitcases, the occasional wail of a child. Emmy was well used to it; she navigated through the sea of people and briskly made her way to the staff room, towards her locker, then stowed away her bag and grabbed her navy blue blazer. She then pushed open the door to the crew briefing room. Judy, her boss, looked over from pouring a coffee at the machines as she walked in.

'Morning, Ems. How you travelling?'

'Morning. Well.'

'How are you?'

'Good, thanks.'

Judy raised her eyebrows. 'Not in your usual spot this morning. Did you get stuck in a traffic spot somewhere?'

'No, no. Callum was at Kev's and he forgot his cricket stuff, so I had to do a detour. The joys of teenage boys.'

'Oh, right.'

'Amazing, what a difference ten or so minutes makes. I had to circle the car park.'

'I know.'

'How long have we been asking for extra parking down our end?'

'I also know that.' Judy laughed and gestured to the coffee machine. 'Coffee?'

'I need about ten to both wake me up and get me through these two shifts.'

Judy laughed. 'You do know the ladies' toilets are out of action in the check-in area?'

'No! I might as well give up and go home now. There'll be some dramatics today, then.'

'We're going to need our wits about us today, yep.'

Emmy joked. 'We have years of experience under our belt. We are well-equipped to handle anything that might come our way. What could today possibly throw at us?'

'Do not even tempt fate.' Judy chuckled. 'That's dangerous.'

'Yup,' Emmy said as she took the coffee and sipped.

'How were your days off?' Judy asked.

'Yeah, busy.'

'How's everything going with the shop? You said you were getting the dressers and doors, that was right, wasn't it?'

'It went well. Actually, it went better than I expected.' Emmy slipped her phone out of her pocket and navigated to the pictures of the mirrored dressers in the shop. She turned her phone screen around to face Judy.

Judy's eyebrows rose, and she blinked exaggeratedly. 'Wow!'

'I know, right? It suddenly sort of came together once everything was in.'

'I should say so. Compared to the ones you showed me before.'

'I'm really pleased.'

'I should think you are. Go you.'

'Not bad for things that were as cheap as chips. I did see an antique shop display cabinet in a commercial antiques shop that I absolutely loved, but it was way out of my price range so this lot had to do. It turned out well.'

Judy enlarged one of the images and then looked up. 'So, this must mean you are close to opening.'

'I know.'

'You don't sound convinced.'

'Truth be told, I'm quite apprehensive. It was all good when it was a plan on my laptop. Now it's here, it's a different story.'

'Right. I get it.'

'Once the flower instalment is in, though, I have no further excuses.' Emmy laughed, shaking her head.

'What are the plans for the opening days?'

'I'm only going to do Fridays and Saturdays, I think, at this point. I'm just not going to make enough money initially.'

'Oh, since when?'

'I decided that a while ago. Because the online sales are so strong, I can do it. Lots of boutiques nowadays only open a couple of days a week. Sort of like a destination thing,' Emmy explained as she took sips of her coffee.

'Hmm. Right. Makes sense. I meant to say to you that my sister went to a workshop thing in a shop the other day. I thought of you when she was telling me about it.'

'What sort of workshop?'

'It was actually about the ins and outs of how mugs are made, and then you could buy them at the end, but I thought about you. Once it's up and running, you could do little lunches and evenings and things, and now I've seen what it looks like, I reckon you'd get people to pay to sit there and have a lovely afternoon tea.'

'Hmm. I like that idea,' Emmy mused.

'You'd probably need to get it all watertight with regulations and stuff.'

'I think that would be covered with the insurance I've already got in place. Yeah, good idea, Judy.'

'I'm full of them.' Judy winked. 'Right, I'll see you out there.'

Once Emmy had read the briefing for the day, she made her way to the gate. As she walked through the concourse, she mulled over what Judy had said and went through her upcoming day. Despite the early morning, the demanding schedule, and the occasional angry passenger, she realised that she loved her job. There wasn't particularly anything special about it, but it gave her structure, security, and made her feel safe to continue with the Love Emmy x dream. She adjusted her scarf, tapped the back of her head to make sure her hair was neat, and with a professional smile plastered onto the front of her face, made her way to the desk.

As her radio buzzed, her day began. She had a double shift ahead of her, but it was funny how she'd got used to it. Plus, these days, she got to go home to Darling Island, and there was no way anyone could complain about that. For Emmy Bardot, just about everything in her life was good. The thing that was niggling away at the back of her head, though, was how long was it going to last?

7

Emmy sat on the train on her way to meet her sister and her mum for one of their regular long and boozy pub lunches. The pub was in the same place where she herself had lived with Kevin before her world had turned upside down. She twiddled the gold and pearl cuff bangle on her left wrist, turning it over and over with the thumb and finger of her right hand as her mind drifted to how the lunches had started many moons before. Their little tradition had first begun when Amy had gone to university, and Emmy and their other sister, Katy – who no one now saw – had both also moved out of home. In those days, they had all met once a month at the pub on a Saturday afternoon, and it had been a tradition ever since. The one main difference being that Katy was no longer around.

Emmy had left her car at home, crossed the Darling floating bridge as a foot passenger, and was now on a train. She would be staying along with Callum at Amy's for the night. She sat with her emails open on her phone, sorting out a refund for a Love Emmy x customer and liaising with a delivery company who'd somehow managed to lose one of her parcels. After finishing her emails, she let her eyes wander out to the backs of houses whizzing past the window. As the motion of the train lulled her, she watched as the landscape stretched away and small towns and villages flew past. As the wheels clattered on rails and the announcements over the intercom told of the next stop, Emmy remembered clambering onto the train with Callum in a pram. Her first flat when she'd split from Kevin had been on the line, and before her mum had given her her car, she'd had to struggle on public transport with a pram to get anywhere. Those days felt like a million miles away from her life on Darling.

Emmy's hand brushed the velvety upholstery of the train seat, and the smell of the coffee of a man sitting in front of her made her zoom back in time. Her brain spiralled backwards, and she remembered the feelings of being alone with Callum, wondering how she was ever going to cope. She recalled the almost desperate feeling of how she was going to get through each day. As she sat there, her brain was an odd mush of different emotions, nostalgia for Callum's little chubby, inno-cent baby days and the sheer desperation that had engulfed her at what had happened after Kevin's gambling addiction had finally come out in the open. Emmy reminisced about the early days with Kevin, when they got married, when Callum had arrived, how it had all felt lovely and as if her life had been waiting to unfold. But reality had chipped away at all of that as the shadow of Kevin's addiction had stolen her dreams. The escalating debts, the fights, and the nights she would cry herself to sleep – all of it now seemed like dark fragments from a different life. Each day had felt like a mountain, a long round of feeding, crying (both her and Callum), and wondering how she was ever going to get back to normal again.

Oh, how she had done it, though. Emmy had not only coped, but she'd done well. Or, at least, she'd thought she had. It looked that way on the outside. But now that she was on Darling, she could see that those years had been about survival. Now she felt no longer in survival mode. Now she had an *actual* life. Her gaze remained fixed on the passing scenery as a patchwork quilt of greens, browns, and gold rolled on endlessly past the window. Hedgerows bordered the fields, and every now and then, an old house or a little cottage would appear and be gone in a second. She smiled as she remembered the baby days. Amidst the chaos, there had been moments of unadulterated joy – Callum's first steps, his baby giggles, his fat little legs, teaching him his alphabet. That feeling of love for Callum triggered her brain to think about loving Tom. She remembered when she'd gone to Darling to pick up Callum's birthday cake. Tom bumping into her in the street had started a domino effect, and now here she was in a lovely relationship.

She smiled at the thought of how Darling Island had worked its magic on her, and as the train began to slow, the announcement for her stop echoed through the compartment. The familiar station of her old town came into view. The platform was abuzz with activity, people waiting for loved ones and others hurriedly making their way out. The once-familiar sights and sounds now felt somewhat alien, a bit of a reminder of how much had changed. Gathering her belongings, Emmy stepped off the train. As she made her way out, her phone buzzed with a message from Amy.

Amy: *I'm in the pub. It's busy. Been looking forward to this. I have our usual table.*

Emmy: *Just got off the train. See you in a bit. Xxx*

Amy: *I'll get you a drink.*

Emmy smiled. Thank goodness for Amy. Despite everything that had gone on, Amy had always been there. She cherished her sister and their bond. As Emmy walked towards the pub with a spring in her step, she felt buoyed by the turnaround in her life.

Getting to the pub, she smiled as she remembered all the times they'd been there – good times, really sad times, celebrations, and all sorts. As she pushed the inner door, she squinted over to the far side where Amy was sitting at their usual table.

'Hi, how are you? Good?' Amy asked.

Emmy wedged her overnight bag under the table. 'Yeah, really good.'

'How was that journey?'

'Not too bad. I'm glad I left the car now.'

'Train okay?'

'Yep.'

'You okay?'

'Ahh, yes. I was just reminiscing on the train. Weird, really.'

'About what?'

Emmy sighed. 'The old days when Callum was a baby. When I first moved into the flat, I was on and off that train with a pram. Now look at me.'

'Now look at Callum. He's ginormous!'

'I know. Time flies, doesn't it?'

'It does.'

'I was thinking about Kevin when we got married and all that.'

'Sad?'

'Aww, yes and no. Bittersweet, right?'

'Yeah. Just blame Kevin,' Amy said, dropping in their age-old joke where they blamed Kevin for everything.

'When I look back now, I realise I was desperate then. And really bloody sad.'

'Yup.' Amy nodded. 'But you didn't give up. Were you the one with an addiction? Did you turn to drink or drugs? No.'

Emmy blinked. 'Blimey Ames! You're on form today. Taking no prisoners.'

Amy sighed. 'Sorry. It just irritates me. Everyone has a problem nowadays. One of the women at work has anxiety, and she is refusing to take phone calls. She's head of the Outbound Sales Team. I don't know...' Amy trailed off, leaving her sentence. 'What do I know? You, though, you put your head down, and you got on with it, and now look at you.'

'True. I had a lot of help, though. I mean, for example, Mum gave me her car, which meant I could get to work, which meant I earned money, which meant we were okay. You helped me *all* the time. A lot of people don't have that. My family were there for me every step of the way.'

'Yeah, I get it. It was still a struggle for you, though. You made it work, Ems. Look at how Cal has turned out. He's such a lovely lad. You should be really proud.'

Emmy laughed. 'A nice happy conversation to set the tone for lunch.'

'Ha. I'll shut up. It just gets my goat, all these people complaining about this, that, and the other. We, on the other hand, put our heads down and get on with it.'

Emmy nodded. She loved Amy and was very grateful for everything she'd done for her, but she had to laugh. Even Amy didn't really get it, despite what she thought she knew. Everything had gone just fine for Amy, and Amy's world had never really had a problem at all. No one's life was perfect, but Amy's was up there with not too bad at all. Apart from what had happened with Katy, their sister, Emmy couldn't think of much at all that had gone pear-shaped in Amy's life. There was no way on earth she'd ever say that, though. Not on your Nelly. 'We do.'

Amy's phone pinged, and she looked down at her screen. 'Mum's running a bit late.'

'Rightio. How was she last week when you spoke to her?' Emmy said, referring to the fact that it had been their estranged sister Katy's birthday.

'Hmm. She didn't really mention it. What about with you?'

'Nothing much.'

Amy let out a huge sigh. 'It's sad.'

'I know. You can't make someone behave properly, Ames.'

'I know.' Amy nodded.

'And you cannot continue to be abused by someone.'

'She's still our sister at the end of the day.'

'I know.'

'She knew the drill. If she got off the drugs...' Amy's voice caught.

'Yep.'

'We just don't even know where she is.'

'I know.' Emmy patted the back of Amy's hand. 'Let's close the subject, or we'll both be in bits when Mum gets here.'

'Yep.'

'Addiction, eh?'

'I know. Speaking of that, how is Kev?'

Emmy tapped the top of the table. 'Touch wood, he's in a good phase at the moment.'

'How long 'til the relapse?' Amy asked.

'Blimey! What's got into you today? You're full of the joys.'

'Sorry.'

'I'm hoping he won't relapse. For Cal's sake.'

'Don't hold your breath,' Amy said resignedly.

'I don't need that in my life. Everything is ticking along very nicely for me. I don't want anything to mess it up.'

'Yes, it is. Let's talk about that and much nicer things. We don't need to be talking about Katy or Kevin when Mum arrives.'

'Yes. Let's. No one needs to be talking about either of those topics.'

Emmy strolled along in silence as she listened to her mum and Amy chatting about how Bob, their dad, had rented another allotment with a bright yellow shed. She smiled to herself as she heard Cherry going on about the fact that she was going to paint the shed a pale oyster pink, string bunting from the guttering, and put floral camping chairs inside. Emmy felt an almost overwhelming feeling of love for her mum and Amy. Their relationship had certainly had its fair share of ups and downs, but overall, she couldn't fathom life without them. They were so close and shared just about everything in life.

Walking side-by-side, Emmy felt grateful as her mum continued to ramble on about the state of the allotment and how she couldn't wait to get her teeth into it and do a makeover. Emmy remembered the countless times over the years Cherry had turned the mundane into something much more bearable. She'd turned up with meals for Callum and her, made weekends feel like mini holidays, and treated everyone to lovely picnics and days out. Cherry was always thinking about somebody else, but woe betide you if you didn't keep in Cherry's line. She liked her life, her husband, and her girls to do things *her* way. Step out of line and she'd come down on you like a tonne of bricks.

As Emmy thought back to her childhood, she realised that Cherry had always been the backbone of their family. Cherry had been through all sorts, especially with Katy. Despite it all, she was always there at the end of the phone, standing in the kitchen with a cup of tea, or generally just being there, making sure everything and everyone was okay.

Emmy thought about Amy as she heard her asking Cherry if she thought pink for the shed really was a good idea. The bond she had with Amy was special, and though they'd had their fair share of teenage squabbles and they still loved quite a good bicker, there was an underlying current of fierce loyalty and unconditional love.

She remembered how when life had decided it might like to throw a few curveballs Emmy's way, it was always Amy she'd leaned on, and vice versa. They had navigated through life's ups and downs, offering shoulders to cry on, listening ears, and more often than not fumbled through all sorts of things being utterly silly. Emmy strolled, listened, and in her head, offered up a silent thankful prayer for her sister. Thank goodness for having Amy on her side and in her life. She never wanted anyone or anything to ever jeopardise that.

8

It was the day after the long, boozy lunch, which had most definitely been both long and absolutely boozy. A light drizzle misted through the air as Emmy stood next to Callum, waiting to cross over the lights near the train station. As the green man buzzed, they ambled along in plenty of time for their train and chatted about how Callum had got on at cricket the day before. Once they'd stepped inside the station, both of them stood with their chins raised, looking for their train. As Emmy's eyes scanned the destinations, and in the hustle and bustle of the station as they stood waiting for the platform to be announced, she was suddenly acutely aware of how different life on Darling was. The pace was slower, the people smilier, and everything just that little less busy. A lot nicer.

When the platform finally emerged, Emmy and Callum followed the trail of passengers through the gates, and just as she had the day before, they got on the train and took a seat on the blue velour seats. As Callum sat engrossed in his phone, Emmy was suddenly struck by how not only they were going home to a new place but how she was actually a homeowner. Emmy Bardot had a home to call her own. It blew her mind. She was no longer ensconced in the rental trap. She was not paying someone else's mortgage. She was not paying *any* mortgage. The flat was small, admittedly, poky even, and the building itself would be a long time before it was finished, but the fact that it was hers was monumental. All of it made her buzz with something she'd never quite felt before. Safe. It felt so nice.

She continued to mull over living on Darling and being a homeowner as she stared out the window, gazing at the scenery slipping past in a blur of colour and shade. Rear gardens, the backs of roofs and fences whizzed past the window as Emmy's brain percolated her new life nearly as quickly as the train sped along. She mused about the flat over the shop and how lucky she was that there was a top room. She couldn't quite believe the fact that she was actually one hundred per cent in possession of a bedroom with a king-size bed, a view to the sea, an admittedly tired bathroom but an en suite nonetheless, and lots of nice touches courtesy of Cherry and her interior design habit. She so loved that she now had a home to call her very own.

Her brain continued to fizz with the happenings in her life. On top of now being a homeowner, she was also the owner of what was looking more and more like quite a serious relationship that had arrived in her life completely out of the blue. Emmy thought of her grandma Emily and chuckled to herself. Emily must have been up there twiddling the knobs of Emmy's life and making it turn around because it sure had. As the train rumbled over the tracks and Callum was lost in a cricket game on his phone, she rested her head back on the headrest and felt a strange tightness inside. A distant but horribly gnawing feeling that this new life of hers and her happiness wouldn't last long. Something would indeed come along, give her a little whack, knock her off her pedestal, and mess things up. Just like it always had.

As the train got nearer and nearer to the coast, Emmy tried

not to think about anything going wrong. She let her brain go over her plans for the flower installation that week and thought about how well Callum had settled into Darling life. She perused how Tom was getting on like a house on fire with Bob and how even the long double shifts at work weren't too bad. The train started to slow down, and she sighed to herself. Hopefully, Emily, up in the sky, was still in charge of the knobs and would continue to twiddle them in the direction of Emmy's new happy trajectory of life.

Callum took his earphones out. 'Alright?'

'Yep. Good. You?'

'Yeah. Can't wait to get home.'

Emmy felt a little blob of pleasure inside. She felt exactly the same. The Old Ticket Office really did feel like home. 'Same. Feet up and a cup of tea.'

'Sandwich?' Callum asked with his eyebrows raised in question.

'You cannot seriously be hungry after that breakfast Aunty Amy made. You had a massive stack of pancakes!'

Callum laughed and wrinkled up his nose. 'That was ages ago.'

'Cal. It was just before we left.'

'I'm thinking cheese and tomato toastie. You know, like we used to have in the flat.'

Emmy felt her heart twinge. 'I'm surprised you can remember that.'

'Of course I can.'

'What, before we moved to the cottage?'

'Yeah. We used to have cheese and tomato toasties all the time. You used to cut mine because sometimes the tomato burned.'

'We did.'

'I could eat at least two rounds.'

Emmy grimaced and screwed her face up. 'I don't think we

have a toasted sandwich maker these days. It blew up, remember?'

Callum nodded. 'I know, but Grandma bought one.'

'What? Did she? What, when she did the kitchen?' Emmy raised her eyebrows. 'Little did I know.'

'Yeah, it's in the far cupboard. It matches the kettle and stuff.'

'News to me. I didn't even see it in there.'

Callum laughed. 'I think she slipped it in when Grandpa wasn't looking.'

'What, along with those little things like a fancy-pants fridge and a dishwasher?'

'She said we're not to mention those.' Callum laughed.

'I know.'

'And that no grandson or daughter of hers was going to be washing up.'

'God love her. Your grandma likes to be in control of everything – luckily for us.'

'So I'll make us toasties then, yeah?'

'Sounds good to me.'

'What about Tom?' Callum asked.

Emmy shook her head and said a silent prayer of thanks. Callum had taken to Tom and seemed to have just got on with it. She'd braced herself for issues, but so far there'd been none. 'What about him?'

'Will he want a sandwich, do you think?'

'Oh, not sure. I don't know where he is at the moment.'

'Shall I message him?'

'Yep, you do that.'

As Callum whipped out his phone, Emmy smiled. She felt a twirl of butterflies at Callum texting Tom. Things were far from messed up in her life. Things were really rather good.

9

A few days or so later, one by one, Emmy dragged boxes of artificial flower garlands from the storeroom to the front of the shop until they were all piled by the front door. She'd first ordered the flowers when she'd been in a rose-tinted, fuzzy dream about being a shopkeeper on Darling Island before reality had taken hold. That had been right at the beginning of her journey, not long after she'd first viewed the place. Now, as she actually owned not just the shop but the building, her dreams weren't quite as tinted with rose. They were, however, still alive.

Emmy took a moment, kneeling next to the boxes as a swirl of emotions filled her. The journey from Love Emmy x the Etsy shop to becoming an *actual* owner of an *actual* store had been anything but easy. Yet, here she was, about to open the doors to her own shop. It was as if the artificial flower garlands were symbolic of years and years of dreams and plans. She remembered the evening she'd spent hours on Pinterest pinning shops with flower garlands on a secret board. She'd envisioned the shop in the summer, drowning in the flowers draped around the windows inviting passers-by to stop in. She'd imagined the flowers as the start of the Love Emmy x experience. Somewhere people could come and forget their worries for a while, a place that was a little bit of a small escape.

Now, making that envisioned experience a reality had set in since the actual hard graft of painting, pulling up carpets, and setting up display units in place was done. Every decision she made, from what pieces of jewellery she included in her shop to how the garlands would drape around the windows, was part of creating the thing that had lived inside her head for so long. She was finally bringing a part of her and her grandma to life.

Emmy began unpacking the boxes, thankful that the flowers were even more beautiful than she remembered. Heaving a stepladder over the floor, she then draped one of the garlands across the top of the window, letting it cascade down the wall to see how the effect might be outside. She plonked three more garlands over a nail, stepped back, tilted her head, gauged the effect, and then looked back at the number of garlands in the boxes. She could tell if they got it right, it was going to be gorgeous and everything like she'd imagined.

As she began to sort through arranging the flowers into hues of pink, she suddenly felt both a surge of pride and a prick of tears. She'd only gone and actually done it. Her shop was no longer a figment of her imagination, but a tangible thing she was completely surrounded by. Crouching amidst the garlands, she was almost fizzing with a mix of excitement and pride. Emmy Bardot was at the helm of a job well done. Boy, did that feel good.

She stepped back and looked at the floor, now a tapestry of petals and leaves. They were so well made, it was easy to forget they weren't real and would be living their life until winter around the front of her shop. In a funny sort of way, the flowers all over the floor reminded Emmy of Emily. She recalled how her Amy and Katy would sit in Emily's garden for hours on end doing not much at all. Emily would bring them out sandwiches and ice cream, and they'd play all sorts of weird and wonderful games. The pink flowers reminded Emmy of summer afternoons and the trellis archway over the gate to Emily's house.

With a sigh, she began to sort further, separating each type of flower and greenery into piles. She missed Emily all the time, but with the money from Emily's house, which had been worth a fortune, Emmy was able to pursue her dream.

While taking a break and waiting for both Bob and Tom to arrive, Emmy went back upstairs and made herself a pot of tea. Callum was sitting on the sofa gaming. Emmy poked her head around the door. 'Tea?'

'Yes, please,' Callum said without looking up.

'What are you doing today?'

'Nothing.'

'Grandpa is coming over to help with the flower installation.'

'I know.'

'Will you be gracing us with your presence?'

Callum still didn't drag his eyes away from his game. It irritated Emmy no end. 'If you want.'

Emmy didn't bother to reply, left him to it, and went back to pour the tea. After hearing Tom and Bob from the lane, she squeezed two more small mugs out of the pot and, with two in her right hand and one in her left, went back down the stairs to the shop.

'Morning,' Tom called out, walked up to her, and kissed her.

Emmy's heart did a somersault. A nuclear reaction in her stomach followed it. 'Hi.'

'Oi, oi. What's cooking with you?' Bob asked cheerfully.

Emmy passed over the mugs of tea. 'Not much. I've been surrounded by flowers. Artificial ones. You must have smelt the teapot.'

'I always do.' Bob chuckled.

Emmy laughed, watching the two of them navigate the

flowers all over the shop floor. 'There are loads of them when they're like this. I think I got the number right.'

Bob nodded. 'Yeah, every single video I've watched on flower arch installation says you need a minimum of double what you think and more if you want it to look amazing.'

Tom widened his eyes at the mountain of garlands. 'Really? There are loads!'

'Yep.' Emmy pointed to the flowers and then the shop door. 'All of those need to go out there.'

'Not a job for the faint of heart,' Bob said, shaking his head.

'Your mission, should you choose to accept it,' Emmy said with a mock-serious tone, 'is to get these flowers, especially the ivy, to adorn the top of the ticket office and make it look as lovely as the rest of this place.'

Bob sighed and drained his tea. 'No rest for the wicked. I'll get the ladders in.'

An hour or so later, all three of them were standing outside the shop with a ladder balanced against the wall.

Tom positioned himself at the base of the ladder and looked up. 'That's most of the fixing bits up then.'

'Yep,' Bob agreed.

Bob held the ladder steady as Tom climbed up, and Emmy, with her arms overflowing with garlands, started to hand up bundles of flowers and strands of ivy, guiding him on where they should go. The three of them fell into a rhythm, with Bob directing, Emmy passing up the flowers, and Tom fixing them into place. As they more or less silently and methodically worked, at first the flower installation wasn't looking good at all. Emmy was *so* disappointed it was untrue. She felt as if she'd poured good money down the drain. She stood with her head cocked to the side. 'Awful.'

Bob sucked air in through his teeth. 'Hold your horses.'

'Dad, it looks terrible! We're going to have to pull the whole lot back down. I can't have that.'

Bob nodded. 'It does, but my video tutorial watching has informed me that this is the bit where you think it will be rubbish. You just have to stick with it and keep adding the flowers. The more, the merrier.'

Emmy looked doubtful. 'It looks cheap and nasty at this stage. If it doesn't improve, there's no way it's staying. Sorry, just no. I really don't like how it looks.'

'Mark my words,' Bob said and pointed to another bundle of flowers. 'Keep passing that lot up, and we'll reassess in a bit.'

After a lot more fixing of garlands to the structure, as if by magic, the installation suddenly started to take on a life of its own. The ivy trailed down either side of the windows, clusters of roses, peonies, and daisies were woven throughout, and white roses adorned the top.

Another hour of fixing, peering, and fiddling went by, and Tom stepped down from the ladder and all three of them, who had now also been joined by Callum, stood staring up over the shop door.

Bob let out a low whistle. 'Who would've thought this old place could look so good?'

Tom nodded. 'Have to say it is quite something. I was with you earlier, Ems. It looked terrible. Good job we listened to your dad.'

Emmy shook her head. 'I really had my doubts at the start of this.'

'You were right, I didn't want to say, but it did look awful,' Bob agreed and chuckled. 'Look at it now. Wow.'

Emmy beamed. 'It just needed a bit of perseverance, as you said. And some manual labour,' she added with a wink in Tom's direction.

Tom laughed, flexing his arms exaggeratedly. 'Anytime you need these muscles, just let me know.'

Emmy swooned inside. Tom's muscles were not the only

thing she wanted. 'Thank you for helping with this. I'm really grateful.'

'Don't be silly,' Tom said.

As the sun dipped slightly in the sky, casting the street in a golden hue, the floral installation popped even more vividly. A tram trundled past, and Emmy touched the edge of one of the peonies. 'It's just how I imagined it,' she commented, her gaze moving over the flowers and trailing ivy.

Callum took a step back and narrowed his eyes in contemplation. 'You know, with the sunlight on it like that, it really does look good, Mum.'

Bob squinted. 'Yeah. It's a showstopper, that's what it is. Your mum is going to love this.'

Emmy sighed. 'A lot of sweat and thought and... flower petals, and we finally got there.'

Tom shook his head. 'In all the time I've lived here, I've never done something quite like this. I didn't see this in my future.'

Bob chuckled, rubbing his hands together. 'Welcome to the family, mate. Get used to this if you're around my girls and my wife. They rope you into all sorts.'

Emmy smiled. 'We get people working for us early on.'

'We'll have the whole town wanting floral installations above their doors,' Bob said. 'You'll be able to start a second business in them, Tom.'

Just then, a couple walked by with a toddler in tow. The little girl's eyes widened in awe, pointing excitedly. 'Look, Mummy! I love flowers. It's so pretty!'

The woman smiled. 'Yes, darling. Very pretty. Just like in your storybooks.'

Emmy felt ridiculously pleased with the comment as she watched the mum and daughter walk away. Tom, sensing Emmy's emotion, nudged her arm. 'Happy?'

Emmy was more than happy. 'Yep, it's amazing.'

Bob, always one to lighten the mood, clapped his hands

together. 'Right then, how about we get this lot cleared up and shoot off for a quick celebratory drink at the pub?'

Tom started to pick up discarded bits of greenery from the floor. 'Works for me.'

Emmy started to sweep the pavement. 'I don't think I've ever had a better offer, Dad.'

10

E mmy tutted as she came off the phone to the bank. The payment dongle for the shop had been sent to the wrong place, and she now had to go and collect it rather than bother with the hassle of the redirection and a delay. She blew a strand of hair out of her face and shook her head. Why and how were some things always so difficult? Things never went smoothly. It wasn't a great start to the day; the dongle situation most definitely threw a spanner in the works.

Despite annoying blunders by other people like the bank, the interior of the shop, along with the sign and the floral installation out the front, had come on in leaps and bounds, but without the payment dongle, progress would come to a halt. She had banked on getting everything sorted before working and her cricket taxi driving responsibilities.

Bob, who had been busy in the back sorting out the storeroom, walked in holding a cup of tea. 'Everything alright, darling?'

Emmy sighed, rubbing her temples. 'I finally got to the bottom of it. The bank messed up the delivery of the payment dongle, which is why Paul, the postman, knew nothing about it.

They've sent it to the old address instead. I mean, really? Now I have to go and pick it up.'

Bob frowned, taking a sip of his tea. 'Banks, I swear, they work on a different timetable to the rest of the world. Always a hiccup. Every single time. If the rest of the world operated their businesses the same way, where would we be? Don't even get me started on the interest rates.'

'I had everything planned for today, and now this. It's so infuriating, and it took me three different tries to actually speak to a human,' Emmy said, her hands fidgeting with the gold bangle on her wrist.

Amy, hearing the commotion, popped her head out of the store room. 'What's happened?'

Emmy relayed the issue. 'Just annoying. The dongle got sent to my old address, even though it's no longer on the system as far as I can see. I changed everything on the day we moved. I'm going to have to go over there. I really want to get it sorted before it gets sent somewhere else. I'll head over to the old place, get the dongle, and be back in no time.'

Tom, who had been fixing the flower installation, walked in, wiping his hands on a cloth. 'I've got to go over that way at some point this week. I'll drive if you like.'

Emmy smiled. 'Sorted.'

Amy clapped her hands. 'I'll have a surprise when you get back.'

Emmy tilted her head. 'A surprise? What kind of surprise?'

Amy beamed, pushing Emmy and Tom towards the door. 'Go! The sooner you leave, the sooner you'll find out.'

'Ames, you've done enough already.'

'It's nothing major. Just go.'

Twenty minutes later, Tom and Emmy were on the ferry and on their way. Tom turned on the radio, and an old tune played. Emmy laughed as Tom began to belt out the lyrics. 'Got to love a bit of Rick Astley.'

'Never gonna give you up,' Tom sang and laughed, tapping his fingers on the steering wheel.

Once they were nearer to Emmy's old house, she directed Tom as they pulled off the dual-carriageway, sat in traffic for a bit, queued at some lights and finally turned into her old road. 'Ahh, that corner shop got me out of a few dinner spots.'

'It seems weird to think you lived here and not on Darling.'

Emmy chuckled. 'Yep, it does to me, too. I really have settled into Darling life.'

As they neared the old address, Emmy felt a gigantic pang of nostalgia. The little row of cottages with their squat, front walls and tiny patches of garden brought back so many memories. Emmy remembered walking Callum to primary school, parking in the same spot and all sorts. Tom parked the car, and they made their way to the front door of the cottage Emmy had rented for years. She rang the bell and stepped back. A woman with curly grey hair greeted them.

'Hello. Sorry to bother you. I used to live here, and a parcel was mistakenly delivered here.'

The woman turned around. 'Ahh, yes. Bardot?'

'Yep.' Emmy noticed how a few things had changed, but most of it remained familiar. She could see into the living room, which still had the same wooden floor, but the old fireplace was now adorned with framed photos, there was a pair of slippers neatly placed by the door, and a little cat sat in the window.

Emmy took the parcel and said thanks as emotion smashed into her like a tidal wave. Once back in the car, she stared out at the cottage.

Tom reached over and put his hand on her leg. 'You okay?'

'Yeah, yeah, sorry, I'm fine.' She shook her head.

'Sure?'

'Yep. It just feels really weird to be back here. *Really* weird.'

'I bet. You had a lot going on here.'

Emmy nodded. 'I did. It's not just that, though.'

'Right, what then?'

Emmy flicked her hand between the two of them. 'Me and you.'

'What about us?'

'It feels strange that I was here without you.'

'I get it.' Tom nodded.

The car went silent for quite a while as Tom navigated back through the traffic. Emmy was lost in thought, and before she knew it, they were back on the ferry. Tom rested his hand on Emmy's leg. 'Good? You're miles away.'

Emmy smiled. 'Ahh, I don't know. Just thinking about everything that's happened...'

Tom leaned over. 'Same.'

Emmy pointed to the water. 'The water and the ferry make you feel better though, don't they?'

'Every single time.'

'It's like you get on and you feel different, or am I losing the plot?'

'Agree.' Tom nodded.

'It's like Darling welcomes you home.'

Tom chuckled. 'Getting soppy on me?'

Emmy nudged him. 'It's true. Darling has got into my blood. Yep.' Emmy nodded and peered out the window where the hazy blue seemed to go on forever. 'Glad to call this home now.'

'Not half as much as I'm glad you're here.'

Emmy felt her insides turn nuclear. 'Thanks.'

A rriving back at the shop, Amy was sitting with Bob in the backyard, drinking tea. 'How was it?'

'Fine.' Emmy wiggled the white envelope with the dongle in front of her. 'Safe and sound. It was weird going back there. I didn't expect to feel the way I did.'

'I bet,' Bob said. 'Full of memories.'

'Yep.'

'Now you're making new ones.' Amy smiled.

'I am.'

'Right, ready for your surprise?' Amy asked. 'I feel I might have oversold it a bit.' She jumped up from her seat. 'Follow me.'

Emmy frowned as she trailed behind Amy to the top room, across the floorboards, down the funny little step, and into the en suite bathroom. She gasped and put her hands to her cheeks as she walked in. 'What? Goodness!'

Amy nodded. 'Mum sorted all the stuff. You know what she's like, always in charge of us. A complete control freak. She instructed me as to what to do. I just put it all in place.'

Emmy was speechless as she looked around. A brushed brass towel rail was on the wall, with matching hooks on the back of the door. Emmy had painted the cladding when she'd moved in and blitzed the bath but not got a lot further. Now, the bath and sink were showing off brushed brass taps, a stack of plush white bath sheets were on a little side table, a toothbrush pot and toilet roll holder matched the taps, and a thick fabric blind was at the window.

Tom leaned in from the door. 'Wow. What a change.'

Amy raised her eyebrows. 'Bit better than those towels you had, Ems. They were grey and threadbare. You had them for years.'

Emmy smiled. 'They were. This is perfect. Thank you. Gosh, I won't know what to do with myself.'

'It was mostly Mum, and good job Dad is handy. He had those taps in place in no time.'

'I'll text her now,' Emmy said, slipping her phone out of her pocket. 'Shame she's not here.'

'Golf comes before everything.' Amy laughed.

Emmy peered in the beautiful antique mirror hanging on the wall after she hit send on a text to her mum. The same new

Emmy smile that had been around was making itself known. She hadn't known this Emmy while she was in the cottage. She did know she liked being friends with her very much. Her family had again come up trumps, and despite thinking that things were going to mess up in her world, it seemed that this time that wasn't going to happen after all.

11

A few days or so later, Emmy was back on the ferry, but this time without Tom and without a car. She shook her head back and forth as she stood in the foot passenger section, leaning over the barrier and looking down at the Darling estuary. The water stretched out beneath her, the shifting colours reflecting the sky. She did a little sigh of pleasure; the changing colours of Darling were one of the things Emmy loved about living on the island. Every day seemed to bring yet another hue of blue or another blend of white from low-lying fog.

Emmy stood just taking it all in as the estuary dappled with shimmers and the sun peeked in and out through moving clouds. She peered down at a couple of birds diving into the water and, every now and then, spotted the arc of a fish or a ripple suggesting something just beneath the surface. As she held her face up to a brisk breeze coming in off the sea and tiny droplets of moisture were in the air, the ferry's engine rumbled beneath her feet and started to make its way to the other side. The ferry itself was another Darling thing she'd come to love. When she'd first moved in, she'd been concerned that the ferry would be tiresome after a long day. What had actually happened was that getting on the ferry, whether on the way home or leaving to get to the other side, was a lovely way to start or finish any journey.

Like before, Emmy was on another journey to go and collect something – a goose chase to collect a cricket helmet for Callum. After discussions with Bob, Kevin, and Tom, she'd decided the quickest way was to go by public transport and take the train as it was a fair way away with notorious traffic spots along the route. She tutted to herself at yet another thing for cricket and let the sounds of the ferry wash over her – the waves against the hull, the seagulls overhead, and the clanging of the chains.

Her phone buzzed with a call from Tom. 'Hey.'

'Hi. How are you?'

Emmy sighed. 'Good. Just annoyed. I can't believe I have to pick up that cricket helmet for Callum from the specialist shop. Of all the times, it had to be today.'

'Yeah, annoying that they couldn't just send it express. It might save his head, so there is that.'

'I know, but why does it have to be from a specialist shop? Everything with cricket is just so blooming expensive and inconvenient. Sorry, I shouldn't whinge. Anyway, I'm going to do Love Emmy x stuff on the train, so at least I'm killing two birds with one stone.'

'Thank goodness for technology, eh?' Tom noted.

'I needed this trip like a hole in the head. It's totally in the opposite direction. Thank goodness for the train, it's much more direct going this way. I have so many mounting to-dos it's untrue.'

'It could be worse. You could be doing a double shift too.'

'True, but buying a cricket helmet hardly qualifies as my idea of fun on my day off,' Emmy shot back and laughed.

'Get a nice coffee, and before you know it, you'll be there.'

'Yeah. When did you become the giver of advice?' Emmy joked.

Tom chuckled. 'Must be the company I keep.'

Emmy looked out over the view as she held her phone to her ear. 'At least I get to be on the floating bridge. There really is something calming about this ferry ride. I was just thinking about how nice it is. Watching the water, feeling the wind. As we said the other day, it's therapeutic.'

'Yep. Even when you're cranky about going on goose chases, it helps.'

Emmy laughed back. 'It really does.'

'Okay, I'll love you and leave you. Happy cricket helmet hunting. See you later.'

About an hour or so later, Emmy was sitting on the train. With the blue velour train seat behind her and a coffee in her hand, she was replying to emails on her phone as the train trundled along. The countryside zipped by the window, and her thoughts were consumed with all things Love Emmy x and the mission to collect the cricket helmet for Callum. She pondered the lengths parents went to for their children and shook her head as the train started to decelerate, indicating that they were pulling into a station. Dropping her phone to her lap for a second, her gaze settled on the people bustling about on the platform. A sea of faces went past the window; a man in a reflective cycling jersey stood with a bike poised, and a woman with a pram was waiting for the train to stop and doors to open. Just as the train was pulling to a stop, Emmy nearly dropped her coffee at the sight of a face she knew. Her whole body felt as if it was shaking. She frowned, squinted, edged her nose closer to the window, and craned her neck backwards as the train inched past. There was no way she'd forget that face. Her sister Katy was walking down the other side of the platform.

The years had made Katy look older, and her hair was long, but she was unmistakable. She was smartly dressed and was walking alongside a similarly dressed woman, laughing at something the woman had said. A blast of emotions surged through Emmy. Surprise. Sadness. Regret. Nostalgia. The weight of absent years whacked her on the back of the head. Her heart rate quickened, and her palms turned clammy. Without thinking, she quickly grabbed her bag, and just as the train halted, she pushed the door button, waited for the beep, and then stepped onto the platform. For a minute, she just stood where she was, looking up and down. She had no idea what to do. She didn't know if she wanted to approach Katy or what. She was *so* shocked, and the sighting had been *so* unexpected, she almost stumbled as she got in the way of someone getting off the train.

Stepping forward and taking a moment, Emmy sort of loitered by a temporary passenger information sign and tried to slow her racing heart. She squinted down the platform where Katy was clearly heading for the stairs. She watched as Katy threw her head back and laughed. Emmy felt her heart jump to her mouth as Katy's fine, baby blonde hair caught in the wind.

Emmy whipped out her phone to call Amy, changed her mind, and started to walk along the platform towards the stairs. She was torn about what to do and clutched her bag tighter. She felt as if her legs were propelling her along the platform without her really being in charge. A torrent of memories flooded through Emmy's mind as Katy reached the top of the stairs, stopped for a second, said goodbye to the other woman, and turned left. Emmy's mind raced. Memories of Katy's drug taking rushed in and out of her head. All Emmy could see was the look on her mum's face when they'd all made the decision to no longer enable Katy, and it had all gone very downhill from there.

Cherry had always said that she'd help Katy, and she'd tried, but in the end, they'd decided as a family that Katy was in danger and the drug-taking had to stop. Katy hadn't been happy with that; there had been a massive fight, Katy had left, and the family had been broken ever since. Katy had wanted nothing to do with them when the family would no longer enable her habit. It had been Amy who had been the most affected by Katy's ghosting. Emmy remembered the countless nights she'd listened to Amy trying to offer some comfort.

Emmy's train of thought was broken by the distant sound of the announcement for the next train as she tapped her card on the gate pad and followed Katy out of the station. Wondering what on earth she was doing, she just kept trailing behind as a million emotions slammed through her head at the same time. Thoughts of Cherry and Amy popped into her mind as Emmy wondered what to do. Would Cherry want her to approach Katy? None of them had seen her or heard from her for years.

Emmy closed her eyes and took a deep breath. As she kept a discreet distance, she thought about her mum's face, of Amy's upset, and her dad's sort of sad resignation. In a trail of commuters, she kept her focus trained on her sister's silhouette, her heart beating so fast she felt as if it was in her mouth. Katy's hair was much longer than the last time Emmy had seen her. It reminded Emmy how the three of them used to sit on the bed, combing each other's hair and trying out different hairstyles. Emmy squinted as Katy moved. Something was different. She seemed to be straighter, more measured somehow. Was her posture more upright? At one point, Katy paused at a small coffee shop and spoke to someone who was standing with a bucket and squeegee cleaning the windows.

For a few minutes, Emmy contemplated turning around and going back to the train station. Another part of her wanted to rush across the road, but something held her back. Instead, she watched as Katy seemed quite jovial with the woman at the coffee shop. She remembered how Katy had taken their mum's credit card. All the lies. All the upset.

Emmy continued to walk at the same pace as Katy on the other side of the road, lost in her thoughts, unsure if what she was doing was even legal, let alone a good idea. Watching Katy's familiar body language was like a strange, upsetting stroll down memory lane, with memories flooding back at every turn.

After what felt like hours but was, in reality, probably only a few minutes, Katy made a left turn and quickened her pace. Emmy felt her heart tug as she watched from a distance as Katy approached the brightly painted façade of a childcare centre. The building, wrapped in sunny yellows and bright blues, was hard to miss in the street. The double front door was painted a bright blue, and a small playground area held a slide and sand-pit. Giggles and laughter echoed across the road as children ran around, swung on the swings, and clambered up the slides.

Emmy's eyes darted to the sign at the entrance: 'Little Dreamers Childcare - Where Children Flourish.' As Katy entered, Emmy squeezed her eyes together as it dawned on her that Katy had a child. Her stomach turned over and over at the thought of her mum and dad not knowing they had a grand-child. At Amy's children and Callum having a cousin.

A pang of emotion hit Emmy like a train, and an over-whelming mix of bewilderment and curiosity zipped up and down her veins. She wondered if Katy's child was one of the ones running around giggling. The thought of a niece or nephew she hadn't met made Emmy's heart ache. Emmy stood rooted to the spot on the far side of the street, just staring as if something unbelievable was unfolding in front of her eyes. She jumped as a man peered at her, and she realised she was blocking his way. She shook her head and moved to her right. 'Sorry.'

'You alright, love? Do you need a hand?'

Emmy blinked. 'Yes, no, sorry, thanks.'

'Sure? You look like you've seen a ghost.'

'Yes, thanks, I'm fine. Just got a lot on my mind.'

'No worries.'

As the man walked past, Emmy looked back over the road where Katy had disappeared into the brightly coloured building. Thoughts swirled in her mind. Why hadn't Katy reached out? Emmy felt nauseous at what she'd learned. She was now unwittingly in the knowledge of something she wasn't sure how to deal with. Part of her somehow wished she didn't know. She leaned against a nearby tree, taking in deep breaths, and tried to calm her racing heart. Emmy's turmoil heightened as Katy seemed to be inside for a long time.

For a few minutes, it dawned on her that perhaps Katy worked in the childcare centre. Just as she was thinking that and still partially concealed behind a tree, the door suddenly opened. Emmy gasped as Katy emerged from the childcare centre, clutching a tiny hand. The little girl and the sight of Katy with her took Emmy's breath away. The tiny tot was the spitting image of Katy, with a froth of blonde hair pulled into bunches on either side of her head. She was wearing a pale pink T-shirt, a white tutu skirt, stripy tights, and bright yellow wellies. The sight made Emmy smile, and her heart clenched. The resemblance was uncanny. The little girl mirrored Katy. Emmy shook her head over and over again. She had a niece. The revelation was staggering.

Not sure whether or not she was doing the right thing, Emmy discreetly trailed them, her insides in absolute turmoil. She took in the way Katy brushed a stray hair from the little girl's face, the way the two of them were clearly chatting as they walked along. Emmy felt as if her heart was breaking in two.

Katy and the little girl then turned into a quaint street with long lines of huge old terraced Victorian villas on either side.

The houses were old but well-maintained, with trimmed hedges and blooming flower beds. Emmy watched as they approached one of the larger houses with a set of steps up to a pale blue front door. Katy bent down, sharing a few words with the little girl, then lifted her up, swinging her into the air, eliciting giggles that floated down the street. Emmy's heart ached as she watched. She wondered about their life as Katy unlatched an iron gate, walked up the steps to the front door, pushed a button on the left, and walked in. Emmy's brain felt as if it had exploded. How had Katy managed? Who was the father? All the questions zoomed in and out of her mind.

After Katy and her daughter disappeared into the house and the blue door closed behind them, Emmy felt her world pause for a moment. She was rooted to the spot, honing in on the blue front door and flooded with a deluge of emotions. Regret, anger, hope, and sadness washed over her in waves. She thought about Cherry and the rift that had kept the sisters apart. Cherry had lost out on years with her granddaughter, years they could never get back.

Taking a deep breath, Emmy shook her head over and over again, not having a clue what to do. She did know that this was going to rock her world. Her life had been going so well but here it was - the thing that was going to mess everything up.

E mmy found herself walking aimlessly away. In a daze, her brain tried to decipher what she'd just seen, but it couldn't quite work it out. The weight of it felt as if it had landed on her head with a thud. The sight of Katy, whom she hadn't seen or spoken to in years, was shocking enough. But to discover Katy had a daughter left her breathless and all out of sorts. As she stepped back along the pavement in the direction of the train station, she could still see the image of the little girl who looked so much like Katy in the front of her mind, blonde bunches bouncing with every step, the cute little tutu, the odd combination of tights and wellies in the sunshine. Emmy's brain swirled at the thought of her mum having missed out on the birth, the Christmases, the family moments. She reeled and winced at what Amy was going to say and do when she was told. The thought of Amy finding out made Emmy feel physically sick.

Feeling the urge to sit, Emmy found a nearby bench and just sat and stared; the world around her continued its hustle and bustle whilst she felt as if the whole planet had stopped turning. Emmy's world had changed the moment she saw Katy through the train window. It was now distant, muted, and nothing felt quite right. It was as if someone had slotted a thick pane of frosted glass in front of her eyes, and everything around her was not quite in focus. She shook her head, trying to make sense of what she'd seen as noises around her continued on their merry way; the distant chime of a church bell, a plane droning above, and an engine from a van with its door open swirled around her head. None of it felt quite real.

Putting her face in her hands, she wondered what in the name of goodness she was going to do. She felt her grandma Emily's ring on her right hand and silently asked Emily for advice. Emily didn't reply. As Emmy thought about calling Amy, her eyes welled up. This was going to open up a whole can of worms. She felt a mixture of anger, sadness, and regret at Katy. How could Katy have had a baby and not told Cherry and Bob? All manner of questions swirled: who was the father, what was the little girl called, how had the birth been, was Katy okay?

Leaning back on the bench and looking up at the sky, she pondered what had happened with Katy. Her mind swirled around what had got them to the point where Cherry, Bob, Emmy, and Amy had decided the only way to help Katy was tough love. It hadn't ended well. Not at all. Ugly, sad, and distressing. Emmy's mind replayed the arguments, the disagreements, the hurtful words. Katy had just taken off and subsequently disappeared. None of it had been pretty. It had all been so very sad.

Closing her eyes, Emmy thought for a second that maybe the little girl wasn't Katy's at all. Then she shook her head at herself. The resemblance had taken her breath away. The hair, the way they moved, the general aura. Like two peas in a pod.

Emmy thought about the little girl, wondered what her name was, and frowned at the thought that she deserved to know her family. She screwed her eyes up and shook her head over and over again. There was no way she could sit on the knowledge. She was going to have to *do* something, no matter how uncomfortable it was or what the outcomes would be.

Gathering her bits from the bench, Emmy pondered so many things at once it felt as if her brain was going to explode. There were loads of wounds, horrible stuff that had happened, and years to catch up on. As she walked in a daze towards the train station, she was totally at a loss for what to do next. She did know it wasn't going to be an easy ride. More, the whole of it made her feel sick to her core.

12

Later, Emmy's mind raced as she sat on the train next to Callum's cricket helmet. She stared blankly out the window, replaying the encounter with Katy like a little line of Instagram stories in her head. The story flicked from first seeing Katy on the platform, to hurrying off the train, to following her out of the station and trailing her along the road. Little fifteen-second snatches of Katy's life. The same Katy she hadn't seen or spoken to in years. Katy, who now had a daughter Emmy never even knew existed.

Emmy's heart ached as she pictured the little girl with her blonde bunches, happily clutching Katy's hand. Emmy had a niece she'd never met. Emmy couldn't quite wrap her head around it all. How was Katy – unreliable, troubled, headstrong Katy – now a mum? Emmy supposed she shouldn't be surprised. She now knew nothing about Katy, and it had been a long time. Maybe the tough love had worked? Maybe Katy had finally got her life together. The shock of it, though, still coursed through Emmy's veins.

And why hadn't Katy reached out about the child? Their mum, Cherry, was now a grandmother to another child and had missed this little girl's entire life. Katy clearly still harboured resentment towards the family for stopping enabling her behaviour. After everything that had happened, Katy was obviously still upset. Emmy's turmoil heightened as she considered Cherry. Cherry had only ever wanted the best for all her daughters and had sacrificed loads for them. Emmy shook her head back and forth and winced at the information she had, not only about Katy's whereabouts but about the little girl. The news would, without a doubt, upset the apple cart. Emmy wondered if she should even tell her mum and Amy at all.

She leant her head back on the train seat and closed her eyes. Could she keep such a monumental secret? Could she look Cherry in the eyes and pretend she knew nothing? The very thought made Emmy's stomach turn. Her mind spun with the possibilities as the train rumbled along. Maybe Katy would eventually reach out herself and reunite with their family. Maybe the chance sighting was the beginning of fate doing its thing. Perhaps it was a sign that the time was right to reconcile. Emmy desperately hoped so. Her heart broke picturing Callum and Amy's children, all growing up without knowing their cousin.

As the train slowed down, Emmy shook her head, still bewildered by it all. She knew a couple of things for certain: she was glad she hadn't acted hastily and phoned Amy right away, and she needed to process her emotions before making any sudden decisions. This news would change everything. It wasn't going to come without complications.

Twenty or so minutes later, she was stepping onto the Pride of Darling ferry. She took a deep breath of the salty air as the rhythmic hum of the engine and now familiar ferry ride home made her feel a *tiny* bit better. Emmy needed Darling's coastline to soften her jagged nerves. She tried to let the view clear her cluttered thoughts as she stood lost in a world of her own. Trying to push aside thoughts of Katy, she took in the scene; a few skinny clouds floated overhead, and a group of seagulls circled, one or two occasionally diving for scraps. The fresh, briny Darling scent filled her nose, and Emmy felt her shoulders relax ever-so-slightly. Settling into her usual spot at the front of the ferry, Emmy leaned over the railing, letting the brisk air wash over her. The humming motor and churning water didn't exactly do a lot, but it did make her feel as if she was home. She tried to focus on the rhythmic sounds and the island scenery coming into sight. But despite the ferry, Emmy's mind spiralled back to Katy.

She thought back to when the situation with Katy had all come to a head. Katy's behaviour had slowly begun to get worse and worse over time, she had lied more or less all the time, and had generally gone downhill fast. She'd lied about where she was going and who she was spending time with, and she'd taken Cherry's credit card. On top of that were the mood swings, aggressive behaviour, and secrecy. The worst thing about it all was how it had all escalated so quickly. Every attempt Cherry, Amy and Emmy had made to help had been met with hostility and denials from Katy until the terrible night when Katy came home high, incoherent, and aggressive and went for Cherry.

Emmy shook her head as if trying to shake the memories loose and sighed, gripping the railing tightly. After everything their family had been through, and how devastated Cherry had been, Emmy wasn't sure about anything. Underneath the shock, she also wasn't sure if she should do anything at all. There was so much to think about: the pain, the estrangement, the child.

She pictured Katy with the little girl in the wellies. Both of them seemed happy and healthy. It sparked the tiniest flicker of hope in Emmy's heart. Maybe there was a sliver of possibility of healing and mending what had been broken. Maybe Katy was better.

As the ferry reached Darling, Emmy disembarked slowly, as if the weight on her shoulders was physically weighing her down. Trudging up the back lane towards the rear of The Old Ticket Office, feeling conflicted and confused as the building glowed in the evening light, she thanked her lucky stars that she now had her own flat. She was beyond grateful she was home. She needed to get inside and decompress. With the box with the cricket helmet hooked over her left arm as Emmy unlocked the back door, she shook her head and had a feeling she would need Darling in the days ahead. She stepped inside and heaved her way up the stairs to the flat. Emotionally exhausted and physically drained from the day's events, she slipped off her shoes, hung her bag on a hook, flicked on the kettle in the kitchen, and forced herself to take a few deep breaths.

As she inhaled and exhaled and listened to the noise from the kettle, the more she thought about it, the more she realised it would be better not to act in haste. She wouldn't do anything yet. She'd muse it for a while and sleep on it. Tomorrow, she would maybe tell Amy. The feelings felt so odd she couldn't process them all at once, raw and fresh with a mix of happiness at seeing Katy along with ugly, sad, horrible regret.

As if Amy had heard her thoughts, Emmy's phone vibrated with an incoming call. The caller ID flashed 'Amy' with a heart emoji next to it. Emmy drew in a breath. The timing was uncanny. Amy had some sort of sixth sense around a lot of things. Emmy was now going to have to lie.

'Hey,' Emmy greeted, trying to keep her voice even.

'Hi! Was just thinking about you. Are your ears burning? Everything okay?' Amy asked.

Emmy's voice was unnaturally bright. 'Yep. Fine!'

'Did you get the cricket helmet, okay? How did all that go? How was the goose chase?' Amy laughed at her little joke.

'I did, yes! All done and dusted.' Emmy's voice was so high in her effort to be happy it came out forced, like an odd sort of chirp.

'Errr, what's wrong?'

'No, no. Nothing's wrong at all. I'm fine.'

'You sure? You sound off?' Amy probed. 'Really quite off.'

Emmy forced a laugh. 'Just one of those days, you know? Busy with work and everything too.'

There was a slight pause on the other end. 'If you say so, but you don't sound right. Are you sure you're okay?'

'I'm fine,' Emmy replied, brushing Amy off but feeling a rush of guilt for not sharing what had happened on the train.

Emmy breathed an inward sigh of relief that Amy didn't continue to ask her if something was up, and they chatted about their respective days: Callum's cricket and Cherry's latest golf escapades. Throughout the conversation, Emmy's thoughts kept drifting back to the train platform, to Katy, to the little girl with the blonde bunches. All the while Amy yabbered on and on, whilst a movie trailer of Katy wouldn't stop playing in Emmy's head.

Emmy plopped a couple of teabags into the teapot and poured boiling water in as she listened to Amy telling her how Amy's neighbour had been bitten by a dangerous dog at the park. She tried to keep her mind on the conversation and was brought back when she heard Amy say she was going to have to go.

'See you, Ems. You seem distant. Sure you're okay?'

'Yep. I'm just tired. I need an early night.'

'Righto. Speak tomorrow then.'

'Yeah. See you later.'

After pressing the button to end the call, Emmy let out a deep sigh. The sighting of Katy felt like a weight on her chest. To add to that, now she felt not only all over the place, but guilty that she hadn't told Amy too. The deceit had begun. She needed time to figure out what to do next. She glanced at her reflection in the mirror in the hallway as she walked towards the sitting room with her mug of tea in hand. What looked back did not look good in any shape or form; her eyes looked odd, questions swirled around her head, and her face seemed grey with the uncertainty of what to do next.

Emmy leaned back into the sofa with her mug of tea in her right hand as images from the day played out in her mind. It was not the image of Katy that had thrown her the most; it was the tiny hand that had clasped onto Katy's. The thought was jarring, as if everything was upside down. Closing her eyes, Emmy remembered how furious Katy had been with Amy, who had been the one to find out about the credit card. Time had blurred the specifics, but the sting of it all remained. They had been close, all of them, with not long separating their ages, but Katy's actions had put a spanner in the works.

Emmy's train of thought moved to the blonde bunches, the sparkly tutu, the funny little wellies. Emmy went over and over the dilemma: should she tell Amy and Cherry? The three of them had been a tight-knit unit after Katy's departure, and they all felt Katy's absence differently. To Cherry, it was pain bordering on despair, for Amy, it was the anguish of a missing piece, and for Emmy, it was the gaping hole left in the family unit. On top of all of that was Bob.

Emmy visualised the scene of telling Cherry. A little part of Emmy wondered about burying what she'd seen. Did she really want to open old wounds and bring up more misunderstandings? They had built a fragile peace over the years, and Emmy wasn't too sure about shattering it. Then of course, there was Katy. What if Katy didn't want to reconnect? What if she wanted her new life with her daughter to remain a secret? So many questions. No idea what to do.

13

It was a few days or so after Emmy had seen Katy, and Emmy's world had tilted on its axis. She hung in the middle of nowhere with no clue as to what to do. Emmy hadn't been able to make a decision about what was for the best, so she'd done absolutely nothing. She was at the beach with Tom gazing at the sea, watching the waves crash and ebb along the shoreline, with her head full of the dilemma of what she was going to do. A breeze whipped strands of hair across her face as she stood with her feet in the water and let her eyes get lost in the horizon. Tom skipped a stone across the water. It bounced over and over before disappearing under the surface.

'Good one,' Emmy said absently, lost mostly in a world of her own. She tried to focus on the present moment, on the beach and on Tom, but kept finding herself drifting off. All she could think about was Katy and the little girl in the wellies.

She hadn't told a soul about what she'd seen, and a few nights of sleep hadn't done what she'd hoped. In fact, there hadn't been much sleep going on at all. She'd spent hours tossing and turning in bed in a complete dilemma. Her main problem with the whole situation was that she didn't feel right to drop such a bombshell until she'd had a chance to process it herself. Then there was Katy to think about. So with everyone around her, Emmy had kept up a façade of normalcy when she'd felt far from normal. She'd thrown herself into work, shop preparation, and ferrying Callum to and from cricket practice. All the while, questions had constantly churned in her mind.

Tom skipped another smooth stone. 'You're a lot better at that than me,' Emmy noted.

Tom leaned down and picked up a flat stone. 'It's all about the one you choose,' he said as he handed it to Emmy. Emmy gripped the stone and made a half-hearted attempt to look interested. She couldn't really have cared less about the stone or choosing one. She felt so detached from Tom it was as if he wasn't really there.

'You have to get the angle just right and snap your wrist,' Tom instructed.

Emmy attempted the motion half-heartedly. The stone plopped into the water, sinking instantly. She watched the ripples on the top of the water. 'Yeah, not my skill set.' Emmy shrugged, her eyes drifting back to the horizon. She didn't give a stuff about the stupid stone. She pictured herself back on the train, glimpsing Katy again. Her niece's little tutu and tiny wellies.

'Ems, is everything okay?' Tom asked and squeezed Emmy's shoulder. 'You've seemed a bit off-colour the last few days. You seem away with the fairies.'

'Hmm?' Emmy turned toward him. She hadn't heard the question.

Tom's eyes were full of concern. 'You've not been yourself. Do you think you've got that virus you said was taking people down at your work? You've been quite odd.'

Emmy's first instinct was to downplay it all. She'd become an expert at putting on a brave face over the years. On the other hand, she was tempted to blurt the whole thing out to Tom, but telling him before her mum and sister would make her feel even more guilty than she already did. 'Sorry, just a bit distracted,' she said vaguely. 'Lots of things to do with Love Emmy x. Callum's been so busy with cricket these last few weeks. Yeah, sorry. Just got a lot on.'

It wasn't a total lie. She *did* have a lot on, but compared to the fact that she'd seen her sister, those things were nothing. Little things with Love Emmy and cricket paled in comparison to the sighting of her sister.

Tom searched her face as if sensing there was more. But he didn't push it. 'I get it. Life pulls us all over the show sometimes, eh?' He slid his arm around her shoulders.

Emmy leaned her head into Tom. He'd picked up on her strange, distant mood right away. How nice and odd at the same time. It had been a long time since Emmy had had a partner in her corner. She considered for a split second going through everything with Tom. There was no way she was going to tell him yet, though. It felt way too big to tell him before her family. For a few minutes, they just stood watching the waves wash in and out, a fizz of bubbles around their ankles and a salty spray on their faces.

Emmy looked along the shoreline. 'Let's walk for a bit.'

Still with a jumbled head and a queasy stomach, they strolled along, holding hands. Emmy loved being with Tom. She'd never been happier, but just as always seemed to happen in her life, something was always around the corner. Her life always, always, *always* messed up. She scooped up a tiny seashell with a pearly sheen and put it in her pocket, and then held up her face up to the sky. 'What a lovely day.'

'Yep. The air does wonders.'

Emmy wished the air would do wonders to clear up her conundrum. She'd need more than a walk on the beach and a bit of salty air to do that. Threading her arm through Tom's, she tried not to think about it. As they walked back up towards the car, she answered a text from Callum and noted that there was another call notification on her screen from her mum. Tom frowned. 'Aren't you going to listen to your messages?'

Emmy nodded. 'I've missed Mum's last few calls.'

'That's not like you. You three are on the phone twenty-four seven usually.'

Emmy swallowed. Was it really that obvious? She blinked rapidly. 'Yeah.' She pressed the message to listen to her mum's message.

'Hi, darling, it's Mum again...' Cherry's voice stated. 'You must be busy with the shop. Just checking in with you. Send me a text when you can. Love you.'

The message ended with a beep, and Emmy felt guilt engulf her whole body. The secrecy was eating away at her. As she brushed sand off her feet and put her trainers back on, she pressed her lips together. She was going to have to go back and find Katy and do something before push came to shove. She would have to speak to Katy and see what was what. The only question was – would Katy want to see her too?

14

The shrill beep of Emmy's phone alarm jolted her awake. She jabbed at her phone to silence it quickly, not wanting to disturb Callum in his room below. As she rubbed the sleep from her eyes and thought about her upcoming day, she faced a double shift at the port, which pleased her immensely. At least at work, her brain would be so focused on a plethora of problems and issues that it wouldn't have time to constantly worry about the Katy thing. Things were grim when a double shift looked attractive, that she knew for a fact.

She hauled herself out of bed, twisted her hair up into a knot on the top of her head, and made her way to the bathroom. After showering and scrubbing her face, she said a silent thank you for the well-honed routine she did without thinking; her uniform was ironed and ready to go, allowing her to mindlessly pull on sheer tights, a pressed white shirt, her navy skirt, and the uniform scarf. Still half asleep, she braided her hair into a low chignon and tied the scarf just so. As she padded down the stairs, she mentally ensured that her uniform jacket was hanging in the back of her car, her spare work bag was in the boot just in case and her makeup bag was under the front seat.

Grabbing her Thermos cup from the kitchen and a breakfast muffin, she tiptoed quietly out of the house, and via a foggy yard, made her way to her car.

There was one thing Emmy loved about the very early morning commutes via the ferry, and that was the fact that it gave her time to think. She most definitely had a lot of thinking to do as she crossed over the estuary. There was only one thing front and centre of her mind – Katy and her little girl.

As she watched the early morning goings-on of the ferry, time ticked on, and the rest of the commute was uneventful. With her brain churning over, she tried to placate it with sips of coffee and little bites of her muffin. Having mulled over the Katy situation most of the way to the port, she parked in her usual spot and walked briskly to the staff entrance. Once inside the staff area, she stowed her things and made her way to the briefing room. Judy, her supervisor, was already there, reviewing the day's roster.

'Morning, Ems,' Judy greeted with a wide smile.

'Morning.'

'How were the roads?'

'Too easy this morning, despite the fog,' Emmy noted. 'There's no rhyme or reason to it some days. I thought the fog would be a nightmare.'

'Good. Yeah, same my end.'

'Long may it last.'

'What have you been up to? How's the shop coming along?'

'Good, thanks.' Emmy kept her tone even. 'Just finalising all the last few things.'

They made small talk about the shop's opening day and when it might be and the new members of staff Judy was interviewing. Emmy nodded along, watching the clock, ready to get out on the floor and lose herself in the monotony of her day. Judy held the door open for her, and they chatted and made their way to the checkpoints. Showtime would take her mind off her dilemma.

Judy frowned and touched Emmy on the arm. 'You okay?'

Emmy forced her voice to be bright. 'Yep, fine.'

'You seem a bit off. That virus is going around like wildfire. Hope you're not coming down with it too. It sounds nasty.'

Emmy knew what was wrong with her. It certainly wasn't a virus. She wished she'd been struck down with a virus rather than having to deal with what was currently going around and around her head. 'Hopefully I haven't got it coming.'

'No. You don't seem right, though. Hope you're okay.'

The morning stretched on in the regular busy blur of boarding problems and customer issues. By midday, Emmy's feet were aching, the small of her back pinched, and her radio constantly buzzed as she plastered a smile as the next passengers with a problem shuffled up to her. She bore the brunt of their travel frustrations and snide sighs calmly with one eye on the clock, ready for lunch. By the time she got to the staff canteen, she realised that Katy hadn't crossed her mind since she'd taken up her post. As she stood in the food queue and the place bustled with staff, Emmy nodded hello to familiar faces and tried to stop Katy from getting back into her head.

'Usual?' asked Rachael from behind the counter when Emmy's turn came. 'Or could I tempt you with the special today? Roast turkey sandwich? They're really nice.'

'Goodness. Not sure.' Emmy chuckled. 'I'm not sure if I'm up for decisions as big as that.'

Rachael smiled. 'Creature of habit, you are. Honestly, try one.'

'Oh, go on then. Why not? I'll have the turkey sandwich. Bit strange for this time of year, but yeah. Go me.'

Rachael chuckled as she pulled a plate with a sandwich from the counter and deftly handed it over. 'Thanks, hon.' Rachael was always cheerful, even on the busiest shifts.

Emmy settled at her usual table, raising her eyebrows at Jessie, her friend who sat at the next table most days. As she sat down, checked her phone, sent a message to Callum, and slipped her heels from the back of her shoes, the din of the cafeteria faded into background noise. She picked at the turkey sandwich, thoughts wandering to Katy again. She couldn't stop thinking about her sister's face and the shock at her niece's existence. Emmy sighed, dropping the uneaten half of her sandwich back on the plate.

'Everything alright?' Rachael, who was now clearing empty dishes from the adjacent table, made Emmy look up.

'Oh yes, all good!' Emmy tried to sound upbeat. 'Just tired, you know. One of those days.'

'Didn't like the sandwich?'

'Oh, no, it's lovely. Just not in the mood, you know?'

Rachael nodded sympathetically. 'You seem a bit out of sorts. Everything okay?'

'Yeah, fine.' Emmy managed a small smile whilst thinking inside that she must have a message on her forehead saying that she wasn't really okay. It was sort of nice that people noticed in a way. Rachael squeezed Emmy's shoulder before pushing her trolley away, and then Emmy watched her stop and chat with a woman a few tables along. Emmy shook her head. Clearly, people could tell she had something on her mind. She forced herself to finish the sandwich and stood to clear her tray. At the rubbish bin, she nearly collided with Rachael again.

'Whoops, sorry!' Rachael steadied Emmy's tray. 'Not looking where I'm going.'

'Oops. My fault,' Emmy assured her. 'How's it been in here? How's your day been?'

'Manic! Just trying to keep everyone fed and happy.' Rachael chuckled. 'Surviving your double? You'll be feeling it later.'

Emmy rolled her neck from side to side. 'So far, so good. You know how it gets. I had a man leave his passport in the taxi this morning, and somehow, it was my fault.'

Rachael nodded. 'That I do. Nothing you haven't heard a million times before though, I'm sure.'

'Tell me about it. I've heard it all.'

'How were your days off?'

'Good. You? What did you get up to on your weekend off the other week? You were going to that pub in the country. I meant to ask you the other day.'

'Bit of a turn-up for the books, actually,' Rachael said, scrunching up her lips and nodding her head.

'What was that then?'

'Remember that long-lost uncle I was telling you about? My mum's half-brother.'

Emmy squinted, remembering their conversation vaguely. 'Oh yep, that's right.'

'Well, he turned up. Hadn't seen him in years. Talk about family drama.'

Emmy widened her eyes. 'How did it go? Didn't he do something really bad? You did tell me.'

'Yeah, he did loads of stuff. Anyway, so he turns up at the pub...'

'Right! How was your mum?'

'Surprisingly good,' Rachael said with wide eyes. 'She said the past is the past and that it was time to move forward. Unbelievable, but true. Blow me down with a feather, I never thought I would hear her say that.'

Emmy absorbed Rachael's words for a second whilst thinking about Katy. If only it was that simple. 'I'm glad it went well. Family is so important.'

Rachael gave her arm a pat. 'That it is. Who would have

thought it would go okay, eh? Plus, there was a distinct lack of fireworks. Not that I'm holding my breath.'

'Interesting.'

'Anyway. Best get on before the next lot come in,' Rachael said, and with that, she bustled off to the kitchen. Emmy watched her disappear through the swinging doors, struck by their exchange. As she headed back, Rachael's words echoed in her mind. *The past was the past. Time to move forward.*

Emmy mulled it over as she stood in the terminal in her usual position. Could it really be that simple with Katy? As the rest of her shift flew by in between passengers, she thought of the resemblance between the little girl and Katy and Rachael's words. Maybe it was time for everyone to move forward. The thing was she was going to have to be the one to initiate it all. She really wished it was down to someone else.

15

Much later that day, the glow of Emmy's laptop illuminated her face as she sat curled on the sofa with a cup of chamomile tea in her hand. Callum was long asleep, and the flat was silent except for the occasional creak and groan of the floorboards and pipes, and the odd trundle of a tram going past the window. Emmy took a sip of her tea, hands wrapped around the warm mug, and stared at her laptop screen, wondering about Katy. Putting her tea down, she pulled up Google, took a deep breath, and typed Little Dreamer Childcare into the search bar.

The results popped up instantly, and she clicked on the website. Navigating to the contact page, she popped the address into Google Maps. The subsequent overview shot showed a green, tree-lined street dotted with Victorian homes. She dropped the little man on the street and clicked the button as if she were walking along the pavement, just as she had when she'd followed Katy. Reaching for her tea with her left hand, she continued to click until she got to the road where Katy had turned. Peachwood Road looked nicer than she remembered, though most of that walk had been a bit of a daze. Emmy zoomed in further until she got to the spot where Katy had opened the gate and walked up the steps.

Emmy sat forward and leaned her chin on her left hand. There it was, right on her computer screen, the pale blue door Katy had disappeared through. Emmy studied the white-framed bay windows on either side of the huge door, the wrought-iron railing along the street, and the steps up to the door. Emmy was so close to her screen, it was as if she was standing across from number 44. The photo quality was surprisingly clear and it looked better than she'd thought when she'd been peering from the other side of the road.

Sitting back again and sipping on her tea, she took in the house – well-kept potted plants on the front steps and pretty curtains in the downstairs basement windows, a little black railing holding window boxes full of flowers on the first floor. She peered up at the upper levels and back again and noted the intercom by the front door. Katy obviously lived in one of the flats. Emmy squinted, wishing she could tell which windows were Katy's. She wondered how much one of the flats would cost. Did Katy live there alone?

She panned the image back and took in the whole building. It was homey and nice with lots of shrubs, brass plates on the door, and clean windows. Glancing at the homes on either side, Emmy zoomed in on the windows, imagining her sister and the little girl inside. Were the flower boxes on the sills Katy's? Emmy smiled faintly. Katy had always loved it in their Grandma Emily's garden. Closing her eyes, Emmy could still envision Amy and Katy in Emily's garden when they were little. A lump formed in her throat. She swallowed hard and blinked away the memories. She scanned over 44 Peachwood Road once more, cementing it in her mind, and then jotted the address down in her phone.

For ages, she just sat there staring out the window, watching the fog swirling around the buildings opposite. Then she opened a new tab and typed "Peachwood Road flats to rent." Her pulse quickened as a website popped up, listing rental properties in the area. She filtered to see only Peachwood Road. Several flats appeared, but none with the exact 44 address. She was about to give up when she noticed number 38, a few doors down from the house she'd seen Katy going into. It had been rented recently. Not really sure what she was doing or why she was doing it, she clicked and found photos of the flat's interior. It boasted hardwood floors, a fancy bathroom, and a modernised kitchen. This wasn't some dodgy area with horrible little bedsits not fit for much. The area was clearly nice. It gave Emmy a sense of where Katy was living and how she was doing in life. She peered closer at the listing details, jotting down the name of the property company. Eton Estates.

She sat back against the couch cushions, her mind churning with questions. There was nothing for it; she was going to have to go back to the road and wait for Katy. She glanced at the clock and let out a ginormous sigh. It was nearing midnight, she'd been up before dawn, but she was so far from sleep it wasn't even funny. Gazing around the flat's sitting room, she felt a pang of gratitude; at least she had a place to call her own when things were sticky in her life.

Deciding that she couldn't sit staring and wondering all night, she shut her laptop, tiptoed to Callum's room, and from outside, listened for a moment as she'd been doing for years. She couldn't hear anything or see a light under the door, so proceeded to the stairs to go up to bed. Hopefully, she'd get a tiny bit of sleep.

The next morning, wishy-washy sunlight filtered through the fabric blind at Emmy's window, casting a pattern on the stripped and stained floor. Having tossed and turned all night, Emmy felt far from refreshed. She sat on the edge of the bed for a moment, letting her eyes adjust and thinking about her day. Her stomach flipped over and over in quick, nervous turns as she thought about whether to take the train or drive over to the town where Katy lived.

After a quick shower, she tiptoed past a still-sleeping Callum to the kitchen and made a cup of tea. As she waited for the tea to brew and popped a couple of crumpets into the toaster, her eyes kept drifting to the notebook on the table. The night before, she'd jotted down things she wanted to say to Katy. As she went over what was in the notebook in her head, she tutted. A terrible, clumsy attempt to make sense of the time that had passed and things that had gone on.

Once the crumpets had popped up and she was spreading thick pats of butter on top, she debated whether to leave a note for Katy if their meeting didn't happen. Her mind went back and forth over and over again. She winced as she sat down and reread what she'd written. It sounded both sad and a bit pathetic. In the end, she decided against it. Things were too fragile, and she certainly didn't want stuff written down in black and white. Emmy slipped the notebook into her handbag anyway and just sat wondering what to do.

The crumpets sat half-eaten on the table as Emmy stirred a teaspoon of sugar into her tea. She knew she should eat, but her nerves made the food and tea seem to curdle in her tummy.

Just as she was forcing another bit of crumpet into her mouth, she heard footsteps, then Callum's voice. 'Morning, Mum. Smells good out here.'

Emmy forced a smile and attempted to sound bright as Callum shuffled into the kitchen, hair tousled from sleep. 'Morning. There are fresh crumpets from the bakery. Tea?'

'Yes, please,' Callum said through a yawn. He collapsed into the chair across from Emmy and snagged one of the abandoned crumpets from Emmy's plate.

Emmy bustled about, pouring tea into a mug for Callum and warming it up in the microwave. Her own tea had gone cold, but she took a sip anyway to distract herself. Out of the corner of her eye, she saw Callum eyeing the notebook peeking from her handbag.

'What's that then? New designs for the shop?' he asked. 'You said you were going to get something for the shop today, didn't you?'

Emmy tensed. 'Oh, nothing important. Yeah, I need to pop into town.' She placed Callum's tea in front of him.

'Oh, right. What for? What do you need for the shop?' Callum bit into the crumpet, and crumbs dropped on the table.

Emmy's mind raced. 'Just picking up some samples from a new supplier,' she lied. 'Boring stuff, really.' She brushed the crumbs away, avoiding Callum's gaze.

Callum reached for another crumpet. 'Cool. Need any help?'

'No, no,' Emmy said quickly. 'I won't be long. Want me to pick up anything on the way back?'

Callum tore the crumpet in half thoughtfully. 'We're almost out of crisps. And I think I used the last of the fish fingers the other night.'

Emmy chuckled. 'Noted. I'll stock up. We wouldn't want you to run out of fish fingers, would we?' Emmy sighed inwardly with relief at the deflection. At least Callum wasn't noticing her lies.

They chatted about Callum's cricket schedule as Callum made short work of the crumpets. Emmy nodded along, making the appropriate comments. Her mind, though, wasn't that interested in cricket training and her thoughts kept drifting to where she was going. Just as she was thinking about making a move, there was the sound of someone coming in the back door. Emmy frowned at Callum.

Callum jerked his thumb towards the stairs and then to his phone. 'Tom. I just messaged him.'

'Oh, right, okay.'

Before Emmy could think much about that, Tom appeared. 'Morning,' Tom said briskly and kissed Emmy. 'I hear you have crumpets in the house.'

'Uh, yes. I'll pop some more in the toaster.'

'Don't mind if I do. I also have this.' Tom placed a jar of marmalade on the table with a flourish.

Emmy raised an eyebrow at the marmalade. 'Someone thinks ahead,' she teased.

'Never know when you might need marmalade. Just call me Paddington.' Tom shot back with a grin. Emmy felt her cheeks grow warm. She still felt a bit odd with Tom when Callum was there.

Callum, however, seemed oblivious, already spreading butter on his next lot of crumpets. 'So you're going into town today, Mum? I need a water bottle. I left mine at training the other night and someone nicked it,' he asked before taking a huge bite of one of the crumpets.

Emmy kept her tone light. 'Yep, as I said.' She avoided Tom's gaze, focusing on buttering a crumpet as if it was going out of fashion.

Tom frowned. 'Oh, you didn't say.'

'I figured I'd get it done so my week's clear.' Emmy's cheery tone sounded forced even to her own ears. She swallowed, glanced at Tom and saw his eyes narrowed.

'I could do with a bit of an expedition. Want some company?'

Emmy's mind raced. She had to diffuse this offer. There was no way she wanted anyone with her. 'Err, I'm fine, actually. I thought you said you were catching up with that proposal this morning.'

Tom waved her off. 'No trouble at all. It's not that urgent.'

'Right.'

'How about we make a day of it? Maybe stop at the pub for

lunch. It's lovely over that way. Interested, Callum?' Tom suggested.

Callum didn't look too interested. 'I...'

Emmy cut him off. 'Don't you have that assignment to do?'

'I do, yep.'

'Just you and me then,' Tom said with a smile.

Emmy was thoroughly trapped. 'I, well, the thing is...' She faltered, grasping for a believable excuse. 'Do you know what? I think I'll just shoot over there and back in a jiffy.' She forced a bright smile that didn't reach her eyes.

Tom held her gaze. 'You okay?' He said it casually enough, but his look conveyed that he didn't believe her.

Emmy had never been good at lying. It made her flustered and weird, and she felt her lips doing a strange thing. Another lot of crumpets popped from the toaster, and she made a big deal of smothering them with marmalade. 'I'm fine.' Emmy blustered. 'To be quite honest, I'd rather just have a cosy roast at home later.'

Tom appeared placated. 'I can sort that.'

Emmy sighed in relief. 'Yeah. That'll be nice later. I'll bring a bottle of wine. Apple pie?'

'Works for me.'

About half an hour later, Tom made moves to leave. 'Right, so we're on for roast later?'

'Yep. What time do you want us?'

'Whenever.' Tom kissed her. 'Have a nice day at your, err, supplier,' he said pointedly.

Emmy murmured something non-committal and followed him to the top of the stairs to the shop. She reached up and kissed him on the cheek. 'See you later.'

As she heard Tom go across the store room and out the back door, her whole body sagged. The guilt of lying sat like a stone in her tummy. Emmy Bardot wasn't great at lies. Would it the first of many more?

16

The streets of Darling Island were going about their morning business. A few dog walkers ambled by, a tram trundled past, and a lone jogger gave Emmy a nod and wave. The now familiar faces and surroundings helped steady Emmy's nerves as she drove down towards the ferry.

Too anxious to sit on a train and wondering how long she might have to wait around for, Emmy decided to drive to Katy's despite the distance and the chance of the traffic not being too pleasant. She settled into the comfort of her little car and kept the radio off, letting silence sit around her as she drove along with a head full of thoughts. Her brain felt fuzzy and sort of muffled somehow. As if she was peering through opaque glass out into a world that was usually clear. She kept shaking her head and had to force herself to concentrate as mundane details slid past the windscreen.

After being lost in a world of her own, what felt like both a few minutes and endless hours, she reached the outskirts of the town where she'd first seen Katy on the train platform. A weird, unfamiliar tightness in her chest kept her company as she listened to her phone telling her which way to merge. Inching along in traffic on the outskirts of the town, she passed along by the train station, went by the bench she'd sat on in a daze, and finally arrived at the tree-lined road where Emmy had glimpsed Katy turning into the childcare centre.

Before she knew it, Emmy was in Peachwood Road. Feeling her heart pounding in her chest and her pulse racing, she drove past, looking to her left towards the house. After going all the way to the end of the street and doing a three-point turn, she drove back up the road and parked across the street, a cautious distance away from the house with the pale blue front door. Gripping the steering wheel, Emmy took in every detail of the house, the road, and the streetscape with fresh eyes. The house looked better than she remembered; the pale blue front door was large and impressive, the flower boxes in the lower windows looked welcoming, and the intercom panel by the front door with residents' names looked well-kept. A bicycle with a child's seat was parked by the entrance. Emmy's heart squeezed.

Emmy glanced at the time on her phone and wondered what Katy's routine was. Holding her breath, she kept her eyes trained on the front entrance. One minute ticked by. Then another. No signs of anyone, let alone Katy. Emmy fidgeted with her necklace clasp, the minutes crawling like hours as she sat in her little car, wondering what on earth she was doing. When twenty-five minutes passed with no Katy, doubts began creeping in. Maybe Katy was going to spend the whole day in her flat. Maybe she was away on holiday. Maybe this was all a foolish whim of Emmy's, futile and pointless. She realised it was both of those things. She was being completely ridiculous.

As she sat staring across the road at the blue door, she suddenly felt more than stupid. Though she'd thought about little else for days, she'd really not planned things very well at all. Katy could be anywhere. For all Emmy knew, she might not even be in the country. She could sit there all day long and not see her. She was on a goose chase of epic proportions. She debated going up to buzz Katy's flat but thought better of it. So she just sat, watching and waiting, taking in the goings-on of the quiet road. The odd person walked by, a cyclist zoomed past and rang his bell, and Emmy nearly jumped out of her skin when a twig landed on the windscreen. The world kept spinning normally around Emmy, whilst she felt far from normal. Adrenaline hummed through her veins, and her brain couldn't quite function as it usually did.

The surge of optimism she'd felt when she'd finally got to the town began to deflate. She shook her head to herself. What had she expected? Sitting alone in her car like a creepy, nosy stalker was a strange, unfamiliar feeling. As the street continued to not show many signs of life, resignation settled over Emmy. She'd not thought her goose chase through properly at all. With a weary sigh, she decided she'd made a silly mistake and questioned being there altogether. As she moved to turn the ignition key and just as she went to indicate and check her mirrors to pull out into the street, a flash of colour caught her eye further down the road. There, crossing from the far side of the street, was Katy with the little girl in pink wellies beside her.

Emmy's breath caught in her throat. She sank back against the seat, half-hidden by a large oak tree she'd parked in front of. She watched as, on the opposite pavement, Katy got closer and closer to her house. Emmy fumbled in the centre console for her glasses and peered over the road. Katy looked mostly the same as she always had, only older, perhaps a bit thinner. The same wisps of white-blonde hair fluffed around Katy's head, and she walked in the same way. The little girl was the same but in miniature.

Emmy watched, frozen, as Katy chatted with the girl, gesturing animatedly with her hands. Then she was scooping the child up in her arms and nuzzling their noses together playfully. The little girl giggled in delight. Emmy's eyes prickled with tears. Before she could overthink it, holding her breath, and without wasting any time, Emmy shoved open her car door. She looked down the road, waited for a car to pass, and then crossed over quickly. Her voice came out in a strange, strangled tone. 'Katy!'

Katy's head snapped up, eyes wide. Emmy was already halfway across the pavement. Katy stood frozen, hesitating. After a suspended moment that seemed to Emmy to last forever, Katy shook her head and fussed with her daughter. 'I wondered how long it would take.'

Emmy frowned and shook her head. 'What do you mean?'

'I saw you the other day.'

'What? You saw me! Why didn't you say something?'

Katy raised her eyebrows. 'I could ask you the same thing.'

'I didn't know what to do,' Emmy said with her heart hammering.

Katy cut to the chase. 'Not being funny, but what do you want?'

Emmy didn't know what to reply. She didn't actually know *what* she wanted.

Katy gesticulated to the house and sighed. She pointed to the little girl and winced. 'I don't really want to stand here in the street.'

'Right.'

'You'll have to come up.'

Emmy followed Katy up the path, up the steps, and waited as Katy pushed open the pale blue front door. As she stepped into the hallway, she was surprised at how lovely the interior of the building was. She followed Katy up a flight of stairs until they got to a landing with two front doors, and Katy keyed a number into a pad by the door on the left. In a strange silence, Katy pushed the door with her shoulder and helped the little girl in.

Emmy, not saying anything, followed and stood on the door-mat. The flat was bright, clean, and cosy. Little lamps stood on either side of an entrance dresser, a large mirror was on the left-hand wall, and the hallway merged into an open-plan living area with huge floor-to-ceiling shuttered windows. Emmy didn't know what to do, say, or think. She coughed and swallowed. 'It's good to see you, Kates.'

Katy nodded as she bent down and pulled off her daughter's wellies and then placed them neatly in a shoe cabinet alongside four other pairs of wellies. Katy smiled and pointed to the line of wellies. 'They're the only thing she'll wear.'

Emmy did a strange thing with her lips, which was some sort of smile as Katy bent down and pointed to Emmy. 'Elodie, this is Emmy.'

No Auntie Emmy, just Emmy. Emmy swallowed and stayed rooted to the spot, not sure what to do. 'Hi, Elodie. How are you?'

'Hello.' Elodie looked up and smiled and then pointed to her wellies. 'I like the pink ones best. With the dots.'

'Aww, right, yes. I think they'd be my favourite too.' Emmy felt her heart squeeze so tight she thought she might pass out.

Elodie then trotted past them both, proceeded to plonk herself down on the sofa, put her thumb in, and leant back on the pillows.

'We've been to the park. It's just a few streets away. She loves the slide,' Katy said by way of explanation. 'Tea?'

Emmy nodded, and their horrid, stilted small talk continued as Emmy followed Katy into a small but gorgeous kitchen. Emmy stood awkwardly by the door as Katy put teabags in two mugs and then held them under a boiling water tap. Emmy watched the steam float up into the air as the tap hissed.

Katy relaxed slightly as she opened a large, fancy-looking fridge and then put milk in the two mugs. 'Look. I'm sorry. I thought it was easier not to…'

Emmy shook her head, blinking back sudden tears. 'It's fine.'

'How did you see me?'

'I saw you from the train. I couldn't not come after you, Kates.'

'Mmm.'

Emmy was totally unsure of what to say. Katy's body language was very hard to read. 'I didn't know what to do.'

'Does Mum know?'

'No. That's why I'm here.'

'Right,' Katy said with a nod. 'Good. I do *not* want you to tell them. About anything,' Katy said firmly as she passed Emmy a mug of tea.

Emmy grimaced and flicked her eyes upwards at the same time as shaking her head. She felt a mix of pure fury and sadness. Katy hadn't changed. No surprise there. 'What? You really want that? You want me to keep a secret?'

Katy's fingers pleated and unpleated the hem of her jumper as she stood against the worktop. 'I didn't ask you to come here.'

'I know.'

'I just don't want to go there, Ems,' she said finally.

'I should have been there for you,' Emmy said softly. 'I should have tried harder to reach you.'

Katy shook her head. 'There's no changing the past now. It's fine.'

'It's not fine! You have a daughter! Mum...'

Katy put her hand up at Emmy mentioning Cherry. 'Don't even go there.'

'Don't say that. Don't be nasty.' Emmy said tersely.

Katy sighed a long, pained exhale. 'Look, we all know I was the black sheep. The bad one out of her three perfect girls.'

'Do you *really* think that?'

Katy looked serious as she took a sip of her tea and nodded. 'Do you really *not?*'

Emmy shook her head. 'You're wrong.' Inside, though, Emmy thought that Katy was a little bit right. Emmy loved her mum dearly and was so grateful both to have her in her life and for their relationship, but it was Cherry's way or the highway, and always had been. All of them had always known that. Katy had taken a different route up the highway, and it hadn't ended well.

'We both know I'm not.' Katy let out a huge sigh. 'I just don't want to get back into it all. I'm settled. I'm happy. I don't want to have to live up to being either the one who didn't match up to Mum's perfect version of life or the fact that I came back with my tail between my legs. I'm really not up for it.'

Emmy sighed. 'So, you're letting that stop you and all of us from, well, you know, from Elodie. Really? That's not nice. Sorry, Katy, you need to think about what that means. You need to think about your family. It's mean. *You're* being mean.'

'I've thought about it, Ems. Sorry. Just no. I don't want to go back there. Always the little witch in the family who did things wrong. The one who spoke up. There's nothing that can change that. I'm not going back to playing that dynamic anymore. I'm not being the witch again. End of.'

Emmy grimaced and screwed up her lips. She got it. Katy had never wanted to play the Perfect Daughter game. She'd spoken up about things many a time. Cherry hadn't ever let her forget it. 'I don't want Elodie around that, either.'

'What do you mean?'

'That generational stuff. As long as we're all good girls and we follow the correct path: have a few nice girlfriends, get a good job, save up for a house, get engaged, and then live happily ever after. The old right way. Only I didn't want to do it like that.' Katy shook her head. 'Plus, I certainly don't want Elodie around that sort of influence.'

Emmy didn't know what to say. A few things Katy was saying were correct, but she was blowing everything out of proportion. She was also forgetting a few things, like the drugs. She paused for a second and squeezed her eyes together. 'You're being very harsh. Mum and Dad have been...'

Katy held up her hand again and interrupted. 'Mum and Dad have been very good *to you*, Ems. Because you toed the line.'

'I did not!' Emmy exclaimed.

'Oh, really? How did you not toe the line, then? Tell me.'

'Err, how about I start with Kevin? That wasn't exactly anyone's version of happy ever after.'

Katy shook her head slowly and made a funny little sound. 'That just made it all the better for good old Cherry Bardot to swoop in and save the day.'

Emmy was way past being angry. She was too sad for that. 'Blimey. Don't hold back.'

'I know you think I'm nasty and mean. The thing is, I don't care if you think that. My opinion is a valid one. I've thought about it a lot. I'm allowed to have an opinion, Ems.'

Emmy shook her head. Deep, deep inside, there was a fair bit of truth in what Katy was saying. 'No. I don't.'

'You don't get it, Ems. You just don't. You were happy to play the game. I had my own thoughts on life, and that's where my problems started. I had my own opinions and thoughts.'

'I *do* get it.'

'You don't, and you won't. We're just different people. I don't...' Katy contemplated her words. 'I don't want to open stuff up either.'

Emmy thought about what Rachael had said in the coffee shop about the past being in the past. She waved her hand a little bit. 'You can't just let it go?'

'I *have* let it go, that's my point. I've moved on. I'm free from all that judgement all the time.'

'I miss you, Kates. A lot.'

'I know. Same. But I don't want to get back into all that.'

Emmy was mostly shocked. She hadn't thought that Katy would be so positive about not being in the family. She'd contemplated Katy being angry, being upset, being bitter, but not being sort of happily resigned. 'Wow. I don't know what to say.'

'I just wish you hadn't seen me. It would have been a lot easier that way.'

'Right. So where does that leave me?'

'What do you mean?'

'What, I'm meant to pretend none of this ever happened? Pretend you don't have Elodie. Lie! Keep secrets.' Emmy waved her hand around the kitchen.

'I don't know.'

'What am I going to do?'

Katy didn't say anything.

'I'm going to have to keep secrets from Mum. Wow.'

'I'm sorry I didn't ask you to follow me and I didn't ask you to come here. You made that choice.'

Emmy nodded. That didn't make it any better. 'Yes, yes, I suppose I did.'

'I don't want you to tell them where I am.'

Emmy didn't know what to say. She did know that things were messed up.

17

The sun filtered through Emmy's car windows as she crossed back over to Darling Island, lost in thought. Her reunion with Katy had not been what she'd been expecting, despite the times she'd replayed a movie of it in her head. She'd anticipated that it might be awkward and strained, that there would have been tears and angry words. What she hadn't counted on was the sort of detached confidence Katy had – that she didn't want to be back in the family. Emmy wasn't sure what to think of it at all.

Katy's insistence on keeping their reconciliation from the rest of the family weighed on Emmy as she navigated to the Pride of Darling entrance. She understood her sister's wariness after so long estranged, even shared it to some degree, but she hadn't foreseen that Katy would be a flat no. It made Emmy all sorts of agitated. Her head just couldn't seem to get itself around it.

As Emmy inched the car onto the ferry and put it into park, the prospect of lying to her mum and Amy again tied her insides in knots. Emmy had agreed not to say anything to Cherry for now at least, but it made her feel so uncomfortable it was untrue. With the ferry quickly making its way to the other side, the foghorn sounding, and a misty fog descending on the island in what felt like double quick time, Emmy made her way on autopilot through the bustle of people heading off. As she bumped her car off the floating bridge with a vision of Katy's face in her head, she felt detached and set apart from the rest of the world.

Arriving at the lane behind the shops, she nudged the car up onto the verge, parked, grabbed her bag and headed in through the back gate. At the back door, she let herself in quietly and then set her keys down on the hallway table with a rattle, emotionally spent.

'Hello,' she called out to Callum.

Callum answered from his bedroom. 'In here.'

Emmy popped her head around the door. 'Good?'

'Yep. I'm nearly finished with the assignment.'

'Well done.'

'How was the supplier?'

Emmy frowned. 'The what?'

'The supplier you were going to see.'

'Oh, yes.' Emmy waved her hand dismissively. 'Yeah, good.'

'Grandma called.'

'Right.'

'She said she didn't realise you were going to town.'

'No, I didn't tell her.'

'She said you haven't messaged her. Something about some curtains?'

'Yeah, I'll text her. Tea?'

Callum nodded. 'Love one. Any possibility of an omelette?'

'Did you not have lunch?'

'Yeah, I had a bacon sandwich.'

Emmy shook her head. 'We're going to Tom's later.'

Callum frowned. 'That's hours away.'

'I'll make you an omelette.'

As Emmy washed her hands, put the kettle on, and broke eggs into a jug, she thought about Cherry. Every thought was like a needle of guilt stabbing into her brain. Sitting on top of that was Katy's wary expression, which was etched behind her eyes. It was more or less all Emmy could see. Once she had deposited a cheese and tomato omelette and a cup of tea on Callum's study desk, she took her tea downstairs to the shop and proceeded to drift through the rest of her day distractedly. She spent most of the afternoon clearing the storeroom at the back of the shop, but all the while, her eyes kept darting to her silent phone as she wondered if she would get a text from Katy.

As the late afternoon came with no word from Katy, Emmy tried not to feel crushed. She busied herself tidying up the shop, rearranging things from one place to the next as her mind tumbled from one thought about Katy to another. As she manically pushed the vacuum cleaner over and over the storeroom floor, she kept envisioning the little line of wellie boots on the dresser. As Emmy vacuumed, she felt a juxtaposition of emotions – anxiety, hope, fear, and at the bottom of it all, sadness. Flashes of memories flooded through her mind: summer holidays, whispers under blankets, dreams, giggles, and aspirations. After that, her mind zoomed to the troubled times: the misunderstandings, the hurt, and the anger. Then the years of silence.

Emmy thought about Elodie, the spitting image of Katy at the same age. The sweetest little face, beautiful skin, bright blue eyes, the same fuzzy mess of white-blonde hair. The way Elodie clutched Katy's hand. From Emmy's side of the table, there was so much lost time to make up for, but Katy clearly wasn't thinking the same *at all*. Not even close. Emmy's emotions swirled. There was so much to think about at the same time as nothing at all. Katy was adamant that Emmy mustn't mention anything to anyone.

Eventually, as late afternoon rolled in, Emmy dragged

herself back upstairs to the top room and ran a bath, hoping the water and the ritual might settle her emotions. She lit a linen-scented candle, got a clean towel ready, and watched the candle flame while the tub slowly filled with water and bubbles. As she eased down into the perfumed water, Emmy closed her eyes and leant her head back, trying to clear her cluttered mind. But behind her eyelids, it was as if Katy was in her head with her. All she saw was Katy. Katy stood leaning against the worktop, mug of tea in hand, with a sort of resigned, contented look on her face.

When the bath water had cooled, Emmy dragged herself out, dried off and wrapped her dressing gown around her. She stood, wiping the fog from the mirror, and peered at the weary woman staring back at her. An estranged sister was not good for one's anti-ageing aspirations. As she stood looking at her reflection, she contemplated the roast at Tom's. Part of her wanted to text him and ask him if he could bring it over. She could quite happily sit with her dressing gown on and eat her dinner from her lap curled up on the sofa. Lazy and comfort eating as the day was long. As Emmy pulled on a clean pair of jeans, she thought about Tom's probing tone that morning. He clearly suspected something was amiss already, now it had got worse. She shut her eyes as she brushed her hair. She really wasn't good at lying, and never had been. Not because of some holier-than-thou attitude that she was genuinely good or genuinely honest, more that it made her flustered and uncom-fortable and one hundred per cent out of sorts. Putting a jumper on, she rummaged through her jewellery box, fastened her grandma Emily's diamond drop necklace on and put the matching bracelet on her right wrist. The diamond had once been Emily's, and Emmy always reached for it when she was stressed. Right now she was really, really, really stressed, and what was worse was she had a feeling this wasn't even the half of it. There was more to come.

18

E mmy called out to Callum as she walked down the stairs to the shop. 'See you there. Don't be ages.'

'Okay. Yep, I won't be. What roast is it?'

Emmy flicked her eyes upwards in irritation. She'd already told Callum what roast it was twice. It was like talking to a wall sometimes. The joys of the teenage years. Things went in one of Callum's ears and straight out the other. 'Pork.'

'Crackling?'

'Yes. Just don't go on the PlayStation, and if you do, don't spend too long on it,' Emmy instructed, knowing full well that was exactly what Callum would do as soon as she was out of the back gate. They both knew it.

'Okay. See you in a bit.'

As she walked down the path at the back of the shop, the sky flamed with the oranges, pinks, and reds of a Darling sunset. Emmy gasped at how beautiful it was as she took the few steps down the lane to the back of Tom's place, reached over the top of the gate, slid the bolt back, and nudged the gate with her shoulder. The sky reminded her of the night she'd gone to Darlings with Tom and they'd ended up dancing and walking on the beach. The smell of roast pork filled her nostrils as she let herself in and went upstairs to Tom's flat. If it wasn't for the slight problem in her life known as a secret meeting with her estranged sister, life really was quite good.

Unlike The Old Ticket Office, Tom's flat had been beautifully renovated. With the same high ceilings and original features as Emmy's, it was different in that a few walls had been knocked out, giving it a more modern feel. The space had been seamlessly updated with contemporary finishes. In the kitchen, a long marble counter sat underneath a row of pendant lights. Open-plan shelving displayed cookbooks, plants and kitchen things. The lighting was low, and something soothing was coming out of the speakers from above. Smooth white walls and blonde wood floors gave a bright, airy feel. In the living area, a low coffee table held a stack of sailing magazines atop a fluffy sheepskin rug. Built-in shelving flanked a stylish gas fireplace, displaying a mix of paraphernalia and picture frames.

Tom gave her a smile, kissed her, and ushered her over to the kitchen island. Something bubbled on the hob, and Emmy could see a joint of pork roasting away in the range oven. Emmy gazed around at how lovely it all was – the back splash was a textured sea green tile, four metal stools were tucked under the island, cabinets with horizontal reeded glass doors showcased Le Creuset cookware. A large bowl of lemons sat on the counter, and a cluster of artichokes was wedged artfully into a shallow dish. Despite its contemporary design, the kitchen was inviting and the smell of roast dinner made Emmy feel better as she watched Tom bent over the oven, basting the meat. For a moment, she simply lingered by the stools, peering around.

Turning down the heat on the hob, Tom caught her eye with a smile. 'Drink?' he offered, moving to the other side of the kitchen and retrieving a bottle of red wine.

'Love one.' *Glug it right down my neck, please.*

Emmy sat down at the island as Tom poured them both a

glass of red wine. She tried to forget about what was on her mind and let the roast smell wrap around her. As Tom took a huge tray of roast potatoes out of the oven, Emmy sipped on her wine and chatted, attempting to relax and let the music and the wine soothe her jumbled brain. She tried to be soothed by Tom and his words. They didn't work.

Tom's eyes crinkled. 'How was your supplier today?'

Emmy lowered her eyes, tracing the wine glass rim with her finger. 'Oh, fine. Yeah, completely uneventful.' She so wanted to blurt the whole lot out. Her words caught in her throat like a big fat ball of hair and dust. She felt as if it was totally obvious that she wasn't quite telling the truth about her day as she tried to rearrange her body language from stressed to full of the joys of spring.

'Good. Did you get what you wanted?'

Emmy felt another lie slip out of her mouth. 'Yep.' Emmy immediately changed the subject as her brain worked at nineteen to the dozen. There was no way she wanted to talk about what she'd been doing. She didn't want any sort of opportunity to either trip up or have to lie again. She hated not telling the truth. 'The roast smells amazing.' She squinted towards the oven. 'How did you do that crackling? It looks amazing. Mum has a competitor.'

Tom laughed. 'I'll have to kill you if I tell you. It's *my* mum's secret recipe. Not that I like secrets, but you know what I mean.'

Emmy gulped. It was as if Tom was reading her thoughts about secrets. She didn't know what to say. 'Ha.'

'I'll tell you, though,' Tom bantered.

Emmy's voice was a strange cross between a squeak and a chirp. 'Thanks.'

Tom pulled open the oven and took out the tray with the joint of pork again. He put the tray on the island and tapped the top of the pork with a slotted spoon. 'That crackling is much researched. You won't find better in the country and, as I said, a secret recipe. You'll have to swear not to divulge it to anyone. Can you keep a secret?' he joked.

Emmy nodded and drew in a breath. She squeaked again, 'Promise.'

'The skin is seasoned first with salt. We're talking a thick layer of the stuff. Like loads of it.'

Emmy wrinkled her nose. 'Won't it be really salty?'

Tom shook his head. 'No, it doesn't stay on there. You salt it first. That's the secret.'

'How do you do it then?' Emmy pretended to be interested. She wasn't.

Tom turned around and took a container of table salt from the cupboard. 'You pour this on liberally. Like half the bottle. Then you let it sit for a few hours or overnight. Then you wipe the whole lot off. It's as simple as that. However, it's also a game changer.'

'What, and wash it? You wash the salt off, do you?' Emmy said, feigning that she was totally curious about the salting of the pork whilst really she just wanted to talk about anything but what she'd been doing in her day.

'Nope. You just make sure you get most of the salt off with kitchen roll.'

'Hmm. Interesting.'

'Trust me. My mum's secret method is the best. Now I've told you, you have to promise to keep that to yourself. Don't let on. You can keep a secret, can't you, Ems?' Tom bantered.

Emmy winced inside at the mention of secrets. The look on her face must have been weird. Tom frowned. 'You okay?'

Emmy quickly sipped her wine. 'Fine.'

'Are you sure there's nothing wrong?' Tom asked earnestly. 'You seem a bit odd.'

Emmy really wanted to tell Tom about Katy, but she'd promised Katy she wouldn't utter anything to anyone about their meeting. 'Fine. Just tired. It's been a busy week.'

'Yeah. It has. Early night for you, I think, young lady,' Tom joked.

Emmy swiftly changed the subject and gesticulated around in the kitchen. 'This is all so lovely. I feel lucky to have you.'

Tom laughed as he topped up Emmy's wine glass. 'Not as lucky as I am. Here's to us, loads more of this.'

Emmy's heart thumped, but inside, she felt awful. There was a horrible feeling rushing around her body. She hated that she hadn't told Tom the truth. She had a gnawing voice telling her that things were not going to end well with the whole Katy thing. It was all going to wind up in a big jumbled web of mess and lies, and here she was already lying through her back teeth.

Later, once she and Callum had gone home, she'd got into bed with a heavy heart. Curling on her side under the covers, she tried to quieten her thoughts, but there wasn't a hope in hell of her brain not galloping around. Lying in the darkness, all she could think about was Katy. Her emotions went up and down like spikes on a chart – sad, angry, so angry, resigned, furious, disappointed, doleful. Part of her was *very* resentful towards Katy. A voice whispered: why did Katy always have to cause trouble? Why couldn't Katy just put up and shut up? What was her problem? Why couldn't Katy just be grateful about having a mum like Cherry? Emmy blinked as she stared across the dark room. She wanted to get all of it out in the open and stop her mind from whirring about it all. Make it someone else's problem. She sighed as she lay on her side and accepted that, for now, she'd have to keep the secret. The rest would unfold in its own time. She hoped.

19

A few weeks or so later, nothing had changed much with the situation, and the only thing Emmy had done was try to put the Katy thing to the back of her mind. The streets of Darling were bustling as Emmy cycled along and made her way to Darlings café. She'd spent the day working on the shop and needed a breath of fresh air. As she weaved along, she took in deep lungfuls of the Darling smell, hoping it would do something to stop her mind from racing. It didn't really work. Her phone chimed with an incoming text. She stopped, glanced down, assuming it would be from either Tom or Callum, but she was more than surprised to see it was from Katy.

Ever since the awkward goose chase ending with the cup of tea in Katy's flat, Emmy and Katy had sent the odd message here and there, but there'd hardly been an avalanche of communication. After much thought and contemplation about what she was going to do about Katy, Emmy had decided to keep schtum for a bit and wait and see what happened. She'd learnt over the years that time simply had a way of working things out. She'd also taken on board what Katy had said about not wanting to be back in the family. Emmy hoped that if she kept things casual, at some point, Katy would change her mind and would begin to slowly open up. In the few text exchanges they'd had, Katy had been slightly less evasive than she'd been at the flat, and had responded here and there to Emmy's tentative messages. It was something, at least. The only way was up.

Emmy had been in two minds about the situation with Katy. Part of her wished she'd never seen Katy at all. Part of her was racked with guilt. She hated keeping secrets, but it was what it was. She stopped on the side of the pavement, pressed the message, and read.

Katy: *Hope you're well. Wondered if you fancy a coffee this afternoon? I've got the day off. Not sure what your movements are? Probably a bit late notice but thought I'd ask. No probs if not.*

Emmy's pulse sped up a bit as she typed out a response. She hadn't expected a message like this. She had a lot of things to do that afternoon. Nothing that couldn't wait.

Emmy: *Love to, that would be really nice. I've got some time this afternoon, yep. Xx*

The back-and-forth continued until they'd settled on a time and place. As Emmy cycled along towards Darlings, she felt buoyed by the small breakthrough. Katy had been the one to text first. Katy was making an effort. Overall, things with the Katy thing were hopefully looking brighter. She hoped all of it would work itself out in the wash.

Ten or so minutes later, Emmy was greeted by the familiar, cosy ambience of the interior of Darlings. She smiled as she looked around. The floor-to-ceiling shelves were rammed with little coffee bowls, and one of the staff was standing on a rung in the middle of a rolling ladder loading huge bags of coffee onto the upper shelves.

Lucie, one of the staff members Emmy had got to know, walked up to the table as Emmy sat down by the window. 'Morning. How are you?'

'Keeping out of trouble,' Emmy joked as she stuffed her bag

under the table. *Oh you know, just keeping secrets and messaging my estranged sister.*

'Good to hear.'

'How about you?' Emmy asked. 'Nice weather we're having for the time of year, even with the fog.'

'Yes. Same. Busy. Morning basket for you?'

'Yes, please.'

'Coffee?' Lucie asked with her eyebrows raised in question.

'Yup. That would be lovely. I think I need a lot of caffeine to get me through the rest of the day.' Emmy laughed.

Lucie smiled. 'Well, you're in the right place. If there's one thing I can do for you, it's a nice shot of caffeine or six.'

A few minutes later, a white basket with a blue and white gingham fabric liner with a knotted top arrived on the table. Emmy pulled open the fabric with a smile on her face. She loved the little Darlings tradition in the coffee shop. The morning baskets were always so delightful and had become something that really brightened her week. She pulled the fabric aside and peered in. A small cinnamon bun was stacked on the right next to a scone. In a small glass jar with a ceramic lid, gooseberry jam and a knife were wedged in beside a napkin. Worked for her.

As she tucked in and then cupped her hands around the little bowl of milky coffee, Emmy thought about Katy and narrowed her eyes, wondering what their meeting would bring. She was surprised by the text. Maybe Katy was softening. She really hoped so. Stranger things had happened at sea.

The rest of the day dragged, minutes crawling by as Emmy forced herself to get on with jobs whilst her mind was totally on meeting up with Katy. After changing a couple of times, she examined herself, not quite believing how the secret she was keeping seemed to have appeared almost overnight by way of worry wrinkles on her face. Slapping on a brightening foundation and a highlighter on top, she added a swipe of lip gloss and hoped for the best. Wrinkles and what she looked like were the last of her worries.

After listening to a podcast in the car on the realities of running a retail business in tough economic times, Emmy checked her map for the meeting point with Katy and parked her car. She felt a flutter of anxiety as she gathered her bag and checked there wasn't anything worth stealing on show in her car. About ten minutes later, she was standing outside a quiet café in the centre of a parade of shops. Pushing open the door, Emmy spotted Katy tucked up in the corner, a coffee steaming on the table in front of her. Katy looked up from her phone as Emmy approached.

'Hey,' Katy said warmly as Emmy sat down across from her. 'Thanks for meeting me.'

'Of course, it's really nice to see you. You okay?' Emmy replied, hoping her smile looked natural. Inside, she felt far from natural. She felt all sorts of strained and odd. The waitress came to take Emmy's order, and Katy made conversation telling her that Elodie was at the childcare centre as Emmy took off her cardigan and put her bag beside her on a spare chair.

Katy was clearly making small talk. Everything felt stilted and awkward, like she was talking to someone she hardly knew at all. Which was kind of true. 'So, how are things with the shop you were telling me about and everything?'

Emmy nodded, thinking inside that small talk wasn't why she was there. 'Oh, yep, fine, coming along.'

'Sounds like it must be a lot of work,' Katy noted.

'Yep. It is. How have you been?' Emmy really tried to sound bright and breezy.

'Can't complain,' Katy said with a smile. She chuckled. 'I've definitely been worse.'

'How's Elodie?'

'She's lovely. Yes, doing well at the moment. You know how it goes.'

'Good. That's nice to hear.'

Katy shifted in her seat, then leant her elbows on the table and crossed her hands into a bridge. 'Listen, Ems, I actually, I umm, I was thinking about when you came to the flat.'

Emmy frowned, unsure where the conversation was headed. 'Yep.'

'There's a bit more than what I said. I've been mulling it over a lot. There was a lot more that went on – stuff you don't know.'

Emmy went cold inside. 'What do you mean? Like what?'

'I should have told you at the time, but it wasn't easy for me,' Katy began haltingly.

Emmy didn't know what to say. 'Right.'

'I don't know if you remember a guy named Aiden that I dated. I was really secretive about it because Mum didn't like him. Well, Mum didn't like where he was from. We were going out right before things got bad with the family. I wasn't exactly forthcoming with it all then, as you're well aware.' Katy stirred her coffee.

'Yep, I remember.'

Katy gave a bitter half-smile. 'Mum thought he was dangerous, into drugs and stuff. But it wasn't true that he was dangerous.' She shook her head, a faraway look in her eyes. 'He wasn't bad. He just didn't fit into her mould.'

Emmy stayed quiet, the waitress put her coffee down, and Katy was silent until the waitress walked away. 'Anyway, to cut a very, very long story short. I found out I was pregnant.' Katy twisted a napkin tightly in her hands. 'We were terrified.'

A lump rose in Emmy's throat. 'What happened?' she asked softly.

'I was already on thin ice with Mum and Dad by then. I didn't tell Mum the real reason. I just said that I wasn't going to live her life and I was dropping out. You know all that. Dad shouted. Said I was throwing my future away. That Aiden would drag me down. Etcetera, etcetera. No point raking over all of that.'

Emmy closed her eyes for a second. 'And you were pregnant? Why didn't you say anything? I can't understand that. I don't get it. I really don't. You always had me and Amy.'

'Because it would have been another thing I had done wrong. I'd already slipped from Mum's perfect path. She acted as if the drug thing was the end of the world. Emmy, it wasn't that bad. Half the middle class live on it.'

Emmy shook her head and sighed out through her nose. 'You seem so het up about that. You make her out to be awful. It's not true. Kates, you really need to let go of it. I don't like it when you talk about Mum like that.'

Katy's back went up. 'We all have different opinions, Ems. Looking back now, I can understand where their reaction came from, even if it felt the opposite at the time,' Katy continued shakily. 'Anyway, you know how that ended up. When I left, and everything. They kept saying that they were no longer enabling me. What a load of rubbish! I was just young and headstrong and did things differently to Mum's perfect world.'

'I really don't like what you think about Mum,' Emmy stated again. 'You're not being nice. Sorry, but I don't want to hear you talk that way about Mum.'

'I know. I am allowed my own opinions in life, Ems.'

Emmy reached across the table and patted Katy's hand. 'I didn't know you were pregnant. I can't believe this! I literally don't know what to say. You were so young.'

Katy shook her head and took a deep, steadying breath before continuing. 'As I told you, I went to Aiden's family flat.'

Emmy was trying to compute the dates in her head with Elodie's age. 'Hang on a minute. Wait. Sorry, I'm confused.'

'I lost the baby.' Tears spilt over the bottom lids of Katy's eyes. 'It was the second trimester. I had to go in and...' Katy cut her sentence off. 'Anyway. That's in the past now. I can't change it.'

Emmy didn't know what to say. Her first response was to say something about Cherry, but she stopped herself. 'I'm so sorry.'

'So, yeah, obviously neither of us had touched drugs, but when that happened, Aiden went off the rails. He was in a terrible place.' Katy screwed her face up at the memory. 'It really wasn't good. Not good at all. The whole time was very traumatic, to say the least.'

Emmy still didn't really know what to say for the best. Katy was very edgy. 'Oh, I'm so sorry. You should have got in touch. You poor thing. I could have helped.'

'Aiden was never the same, drinking to numb the grief,' Katy continued in a monotone. 'He left not long after. I was totally alone, trying to cope with it all. I didn't know what to do. Aiden's parents gave me money, and I studied online, plus I got a job. I just slowly got myself back on my feet. Getting back to studying turned out to be the best thing.'

Emmy let out a shaky exhale. 'I'm so sorry, Katy. I actually don't know what to say.'

With a sad half-smile, Katy sat back in her chair and picked up her coffee. 'I'm actually fine now. It feels like it was a long time ago. But I needed you to know I wasn't just being a little brat. I was dealing with a lot at the time. Since then, too, but as I said, I'm fine.'

'Oh, Kates.'

'I know it's a lot to process.' Katy wiped under her eyes, composing herself. 'I don't want your sympathy. Just, hopefully, your understanding. Why I had to stay away back then. And why I'm so cautious now about letting anyone in again. It's been hard, Ems.'

Emmy's mind was reeling. 'It must have been awful, not just hard.'

Katy shrugged. 'I'm fine.'

Emmy felt as if she had countless questions at the same time, as if someone had poured a long stream of sawdust mixed with sadness in her mouth. She could barely get her words out. 'What about Elodie?'

'Elodie came along as a surprise.'

'Sorry, with Aiden?'

'Oh no! No, no, I haven't seen him for years. I wouldn't have a clue where he was now.'

'Hang on. So you live with Elodie's dad, do you?'

Katy chuckled. 'God, no!'

'Oh, right.' Emmy shook her head, trying to make sense of the information about Katy's past. 'I'm sorry to be a bit dense here. It's a lot to take on. I'm just trying to understand the time-line. So, Elodie?'

Katy traced the handle of her coffee mug. 'I sort of stumbled into a reckless relationship with someone I met in the pub. We were always fighting and making up. It was a bit toxic, really, when I look back. Nothing bad, just put it this way, we weren't made for each other.' Katy did a funny, wry chuckle.

'Oh, okay.'

Katy looked down, speaking softly. 'So when I found out I was pregnant, I ended things for good with him, but sort of in a nice way. Told him it was over and it was up to him if he wanted to be involved.'

Emmy nodded, picturing fiercely independent Katy taking control over such difficult circumstances. 'And what did he say? How did that turn out?'

Katy continued, 'He was happy from the get-go. It's all been bizarre. Yeah, so we sort of co-parent and it works so well apart from the fact that he travels for business quite a bit. He's bril-liant, actually. The best dad ever. He worships Elodie. Yep, it's great.'

'Wow, that's amazing,' Emmy interjected.

Katy's face shifted, softening. 'Yeah, and when he held Elodie for the first time, seeing her tiny little face, I knew it was going to be okay. It's gone better than I hoped. He adores her. He's such a good dad. Well, most of the time.'

Emmy felt a prick at the corner of her eyes. 'She seems like the most perfect, beautiful little girl,' she said earnestly.

'Well, not perfect.' Katy laughed. 'She's positively feral some days, won't listen to a word I say on others. The colic when she was a baby wasn't pleasant either. Neither were the sleepless nights. But yes, she's my everything.' Her smile faded slightly. 'I suppose that's why all of this' – Katy gestured between them – 'scares me so much.' She trailed off with an anxious frown and seemed to close up again.

Emmy chose her words carefully, leaning forward. 'I know the idea of facing Mum is hard. But maybe just start with baby steps?' Emmy spoke before she'd thought properly about what she was saying. 'Or, I don't know. I could come round again, spend a bit more time with Elodie.'

Katy's shoulders relaxed a bit as she considered. She then grimaced. 'Sorry, Ems. I don't know. I wanted to meet up again so I could tell you the truth. Just so you know.'

'No pressure,' Emmy added gently. 'We can take things one day at a time, do this at your pace.'

Emmy felt Katy's mood shift. She lightened the topic. 'So, does she really only wear wellies?'

'Yup, plus anything pink. So much for gender neutrality.' Katy's face lit up as she chuckled about Elodie. 'She's obsessed with anything that sparkles. She's like a little magpie child! She adores dollies and sticker jewels and rings. Plus, she's crazy for glittery nail varnish for her fingers and toes. I've been vacuuming glitter off the furniture for weeks...'

Emmy giggled and felt a huge wave of nostalgia for their lost closeness. She touched Emily's diamond at her throat. 'God help you. She sounds just like me if she likes sparkly things.'

Katy shook her head and her eyes went wide. 'I've never realised. Yes! She's just like you! Remember your obsession with your jewellery boxes? Drove Mum mad.'

'Oh God, and the glitter! Wasn't there a solid year where we just dumped it in everything? Crafts, makeup. I think it's still ground permanently into the carpet in my old bedroom.' Emmy laughed. 'Mum says it will be there until the end of time. An eternal reminder.' Emmy rolled her eyes in mock annoyance.

They continued to reminisce for a bit, and Emmy realised how much she'd missed Katy. Katy was sharp and funny with a wicked sense of humour and didn't take fools gladly. It had often got her into trouble, but she'd always made Emmy laugh.

All too soon, Katy was glancing at her watch. 'I'd better run. I've got to pick Elodie up. Thank you for listening. And understanding.'

Impulsively, Emmy went around to Katy's side of the table and folded her into a fierce hug.

'I meant what I said about going at your pace,' Emmy said. 'I'm not losing you again, even if we're not, well, you know. I'm on the end of the phone if you want me.'

Katy pulled back, dabbing at her eyes with a napkin. 'Yep, thanks. Look, I'm just not ready for that, Ems. I'm sorry.'

'Think about it?'

'I will. Right, I'm off before I'm a complete mess.'

'Yeah, make sure you keep in touch.'

20

Emmy stayed in the coffee shop, ordered another drink, and sat for a bit, letting the conversation filter down through her mind. She felt a tiny bit of hope somewhere inside. Another part of her felt the opposite. The whole situation was very fragile, especially with the further information she'd now garnered. She thought about her mum and Amy, and the fact that she now not only knew where Katy was but that she'd met up with her and knew about Elodie. Her mum and Amy would not be happy if they found out. Emmy hoped she was doing the right thing. If she met up with Katy and took things step by step, maybe they could start to bridge the distance, but she wasn't going to hold her breath.

Emmy wrapped her hands tightly around the mug as the situation with Katy zoomed around her brain. The coffee shop suddenly felt cavernous and empty as she sat with their emotional conversation replaying and her thoughts spinning. She stared blankly out the window, noticing details of the street scene without absorbing them – a laughing couple holding hands, a dog tracking a stray leaf blowing along the gutter, a mum hurrying past dragging a crying toddler behind her. All of it faded into the background of Emmy's churning emotions.

On the table in front of Emmy, Katy's mug was still there on the opposite side. Emmy stared at it for ages, feeling sad about the whole situation. There were so many horrible old wounds, so much anger and nasty words. It all seemed so murky and gross. She could see why Katy would much rather leave it alone. Who would want to dive back into that? Emmy had seen Katy's wariness, and Emmy understood her instinct to protect herself and Elodie, especially after what she now knew Katy had been through. She'd also seen the other side of Cherry a few times. The side Katy had always been on. Even though Emmy hated to admit it to herself, her mum wasn't all roses when things didn't go her way. Cherry was fine and lovely and perfect as long as she got what she wanted. If that didn't happen – watch out. All of them knew that too. It was like an unspoken Bardot family code.

Just as Emmy was wondering how the whole situation would pan out, her phone buzzed, jolting her from her contemplation. Glancing down, she saw Amy's smiling face lighting up the screen. Instantly, a slam dunk of guilt like nothing else whacked her on the head. The picture had been taken at their last boozy lunch. Amy and Emmy's heads were pressed together, faces flushed with laughter. Emmy's finger hovered over the button as she hesitated. If she spoke to Amy, she'd have to lie. She swiped to accept the call. *Here we go.*

'Hey, Ames, what's up?' Emmy tried to make her tone bright, but even she could hear that she was putting on her happy voice. She really did feel and sound all out of sorts.

'That's what I was going to ask you,' Amy replied. 'You're not answering my calls, and Mum said you seemed off this weekend and didn't want to chat for long.'

Emmy winced as she pictured Cherry. She'd definitely been avoiding speaking to her mum, there was no doubt about that, and when she had spoken to her, she'd got off the call pronto. The deceit sat like a lead weight in Emmy's tummy. 'Ahh, yeah. I'm not *not* answering them. I've just been manic! I've been getting the shop ready. I meant to ring you back, and then I had to sort out all that cricket stuff with Callum. The weekend has flown by in a flash.' Emmy shuddered as she heard the falseness in her breezy reply.

Predictably, Amy saw right through it. 'Come off it, Ems. I know when something's bothering you. You always pick up. What's going on? Has something happened with Kevin? What has he done this time? Spill.'

'No, no. Honestly. It's just the shop. I'm really busy. You know what it's been like.'

Amy wasn't going to let it go. She pressed on. 'Is everything okay with you and Tom still? Or is it about...' She lowered her voice. 'Kevin and money stuff? Just blame Kevin, eh?'

'God, no,' Emmy cut in hastily. She took a gulp of lukewarm coffee before answering properly. 'Couldn't be better with Tom. Honestly, I'm fine. Just have a lot swirling around with the renovations and work. Nothing to worry about. Absolutely nothing.'

There was a weighted pause on Amy's end. Emmy could picture Amy with her eyes squinted and the line between her eyebrows she was always threatening to have softened with an injectable wrinkled into a frown. The frown would be saying that it wasn't fully convinced. Nothing got past Amy. 'Well, alright, if you're sure nothing's wrong...' Amy trailed off.

'Everything is fine. More than fine,' Emmy said, hoping she sounded convincing. She didn't, far from it.

'Anyway. I was thinking we're overdue for a long chat, just you and me. We haven't done that for ages, what with the shop, and Tom and everything. We haven't been out, just us two for so long apart from that beach day. We could meet in town this week? I'll come to you, get lunch, have a moan about life, Kev, Mum, or whatever's going on. Fancy it?'

A lump rose in Emmy's throat. She'd feel even worse if she sat with Amy putting the world to rights, nattering on with their usual complaints and confessions and talking about the ins and outs of their lives while she sat there totally keeping the Katy secret. She winced and screwed her eyes shut as she lied. 'I'd love that, but I'm working loads this week. Just crazy busy. Rain check?'

Amy sighed down the line, clearly unconvinced. 'Sure.'

Neither of them spoke for an awkward beat. 'Right, well, I'll see you with Dad for the shop.'

'Yep.'

'Will do. Thank you,' Emmy said. She blinked back a press of tears in the corners of her eyes.

'Oh, and we have dinner at Mum's. Has Callum got cricket? Is Tom coming?'

'I'm not sure because it's a rained-off day, and I'm rostered for an early shift. Tom and Cal might come together, and I'll come from work.'

'Right. At least we have that to look forward to, though we won't get a chance to chat properly in peace. It will be the usual chaos.'

'Yep. Fab. We can have a good old chat then.'

'Rightio, then see you later. Love you, Ems.'

'Yeah, see you later.'

Emmy put her phone face down on the table, feeling a million times worse than she had when she'd answered her phone. Not only was she keeping secrets, but she'd lied too. Fabulous. Not. She sat unmoving with a grimace on her face as guilt churned inside her. The cheery café soundtrack of clinking china and chatter suddenly felt jarringly at odds with her mood. Emmy grabbed her phone, pushed up from the table, paid the bill at the counter, and hurried out the door. Out on the pavement, sunshine didn't make her feel any better in the least. In fact, it seemed to make her tangled emotions feel all the more worse. She walked aimlessly in the direction of her car and tried to convince herself that it would all work out in the wash. Katy would come around, and they'd all get back together again. Simple. Except that she knew Katy, and she knew Cherry. It would be far from simple.

After getting in her car, she just sat for ages with her head leant back on the headrest and her eyes closed. As the sun beamed through the windscreen, she backtracked over the conversation and thought for a bit. She'd have to just go with it. The past was done. All she could do was move forward and try to rebuild something new. She had to hope a fresh start with Katy was possible.

Emmy was startled when her phone buzzed again, yanking her back to the front seat of her car. Expecting Cherry, she turned her phone over with a grimace, but instead, Tom's name flashed on her screen.

'Hey, you,' she answered with a smile. She could hear the strain in her voice.

'Just wanted to check in, see how your day's going,' Tom asked, sounding relaxed and happy.

Emmy felt a nuclear reaction going on inside as she revelled in Tom calling her to see how she was. It had been a long time since she'd had a partner who cared. Part of her was still getting used to having him in her life. She couldn't quite get her head around how deep her feelings for him actually were. How much she loved him. She flinched as she didn't quite lie but omitted the truth. 'Nothing exciting to report,' she replied, aiming for casual.

'Up to anything exciting?'

Emmy raised her eyebrows, took a deep inhale and shook her head all at the same time, 'Nup.' *Oh, you know, just secretly meeting the sister none of us have seen for years. Nothing that exciting at all.*

'Another regular old day in Emmy Bardot's life?' Tom joked.

Far from it. 'Indeed. You nailed it. Are you working on that big commission?'

'I am. It's definitely another regular old day here. Long too, throw in a bit of boring, and you've pretty much summed up my day. Not much going on at all.'

'Hmm. Same,' Emmy replied, putting on her best breezy tone, skirting around anything weighty.

Tom paused thoughtfully. 'You sure there's nothing new or… unexpected happening lately?'

Emmy smiled at Tom's way of probing. He clearly knew something was going on. There was no way she was going to tell him. Part of her wanted to spill everything and unload the secret. But the whole Katy thing and the situation with Cherry was fragile, and though she hated how it made her feel, it was not her story to tell.

'Nothing I can't handle. Just stuff with the shop. Just busy,' she said lightly instead. 'See you tonight?'

'Rightio. Yeah. See you later.'

Emmy slotted her phone back into the centre console. She'd now omitted the truth from two people she loved in her life. She shook her head. Tom knew she wasn't right. She'd heard it in his voice as he had hers. Like Amy, he was far from a fool. All of it made Emmy feel as if she was adrift. She sat a while longer, staring out the windscreen as a stream of cars went past. This was not good. It did not bode well at all.

21

Morning sunlight filtered into Emmy's bedroom, stirring her from a horrible, groggy night of tossing and turning. She blinked up at the ceiling, the day before's conversation with Katy already replaying in her mind. Learning about Katy's pregnancy, the lost baby; all of it had shifted something in Emmy's understanding of her sister and everything that had gone on.

There were still a lot of mixed feelings in Emmy's head – angst over the years lost and the pain caused by Katy's disappearance. But beneath that, Emmy now felt sad on top of it all, and goodness knows how her mum Cherry was going to feel when she eventually found out the truth. However terribly Katy had behaved and whatever had happened, she clearly had a lot of wounds after a very traumatic time. Emmy was now grasping the extent of what had gone on.

With a groan, she forced herself upright, turned off her alarm, and shuffled to the bathroom. As she waited for the shower water to heat up, she caught a glimpse of her reflection and paused. She was not looking great. The worry showed all over the place. It wasn't just tiredness from the previous night, chock-full of tossing and turning. There was something else in her face. It didn't take long to work it out. Guilt. Which was now coming from every avenue. Guilt about the secrecy and guilt about not being there for Katy. Just guilt all around, really.

Emmy stepped under the hot shower with a sigh, letting the water wash over her. She tried focusing on the mundane tasks ahead of her that day – Love Emmy x order emails in her break at work, tidying up the flat when she got home, plus she needed to stop in the supermarket before she got on the ferry, she wanted to make a steak and kidney pie, and the car needed to be cleaned. After years of practice putting her head down and getting jobs done, compartmentalising came easily to her, and she was normally quite good at putting things aside and burying herself in the humdrum of life, she had enough practice. But today, thoughts of Katy lingered, no matter how hard she tried to ignore them. She kept replaying Katy walking out of the hospital without a baby. Emmy's heart felt as if someone had squeezed it closed.

As she poured shampoo into her right hand, rubbed both hands together, and then scrubbed the shampoo onto her scalp, she thought about Katy's face as Katy had told her about the baby. Katy's anguish had been so raw and so painful when she'd mentioned the baby she'd lost, it was almost as if it was actually written on her face. Emmy shook her head as she washed off the shampoo suds; she couldn't even fathom the pain of having that happen, let alone going through it alone.

On top of the dreadful thing itself, Katy had endured it without either of her sisters to help shoulder some of the grief. Emmy felt awful, and she knew Amy would feel the same way. Katy had felt so judged and so unwelcome, she'd not been able to get in contact with her own family when bad stuff had hit the fan. What a terrible state of affairs. So much for the Bardots being close.

Emmy's heart ached as she comprehended the extent of

Katy's situation. Lots of things now made sense, not just what had happened with the family but also the look on Katy's face that was different. Katy looked scarred, broken by something she'd never be able to change. Emmy felt terrible that she'd not been there to help.

Stepping out of the shower, Emmy swiped the fog from the mirror, taking in her weary expression. Dressing for her shift, she moved through the familiar routine automatically, tucking her hair into a chignon and dabbing on her base makeup with a foundation brush. As she then went downstairs and bustled about the kitchen, she waited for the kettle to boil and took the breakfast roll she'd made the night before out of the fridge. She could barely face anything to eat, her stomach was that unsettled. Just looking at food made her slightly nauseous. As she was pouring hot water into her travel mug, Callum, in pyjama bottoms and no shirt, shuffled into the room ruffling the hair at the back of his head.

'Morning,' Callum said and squinted at Emmy. 'I thought you were on the other shift this week.'

'It got changed.'

'Right.'

Emmy pointed to the fridge and then grabbed a mug out of the cupboard and made Callum a cup of tea. 'There's an egg and bacon roll there for you. Microwave it if you want it warmed up.'

'Thanks. Lifesaver.' Callum squinted again and shook his head. 'Are you okay?'

Emmy frowned. 'Yeah, why?'

'You look *terrible*.'

'Do I?'

'Yeah.' Callum screwed the whole of his face up and held his head away for a second. 'Sort of green or something. Are you sure you're okay? Do you feel sick?'

Emmy shook her head and swiped the roll from the worktop. If Callum had noticed she must be looking bad. 'I'm fine. I just had a bit of a restless night.'

'Did you hear the foghorn?'

'How could I not?' Emmy smiled.

Callum peered out the window. 'It's still quite thick out there.'

'Yep, be careful on the way to school. Make sure you text me.'

'Will do.'

'See you later.'

Emmy glanced at the time as she hurried out into the foggy, salty morning air, got into her car, and headed for the ferry. It was second nature now, the early morning trek from Darling Island over the estuary. Now she'd got her routine down pat and did her breakfast the night before, she found the routine of getting on the ferry not a bad way to start the day. But today, as she loaded on with all the commuters, put the car in park and slipped the beeswax wrap from her breakfast roll, Katy was occupying her thoughts. By the time the ferry reached the other side, Emmy's head felt full to bursting.

She drove to work through various bottlenecks of traffic, feeling strangely removed from it all. Arriving at the staff entrance, Emmy waved her badge to pass through security in a daze. The usual port sounds washed over her: blaring announcements, rolling suitcases, crying toddlers. It blended around her as she went through to the staff room. She then floated through the briefing session on autopilot, not really retaining a word. When she was asked a question, she hadn't heard anything that had been said. Judy shot her a concerned glance as Emmy scrambled to bring herself into the room.

Only when she reached the main concourse did Emmy shake herself back to reality. She pasted on her professional work smile and tried to get a grip. Time to focus and get on with the job at hand. Her radio beeped from her shoulder, informing her that someone with a bee in their bonnet about the parking situation was on their way. Emmy felt as if complaining passengers were the last of her worries as she stood directing people to the correct queues. Thankfully, hours flew by in a blur of passports, gate directions, whingeing passengers, and lost children.

'Enjoy your travels,' she told an elderly couple shuffling in the queue. As soon as they passed, Emmy's fixed smile faded, and she tried to roll the tension from her shoulders while she dealt with another problem. She attempted to focus, but her thoughts kept drifting back to Katy no matter how many times she re-centred herself. She blinked against the sting of tiredness and the long night spent turning over and back dissecting each fragment of her conversation with Katy. When one passenger barked something at her, she mumbled an apology robotically. Irritation simmered right below her surface. She really couldn't be doing with anything, let alone the usual complaining passengers that were the nuts and bolts of her job.

Emmy tutted to herself as she made her way to the loo. How long could she maintain the charade that everything was fine? At her mid-shift break, she collapsed into the canteen with a coffee. Her eyes seemed to be burning, and her temples pulsed. She pressed the heels of her palms against her eye sockets and inhaled deeply.

By the afternoon lull, when the check-in area was much quieter, she was really feeling the bad night everywhere. Her heels throbbed in her shoes, and her eyes strained against the harsh lighting. She nearly jumped when a voice spoke at her shoulder.

'How're you holding up?' Judy asked with a concerned look on her face, handing Emmy a cup of coffee. 'You look like I feel. Are you okay?'

'Oh, I'm fine,' Emmy replied vaguely.

Judy's expression remained concerned. 'You look right off-colour. Is there something wrong? You've been strange all day. Not your usual self at all.'

Emmy cut her off, bristling at the insinuation a little bit. 'Honestly, I'm fine, just didn't sleep well. But thank you.' Her tone came out sharper than intended.

Judy looked taken aback and raised her eyebrows in surprise at Emmy's short tone. 'Okay, well, if you need to take the afternoon off…,' Judy said after an awkward pause.

'No, I'm fine, thanks,' Emmy sighed, sipped the coffee and tried to shake off the guilt twisting her stomach. She was barely keeping it together. How long could she keep thoughts of Katy compartmentalised and not tell her family what she knew? How long before everything unravelled? The whole feeling was why she hated secrets and lying. It wasn't her skillset in any shape or form.

When her shift finally ended, Emmy couldn't wait to get back to her car. She felt bad about brushing Judy off, and she realised that Judy must have seen right through her and known something was wrong. She really must be that transparent. By the time she got back to Darling, the sun was sinking towards the horizon as Emmy made the crossing. She sighed as she leant over the railing at everything appearing as if it had been spun in gold. She closed her eyes, letting the gulls overhead, the chatter of passengers and the engine hum fade to background noise. By the time she was stepping down the path at The Old Ticket Office, she felt a bit better. She knew one thing – that she was very glad to be home.

As Emmy walked in, slipped off her shoes, and pottered around the flat, gradually, some of her muscles began to uncoil. The comfort of the flat and the light outside worked its magic, as Darling Island always seemed to do. Her mobile ringing made her jump as she stood peering into the fridge, wondering if it was too early to pour a glass of wine.

'Evening, beautiful. How was your day?' Tom asked.

'Err, everything hurts,' Emmy joked. 'My head, my cheeks, my feet, and my hips.'

'Oh dear. That doesn't sound too healthy.'

'Ahh, I'm fine, the usual chaos,' Emmy replied breezily as she decided it *was* too early, but she didn't care, and pulled the bottle of wine out of the fridge.

'Still on for dinner?'

Emmy's heart sank. There was no way she was making a steak and kidney pie. She really couldn't be faffed to cook. 'Yep.'

Tom laughed out loud. 'You don't sound too up for it.'

'Just a bit full on today.'

'How about I come and make us pizza instead? Homemade.'

Emmy sighed in relief. 'Sounds *very* good to me. It's been a long day.'

By the time Tom arrived later with all the stuff for homemade pizzas, Emmy felt almost like herself again. She'd had a bath, washed and dried her hair, and was in soft clothes. They stood in the kitchen prepping the pizza and drinking wine. Once it was cooked, they sat in the sitting room with the pizzas on the coffee table in front of them.

'Feeling a bit better now you're fed?' Tom asked.

Emmy nodded, swallowing a bite of pizza. 'Work was just a lot today.' She hoped she sounded convincing. She didn't.

'You know you can tell me stuff. I'm not fragile like, err, Kevin.' Tom's tone was a mix of funny and earnest.

Emmy felt herself go nuclear. 'I know. Thanks.'

Tom slid another pizza slice from the board. 'You never know, I might be able to help, too. A problem shared and all that.'

'Why would you be able to help if there's nothing wrong?' Emmy countered as quick as a flash and added a silly smile.

She could tell, though, that Tom P Carter wasn't convinced, but he brushed it off.

Once they'd finished the pizza, cleared up, and Tom had

gone home, part of Emmy was relieved. The pretence of pretending everything was fine had got old very quickly. Lying in bed later that night, yet again, she found herself exhausted but wide awake. The day's events replayed in her head on an endless loop: Judy's worried frown, thoughts about Katy, then Tom. Frustration jolted inside Emmy, and she punched her pillow, trying to fluff it into a more comfortable position. Katy's re-emergence had tipped everything upside down in her world. Just as everything had been so good, too. With a huff, she turned onto her other side, staring listlessly out the window. She had a horrible, morose feeling that things were only going to get worse.

22

Emmy had been on a three-day stint of double shifts. She'd also spent way too much time for her liking ferrying Callum hither and thither for cricket. On top of the general stresses of mum life and life life, she'd WhatsApp messaged back and forth with Katy multiple times and still felt very guilty about the secret she was having to keep.

In soft blue tracksuit bottoms, a white T-shirt, trainers, and with her hair in a bun knot on the top of her head, she stood in the Love Emmy x shop with a mug of tea in her hand and assessed what was what. She hummed to herself as she ran her hand over the mirrored dresser and smiled at a group of dainty gold lockets in the display cabinet. Things were taking shape. Sunlight streamed through the large front windows, a tram trundled past, and apart from the Katy thing constantly in the back of her mind, life felt quite okay. She fussed with one of the lockets, moved a little pale pink velvet pouch into place, and leaned back to scrutinise the effect. All of it was looking lovely.

As she stood just staring around for a bit whilst she drank her tea, the hush was broken by the back door opening. Emmy poked her head around the door and peered through the store-room to see Tom sauntering in with a toolbox in his hand.

'Morning!' Tom called out cheerily.

Emmy frowned. 'What are you doing here? I thought you had meetings all day. I didn't expect to see you.'

'Why? What are you trying to hide from me?' Tom joked. 'Got my replacement upstairs?'

Emmy joked back as her insides shuddered. If only he knew she was keeping secrets. She laughed *way* too cheerfully. 'Ha ha. Yep, totally got my boyfriend upstairs hiding. Don't go up there. You don't know what you might find.'

Tom chuckled and flourished his hand around. 'I come bearing gifts.'

'What kind of gifts?'

'I have got a little delivery for you today.'

'Oh?' Emmy replied, intrigued. She wasn't expecting any packages. 'Like what?'

'Yep, I've got a van parked just down the lane. I was just checking to see where you were. Follow me,' Tom said, gesturing with his hand for Emmy to follow him.

Emmy's curiosity was piqued. 'What in the world?' She grabbed her phone from the counter and followed Tom out through the back and down the path at the side of the small courtyard garden. A nondescript white van was idling by the gate.

Seeing her questioning look, Tom gave a conspiratorial wink. 'Trust me, you're going to love this surprise. I'm going to be the best bloke on Darling. Possibly the whole planet.'

Emmy thought it must be another e-bike. 'Ahh, you got a bike for yourself. Excellent.'

Tom raised his eyebrows as he opened the van's back doors with a flourish. Nestled inside was a large object covered by a grey paint-splodged dust sheet.

'What on earth have you got there?' Emmy asked, laughing.

The shape was bulky and long. 'It looks nothing like a bike unless it has a sidecar. What is it?'

'Remember, you were looking at that nice antique display cabinet on that website?' Tom said, grin widening. He whisked the sheet away with a dramatic flair. 'Ta-da!'

Emmy's jaw dropped. Before her sat an ornate mahogany glass display cabinet atop clawed feet. Intricate geometric detailing accented the frame. Glass shone. It was absolutely magnificent. 'Oh my goodness! What? You didn't? It's stunning!' Emmy breathed, hands clasped to her chest. She stood looking up into the van. 'I can't believe it.'

'I knew it would be perfect,' Tom explained, looking pleased by Emmy's awestruck reaction.

Emmy shook her head as she remembered how long she'd stared at the pictures of the cabinet in the gallery of an online specialist antique shop. She also recalled how much the cabinet cost. 'I can't believe you did this,' she stammered. 'I don't know what to say.'

'I wanted to. After how hard you worked and everything. I spoke to your dad and Amy, and they reckoned you'd be well happy.'

That was the understatement of the year. Emmy was so happy, she was actually at a loss for words. It wasn't just about the cabinet, more that Tom was such a sweetheart. It felt so nice to be treated. Emmy felt bowled over at his thoughtfulness. She'd lusted over the antique cabinet multiple times, but never in a million years expected it would be part of Love Emmy x. It had been way out of her budget but had remained in her little imaginary vision for her shop in her mind.

'So, I take it you like it? Shall we get her inside?' Tom asked.

About ten minutes later, they carefully manoeuvred the cabinet up the garden path and through the back door into the shop. Tom stood back once the unit was in place. 'I measured it about six times, wondering. It fits like it was made for this spot. What do you reckon?'

'It's absolutely perfect,' Emmy gushed and clapped her hands to her face. 'I can't wait to style it up.' Her mind was already racing with ideas about how to display things. Impulsively, she threw her arms around Tom's neck. 'Thank you so much! I can't tell you how much I love it. I love you, in fact.'

Tom's eyes crinkled. 'Just glad you like it in the flesh, as it were.'

Emmy's pulse fluttered. She gazed up at him, suddenly lost for words. 'I can't believe you'd do this for me.'

Tom looked confused. 'Why wouldn't I?'

Emmy thought about her ex, Kevin. He'd hardly been there for her, even before his gambling addiction. Tom was a whole other ball game. She brushed off the thought, unwound her arms from Tom's neck and bustled behind the counter. She took a few pieces from one of her storage tubs holding her stock and nestled them into the new cabinet. Then she put a couple of pairs of earrings on the top shelf and a delicate silver necklace on one of the lower trays.

Stepping back with a nod, she could already envision shoppers oohing and ahing over its contents. 'Thank you again. It's beyond what I could've hoped for. It was so expensive! Ahh, I'm so pleased!'

'Happy to play a part in making your dream a reality,' Tom said with a crinkle-eyed smile. 'You've worked hard with all this. It deserves to dazzle.'

Emmy flushed with pleasure. She was suddenly zoomed back to outside the shop when Tom had bumped into her while she was carrying Callum's birthday cake. She slipped her phone out of her pocket and navigated to the bookmarked page for the cabinet. She held her phone up alongside the cabinet. 'Better in real life, actually.'

Tom squinted at the photos. 'Yeah, it is.'

Emmy read out the wording. 'This stunning Allderley cabinet is not just a piece of furniture; it's an exquisite piece of art that has stood the test of time. Acquired many years ago, it's a true testament to craftsmanship at its finest. It's designed with an unparalleled level of quality that's synonymous with the Allderley name, lending a touch of elegance and sophistication to any room it graces. The framework, masterfully crafted, exudes a rich patina that gives the cabinet its vintage allure, and the intricate detailing adds an extra layer of luxury. Each leg is carved with utmost precision, featuring graceful curves that lend the piece a timeless beauty.

Functionality marries form here, as the cabinet is complete with lockable doors for added security and a series of removable trays. In summary, this Allderley cabinet is not just a storage solution; it's an investment in aesthetic beauty and craftsmanship.'

'Well, there you are.'

'Yes, here I am.' Emmy nodded. 'Thank you. I'm absolutely over the moon.'

Emmy felt buzzy and flushed with a warm feeling. Everything with the shop was working out okay, and Tom P Carter was more than okay. There was just one little mar in her world that was definitely not in any way okay. It was one she had not a clue how she was going to change, and she didn't really want to have to work it out.

23

Emmy had been busy with all sorts and had tried not to think about the Katy dilemma too much. She attempted to convince herself that just keeping in touch with Katy was fine for now. It didn't need to be a problem. She tried to tell herself it was okay to have secrets in some cases in life. Millions of people did it every day of the week, all over the world. Secrets were part of real life, weren't they? She'd just finished cleaning the bathroom, where she'd been mulling over the Katy situation. Deciding to send a text, she slipped her phone out of her pocket and typed out a message to Katy.

Emmy: *Hey! How are you? Hope you're doing okay. Any chance you fancy meeting up this week?*

Emmy instantly saw the little dots flashing on the screen indicating that Katy was typing back. She stood staring at her phone, waiting for Katy's reply to come through.

Katy: *Hey, Ems. Sorry, I've been quiet. Just trying to figure things out, I guess.*

Emmy: *No need to apologise! I know this is a lot. No pressure.*

Katy: *Lunch later this week? My treat this time.*

Emmy inhaled and let the air out in a whoosh through her

nose. Her mind zoomed straight to when Amy had asked her to lunch, and she'd pretended she was too busy and needed a rain check. Too busy for Amy, but not for Katy. Ouch. This is why she didn't like lying. Everything got complicated and weird and swirled around in her head.

Emmy: *Lunch sounds perfect!*

Katy: *How about Thursday? Is that good for you? There's a bakery café near my place we could try. I'm not happy to come over your way.*

Emmy quickly ran through her week. She wasn't at the port and had earmarked the morning for Love Emmy x stuff, and it was a hefty trek to Katy's. She buried the fact that she was busy.

Emmy: *Thursday is great! Send me the address and I'll meet you there.*

Katy: *Will do. Oh, Ems, btw thx for texting. I know I haven't made it easy. It means a lot, you know.*

Emmy felt her stomach lurch. She had no clue if she was doing the right thing or not.

Emmy: *Don't be silly. See you Thursday!*

Katy: *See you then.*

Emmy: *Looking forward to it! xxx*

~

Thursday had rolled around in a whirl of cricket, Tom, and work. Emmy had patted herself on the back for not letting anyone around her know what was going on inside. Or so she thought. She'd spent the morning doing Love Emmy x orders, had gone to the post office and then, having told no one where she was going, she'd driven onto the ferry and made her way to the coffee shop Katy had sent her directions to. Deliberately early, she parked, then answered a few emails on her phone, added some new products to the Love Emmy x store, and then sat in her car thinking.

She sank further into the upholstery of the driver's seat, her eyes half-shut, and with the sun beating through the wind-screen, the world seemed nicely muffled. She felt as if she could just stay in the car locked away from the outside, have a little nap, and when she woke up, everything would be better. It was as if the world outside had all melded into one: the birds, the sway of the trees in the breeze, the occasional car that passed by. She was in an odd little pocket of time with her tangled thoughts. With her bag on the front seat beside her, and the emotional baggage she had been carrying since spotting Katy in the train station and the sun, she felt drowsy. As if her bones were a weight inside her skin – heavy with worry.

She followed the swaying trees in front of her and thought about how if Amy and Cherry found out that she was in contact with Katy and hadn't told them, the whole family unit could turn upside down. She pondered what she was going to do, and closing her eyes fully for a moment, she visualised Katy's face and then Elodie's. She nodded to herself. She was going to have to say something to Katy about telling the others. It really was as simple and as cut and dried as that. She couldn't continue with the secret texts and phone calls. She sat up in her seat, checked her face in the rearview mirror, and gathered her bag with a bit of resolve. Yes, she was going to have to tell Katy it was time to think about Emmy in all of this.

Once Emmy arrived at the coffee shop, she faltered in her resolve. The cosy warmth of the café wrapped Emmy up as she stepped inside, as she scanned the cluster of mismatched tables, looking for Katy. She felt a pang as she spotted Katy tucked away in a corner, staring pensively out the window with her hands wrapped around a mug.

Emmy weaved her way through the tables and forced herself to beam. 'Hi.'

'Hi Ems. Sorry, I was off in my own little world.' Katy stood and kissed Emmy on the cheek.

'It's good to see you. How've you been holding up?' Emmy asked. 'How's Elodie?'

Katy sat back down. 'Fine. The usual ups and downs of mum life.' She smiled a funny, wry smile.

Emmy nodded. 'You're talking to the right person. It gets overwhelming sometimes. If you ever need help or just someone to vent to.'

'I appreciate that...' Katy trailed off, staring down into her coffee for a second. 'It's hard not having any support from, well, you know. It could be a lot worse.'

Emmy paused for a second. 'You could change that.'

'I'm well aware of that.'

Emmy could sense a wall going up in front of Katy at the mention of help. She hesitated before speaking again, but the secrecy was eating away at her. 'Kates, I know neither of us wants to rush things, but...' She faltered, mouth dry. Katy's shoulders immediately tensed, eyes narrowing warily. Pushing forward, Emmy continued haltingly, 'Don't you think maybe it's time to at least tell Mum? I know she would want to know about Elodie. It really is eating away at me.'

Katy's mug hit the table with a jolt, sloshing coffee over the sides. Emmy shrank back as Katy's head snapped up, eyes flashing. 'Absolutely not. I told you, I'm not ready. Not even near it. Please drop it.'

Emmy held up both hands. 'You're right. Sorry. I shouldn't have pressed it.' The café's cosy atmosphere now felt stifling, as Emmy shook her head and blinked repeatedly. 'Sorry. No pressure.'

'You say no pressure, but then you ask to tell. I already told you I don't want that. Sorry, I thought I made that clear. It's probably not fair on you, you're right. We shouldn't have met up again. It's definitely not fair. Sorry. Yeah, this is all wrong. I should have stuck to my guns in the first place. Sorry.'

Emmy shook her head and back-pedalled like crazy. 'No, no.

It's fine. We move at your pace, however long you need. I just hate keeping this enormous secret from Mum. Remember how crap I am at secrets?' She trailed off at Katy's withering look.

Katy's face softened a degree. 'I know it's a lot to handle. You knew the score, though. I did make that clear right at the start. It's up to you. I have to do this in my own time.'

Inside, Emmy's guilt mixed with frustration. Katy annoyed her immensely. She'd always been stubborn. Emmy buried the urge to argue. 'You're right. I shouldn't have said anything.'

Katy busied herself, mopping up her spilt coffee. 'It's fine.'

Emmy cast about for safer conversational ground. 'What's Elodie been up to?'

'I've been teaching her the alphabet. She loves it.' Katy seemed distracted. She pushed her coffee cup away. 'I should actually get going. This probably wasn't a good idea. Sorry you made the effort to come all the way here. What you said – you're right. It's not fair on you, Ems. You've got enough on your plate. I made my bed. I'm sorry. I don't want you to feel uncomfortable.'

Emmy's heart sank. 'Up to you.' Her brightness sounded false even to herself.

Katy just made a non-committal noise. 'Sorry, Ems. I'll message you.'

Before she could really object, Emmy was sitting alone amid the cheerful babble and clinks of cups all around her. Emmy unclenched her fist, realising she'd crushed her napkin into a tight ball on her lap. She brushed a few crumbs from her jeans. Her throat was so tight she felt almost panicky. She shook her head over and over again, berating herself. Why had she pushed Katy about Cherry? She should have known better. There was a lot of water under the bridge, and she'd tried to rush things. Emmy touched Grandma Emily's diamond and closed her eyes. As usual, she'd messed things up. No surprise there. Not at all.

24

Later that night, Emmy sank onto the sofa, tucking her feet beneath her. The sea breeze through the open window carried salty Darling air into the room. At least there was that. She took a grateful sip of wine, hoping it might ease the tight knot lingering in her chest after the tense exchange with Katy. The wine had a lot of work to do.

Leaning her head back against the cushion, she forced herself to focus on the sounds outside the window instead of replaying the conversation's words over and over in her head. She sat staring up at the ceiling for ages, listening to the odd tapping away from Callum on the computer in his room and taking sips of her wine. Emmy's phone buzzing made her jolt, nearly spilling her wine in her lap. Fumbling to steady the glass, she glanced at the screen. Amy's number showed. Emmy just stared at it until it rang out. Amy wasn't going to give up, and it went again. Guilt flickered through Emmy. Amy had called her twice that day already, and she'd not answered.

Hesitating for another quick second, she swiped to accept the FaceTime call. Amy's smiling face instantly filled the screen.

Emmy painted on a matching grin, hoping she looked relaxed and not twisted into knots and consumed by guilt and lies.

'Well, if it isn't the most elusive sister in England!' Amy shook her head in mock annoyance. 'I was starting to wonder if you'd changed your number on me.'

Emmy feigned an eye roll and joked. 'Oh please, you know I can't resist your witty self for long.' She rearranged the phone to prop it against a cushion in front of her. 'How's your day been then?'

'More of the usual chaos wrangling the children and clients.' Amy launched into an account of her hectic day juggling work meetings and school pickups.

Emmy made the appropriate reactions in the right places, but she was definitely a bit absent. Her free hand crept up to fiddle with Emily's diamond. She didn't even realise she was doing it until Amy abruptly paused mid-story.

'Wait, Ems, are you wearing Grandma's diamond?'

Caught off guard, Emmy's hand jerked self-consciously down to her lap. 'What?'

'The diamond. You are. What's wrong?'

Emmy forced an offhand laugh. 'Just fancied taking it out for a spin rather than it sitting in my jewellery box all the time. I thought about it when I was getting the new display set up in the shop.'

Amy clearly wasn't buying it; her forehead creased into a frown. Amy rolled her eyes and tutted, 'Oh, come on, Ems! I know your "comfort necklace" when I see it.'

'Don't be ridiculous! It's not.'

Amy pressed. 'You've been acting so off lately, and now you've got that on. You haven't worn that for ages. Like, a *really* long time. When you twiddle it like that.'

Emmy chewed her lip, cursing internally. She should have known nothing got past Amy. She hadn't even really noticed she'd reached for the necklace. Both of them, though, knew she wore it when emotions were running high. Amy was observant, she had to give her that. Scrambling for some plausible reason that had nothing to do with Katy, Emmy offered weakly, 'It's nothing, really. Just stress about getting the shop ready on time...'

'Is everything okay with you and Tom? Because you wore that necklace all the time when Kevin started gambling,' Amy asked pointedly.

'God no, nothing like that,' Emmy cut in hastily. 'Tom's wonderful as always,' she joked. 'So far, anyway.'

Amy looked slightly mollified. 'Well, something's clearly bothering you, even if you won't say what. You know, bottling it up inside helps no one. Look what happened last time. That didn't end well.'

Emmy just shook her head mutely.

Amy tried another tack. 'Is it money stuff again? I know the shop renovations have been costly and slower than you hoped. You know I'm always here if you need...'

'Honestly, I promise this isn't about money or Tom or the shop, really.' Emmy said, shaking her head and flitting her hand in front of her face as if to dismiss Amy's concern. The lies sat bitterly on her tongue. She hated the secret. She hated shutting Amy out. She felt trapped with no clue what to do.

'My offer stands. If you're worried about money, just say the word. You know Mum and Dad will help too. That's what family is for. They've always been here for us. I always feel so lucky to have that, you know?'

Emmy nodded, a gigantic lump lodging in her throat. Boy did she know how good Bob and Cherry were. Talk about feeling wretched.

Sensing Emmy's mood, Amy seamlessly changed the subject. 'Oh, did I tell you what the teacher said the other day? Proud mum moment.'

As Amy started to ramble on and chatted about her daughter's latest milestones, the knot inside Emmy's chest eased a bit, though she was not fully in the conversation at all. She smiled as she heard Amy say she needed to go.

'See you later, then,' Emmy said.

'Yeah, have a good shift at work tomorrow. Hope the traffic's not too bad on the way home.'

'Same to you. Love you, Ames.'

'Yep. Love you.'

Emmy let the phone drop to her lap, and she stared absently out the window as it began to rain. She watched little shiny rivulets slide down the glass. The weather matched her mood exactly. She thought about the lies and about Katy, and replayed their coffee shop conversation on an endless loop. No matter how she analysed it, she had no idea how it was going to turn out.

With a sigh, she shuffled out to the kitchen to top up her wine, stopped in to talk to Callum, who was knee-deep on the computer, and settled back on the sofa. She curled against the sofa arm, plumped a cushion under her head, and felt herself relax a bit.

She must have dozed off because about an hour later, suddenly, Emmy jerked awake, disoriented. The wine glass teetered dangerously before she rescued it. Groggy and bleary-eyed, she groped for her phone to check the time. The rain had stopped, the sitting room was dark, and she could see a light in the hallway from under Callum's door. She contemplated staying right where she was and staying on the sofa for the night, but her neck already felt the awkward angle, and her lower back was stiff.

Wincing, she hauled herself upright, joints cracking as she shuffled to the kitchen for a glass of water. As she passed Callum's room on the way to the bathroom, she poked her head around the door. 'Just popping up for a shower and to get my pyjamas on.'

Callum looked up, nodded, and smiled. 'You okay, Mum?'

'Fine, just tired.'

'Want me to make you a cup of tea?'

'Love one.'

'I'll put it in the pot and get it ready for you when you come down,' Callum said with a smile.

Emmy raised her eyebrows, and as she made her way up the steep back stairs to the top room, she was thankful for Callum. He definitely had his teenage boy moments, but she could tell that *he* could tell that there was something wrong.

As Emmy stood under the shower, she began to feel angry at Katy. All the secrets and lies. How dare Katy make her keep this secret and think she could call all the shots? How could she be so selfish, denying her daughter the family?

Emmy shook her head. Maybe she'd just come out with it and tell everyone. Her patience was wearing thin. Maybe it was time for the truth.

25

The scent of roast chicken and baking pastry enveloped Emmy as she stepped through the front door of her childhood home. Her mum's voice sounded from the kitchen, mingling with the clatter of dishes and Amy's laughter. Emmy immediately felt her stomach tense. Neither Cherry nor Amy had a clue what was going on, but Emmy was more than aware that she wasn't being truthful. It made her feel *dreadful*. She'd always convinced herself that they were so close. What a joke that now was.

Following the sounds down the hall, Emmy paused in the kitchen doorway, taking in the scene. Cherry and Amy stood side-by-side at the counter, making an apple crumble. Across the room, Bob sat at the kitchen table chatting with Tom and Callum, a spread of vegetable crudités and cheese on a circular spinning board in front of them. Emmy's heart flipped at the sight of Tom sitting with Callum and her dad. She soaked up the familiarity of the place, the comfort of the scene and the memories that seemed to drift in the air. Everything in her life had been going so well until something had reared its head to send her into a spin and mess things up. As it always seemed to do.

'There she is, our missing piece!' Amy exclaimed, spotting Emmy hovering by the door. Amy held her arms out, folding Emmy in a hug that left faint streaks of flour on Emmy's shirt. 'How was your shift?'

'Early!' Emmy replied. 'No huge dramas today, so that was good, just the usual queue of issues.'

Cherry kissed Emmy next, smoothing back the hair from Emmy's face affectionately. 'Hello, darling. Feels like ages since your last visit.'

'I know! I've been so busy.' Inside, Emmy shuddered at the other reason she'd been a little bit distant from both Cherry and Amy. It began with a 'K.'

If Cherry noticed what was going on, she breezed past it cheerfully. 'No matter, you're here now! Go and relax, dinner's doing well. Put your feet up.'

Tom jumped up from the table and kissed Emmy on the cheek. 'All good?'

'Yep.'

'You look tired,' Tom noted.

Emmy flicked her hand to dismiss Tom's words. 'Just a few problems today. I'm glad to be out of there.'

Bob also rose and kissed Emmy on the cheek. 'How's my girl?'

'Great, Dad, thanks,' Emmy replied a little too enthusiastically. She tried and failed to push aside the lingering unease below her façade. If anyone could sense something off in her, it would be her dad. Like Amy, he always sensed when all was not well.

Bob just squeezed affectionately. 'Glad to hear it.'

Before Emmy could over analyse anything, Callum went to pass her a cracker heaped with some sort of fancy cheese. 'You've got to try this,' he insisted.

Emmy took a few steps towards the sink, washed her hands,

and then sat down. She took the cracker and popped it into her mouth. 'Mmm, yes, yum.'

A couple of hours later, the dinner was done and dusted. Emmy had thoroughly enjoyed it all. Her mum was an expert at comfort food, and she'd wallowed in the food and drink. After topping up their glasses, Bob raised his wine glass. 'To family dinners like these,' he pronounced with a chuckle.

Emmy swallowed as glasses clinked all around. She tapped her glass to Amy's and crossed her fingers in her lap. 'To family dinners!' Emmy said, gripping the stem of her wine glass tight and managing a weak smile.

As Bob, Tom and Callum started to clear up, Cherry leant forward. 'Are you okay, Ems? You've been awfully quiet tonight.'

Emmy flicked her eyes to Amy, who was also looking at her curiously. 'Have I? Oh, sorry... Just had a long day. The port was a madhouse early on.' She offered an apologetic smile that didn't quite reach her eyes.

Thankfully, Amy jumped in to complain about her own terribly busy week, and the moment passed. After Bob and Tom had gone out to the garden, Emmy was standing in the kitchen making a cup of tea while Cherry tidied up. 'That was nice, wasn't it?' Emmy said. 'I needed that.'

'Lovely,' Cherry replied as she shuttled glasses into the drying rack. 'Callum helped with the veg before you got here. Sweet.'

'He's good for some things,' Emmy joked.

Cherry laughed. 'Remember his phase when he was little when he wanted to help you cook dinner each night?'

'Oh God, yes! The weeks of just eating salads because that's all he could make.'

'Those were the days. When my grandbabies were little,' Cherry said wistfully.

Emmy's heart raced as her mum brought up memories. She swiftly steered the conversation to cricket and asked how Cherry's golf was. Cherry replied as she put some forks into the cutlery drawer. 'Great. I'm not looking forward to the cold weather. You know how much I love my golf.'

'Yeah. It's good you have that. Good to have hobbies,' Emmy agreed.

'It is,' Cherry said as she whipped a tea towel from the drawer and started to wipe it over a pan. Emmy found herself lost in thought as she looked around the kitchen. The next thing she knew, Cherry was touching Emmy's arm and holding a mug in front of her. 'There you go.'

'Sorry. Miles away.'

'Darling, are you sure everything is alright? Truly?' Her eyes probed Emmy's intently. 'You seem not yourself tonight. More distant than usual. Are things okay with Tom?' Cherry nodded her head towards the door. 'Him and Callum seem good.'

Emmy's gut tightened. She managed what she hoped was a bemused head shake. 'I'm fine, Mum. You worry too much.' She squeezed Cherry's hand and kissed her cheek.

'I don't,' Cherry said. 'You're reminding me of when you found out Kevin was gambling, but you hadn't told us yet.' Cherry wrinkled up her lips. 'Yeah, you were secretive then, too. You had an odd look on your face then. It's back.'

'No, no. Don't be silly!' Emmy shook her head quickly and inclined her chin towards the garden. 'Come on. Let's take the tea out.'

Ensconced on the outdoor sofa between Tom and Callum, Emmy tried focusing on the meandering conversation about Bob's latest garden mishap. All she could think was that she knew where Katy was and that she'd lied through her teeth. Worse was that people had noticed, and she'd said it was nothing. There was a saying about lying and getting caught up in it. How one lie led to another. How it never ended well. Emmy couldn't think what exactly the saying was, but she knew how apt it was in her case.

As she tried to keep her mind on the conversation, little tears pricked at the corner of her eyes. It was Katy's decision to make on her own terms if and when she was ready to contact the family, she reminded herself. But how many more strained family visits would Emmy have to sit through? The pretence hung over her like a horrible, dark, suffocating cloud. She watched as Tom stood by the fence, talking to Bob about the ins and outs of making a raised bed. Here she was, finally with a happy relationship status, and things had been going so well in her world. Now this. Emmy felt exponentially guilty as her family chatted away around her. She nodded to herself. She was going to have to do something. She'd try to persuade Katy to contact Cherry and Bob before the lying by omission warped everything in her life. Yes, she would do that.

26

A few days later, Emmy hadn't done anything about the situation at all apart from let it fester. She sank into the chair in the sitting room and let out a long, possibly overly dramatic, but definitely weary sigh, and attempted to let the day's tension ease from her shoulders. It didn't really work. She closed her eyes as she listened to the sounds of Tom pottering in the kitchen and loading up the dishwasher with their dinner dishes.

She shook her head as she thought about Katy. It was weird to have Katy back in her life after so many years apart. Weird and fraught with lots of issues. Keeping their reconciliation from the family weighed heavily on Emmy, though she was more than aware of the reasons Katy wanted to keep it that way. Emmy forced her mind away from Katy, trying to stay present, but ever since she'd first seen Katy from the train window, staying focused had become a challenge. Tom's voice startled her from her pondering.

'Penny for your thoughts?' Tom said in a joking manner. He was leaning against the sitting room doorway, drying his hands on a towel. 'You've seemed somewhere else all night.'

Emmy shivered inside. How she was feeling was clearly obvious. Amy, Cherry, Tom, and Bob, even Callum had noticed it. 'Oh, sorry about that.' Emmy waved a hand, aiming for casual and unconcerned.

'Are you thinking how lucky you are to have me in the house? Unloading the dishwasher,' Tom joked.

'Well, Callum wasn't going to do it,' Emmy fired back. 'Nah, just daydreaming, I suppose.'

Tom moved behind the sofa. 'How about I do your shoulders for a bit?'

'Thought you'd never ask.'

Tom gripped the muscles across the top of Emmy's shoulders and started to massage the knots. 'Blimey, you *are* tight!'

'I am.'

'So, what were you thinking about? Daydreaming about anything interesting?'

'Fascinating! So interesting,' Emmy said sarcastically, with a smile and heard herself lie. 'Totally the opposite. What I still need to finish at the shop and such. I keep thinking I'm ready to go, and then boom, another hurdle slams down at the last minute. I feel like I'm never going to get there.'

'Mmm. Busy time coming up,' Tom replied as his fingers pushed into Emmy's neck. 'You seem run off your feet lately.'

Guilt pricked at Emmy. It didn't just prick; it poked her like a hot stick. If only Tom knew what she was really up to and what she was concealing from not just him, but just about everyone around her. She turned sideways to face him, smoothing non-existent wrinkles from her shirt to avoid meeting his gaze directly.

'I'm fine, honestly. I just think getting everything ready for the shop has stressed me more than I realised. But it will all be worth it soon.'

Tom looked unconvinced, but simply dropped a kiss on her

forehead. 'Well, don't overdo it. I can always lend a hand if you need me.'

Emmy swooned and turned into a nuclear reactor inside as she turned back, and Tom continued to knead the tops of her shoulder. She wished that the shop was the only thing causing her to be distracted in just about every area of her life. Having Katy back in her orbit had stirred up a tornado of emotions, old and new.

Tom leant down. 'How about a nice hot chocolate? It helps shopkeepers with their worries.'

'Ha. Yeah, love one. I need a lug of something in it, I reckon.'

'Happy to help with that.'

Later, as Emmy cuddled close to Tom with her feet on his lap and her hot chocolate in her hand, Tom looked towards her. 'I know you're not used to it because of what happened with Kevin, but, you know, if you need to talk or want to unload anything on your mind...'

'Thank you, but I'm fine.'

'I can tell there's something on your mind.'

Emmy tilted her face up to meet Tom's earnest gaze. 'Thank you,' she said softly. 'It's nothing, really. I promise I'd tell you if it was serious.' Emmy felt sick to her stomach, and a vile, sour taste was in her mouth. Lying did not suit her at all.

Tom tapped her legs and changed the subject. Emmy sighed inside. When was this going to end?

O ver the next week, Emmy didn't know one end of herself from the other. Someone at work had called in sick, there'd been a leak in the flat and the need for an emergency plumber, Callum had had more than one cricket match and training, and she'd been to meet Katy again. On the day she'd gone to see Katy, Tom had frowned when she'd totally lied and told him she was going to pick up something for Callum.

Since then, she'd felt Tom's body language change. He was now clearly suspicious about the way she was acting. He'd asked a few loaded questions about the cricket errand, and it was clear he remained unconvinced by her vague excuses that all was fine. Emmy was all a quandary. She knew she needed to be more careful until she was ready for the truth about Katy to come out, but secrecy had never come naturally to her, and the weight of lying by omission was getting more and more difficult to pull off.

Around her family, Tom, and Callum, she doubled down on keeping up casual appearances, kept laughing brightly and steering conversations to superficial topics. Inside, however, she was in turmoil. She did, in fact, feel almost like an imposter in her own life.

She was just on her way back to the car from meeting Katy again when she got a text from Callum asking her if she was going shopping. She rolled her eyes at his comment that there was nothing to eat in the fridge, but she had to admit Mother Hubbard was in the house. She sighed as she got in the car, and instead of starting straight away on the trek back to Darling, she looked for a supermarket nearby. She clicked on a Waitrose on the map, followed the directions coming out of her phone, and parked in the car park. Half an hour or so later, she had most of Callum's favourites in her trolley. A load of mince to make a vat of chilli for enchiladas to put in the freezer, and more carbohydrates for Callum than anyone would believe he could eat. She'd whizzed around and stocked up as if her life depended on it.

Emmy began unloading her groceries onto the conveyor belt at the checkout counter. The cashier, a cheery woman with silver hair pulled back in a plaited ponytail, started scanning the items. The machine beeped as the woman passed the items over the scanner.

'Looks like you're stocking up for a big cooking day!' the cashier remarked as she scanned two huge loads of mince.

Emmy smiled. 'My son informed me just now that there's 'nothing to eat' at home, so I figured I'd better do a proper shop. I've whizzed around here, and I'm going to do a cook-up. He eats me out of house and home,' Emmy joked. 'This should keep him going for a bit.'

'Ah, I remember those days well.' The cashier chuckled. 'My two boys were bottomless pits when they were teenagers. The milk we got through alone!' As she scanned one of the packages of mince, she added, 'Good thing the weather's cooled down a bit. Makes cooking big meals more bearable.'

Emmy nodded in agreement. 'Yes, this little cold snap has been nice, actually. I was wilting in that heat wave the other week! The weather's all of a sudden turned, though.'

The two women carried on small talk about the weather as the rest of Emmy's items were scanned. When everything had been totalled up, the cashier told her the amount and looked up. Emmy opened her bag to get her phone and suddenly realised she didn't have it. A wave of panic washed over her as she frantically searched through her bag.

'Oh no. I must have left my phone in the car! Sorry, I need that to pay,' Emmy exclaimed, then swore, then sighed. She shuffled item after item around her cluttered handbag fruitlessly, offered the queue behind her an apologetic grimace, and turned back to the cashier. 'I'll just run out and grab it quickly. Sorry about that.'

The cashier gave her a sympathetic smile. 'No problem, take your time.'

As she hot-footed it out the automatic doors to the car park, Emmy swore again. She muttered under her breath, spinning on her heel to hurry back the way she came. So much for a quick errand. She hurried out, berating herself for being so scatter-brained. It wasn't like her, but she knew precisely why she'd left her phone in the car, Katy and everything going on. She rummaged around in the car and finally found it staring her in the face by the gearstick. Relief flooded through her as she grabbed it and rushed back inside.

As Emmy hurried back into Waitrose, her heels clicking against the shiny tiled floor, she couldn't shake the feeling of embarrassment. 'What a mess,' she muttered to herself, hoping the queue she'd left behind wasn't too disrupted. When she reached the checkout, she found the cashier chatting away to another customer. Emmy's shopping was placed to the side on an empty section of the counter.

She caught the cashier's eye. 'Sorry. Brain like a sieve.'

'All bagged up and ready for you. Don't worry about it.'

'Thank you so much,' Emmy said, feeling herself blush. She quickly pulled out her phone, tapped on the wallet, and then held it over the contactless payment device. The machine beeped approvingly, and Emmy sighed in relief.

'Thank you for being so understanding,' Emmy said gratefully as she gathered her bags.

'Not a problem at all,' the cashier replied. 'Happens to the best of us. Especially when we've got a lot on our minds. You see it all in here, that I can tell you for free. Happens many times a week. You're certainly not the only one. We have our whole life on our phones and when we leave them somewhere, God help us. You have to wonder how we managed to live in the old days.'

Emmy looked up, surprised. The cashier's words had struck a chord. She most certainly had a lot on her mind. The shop, lying to Amy and her mum, work, Callum, annoying Kevin, guilt. Yes, her brain was at capacity, and the Katy situation loomed in the backdrop of her thoughts nearly twenty-four-seven. The cashier, intuitive as she was, seemed to grasp that Emmy's forgetfulness wasn't just about leaving her phone in the car. 'You have no idea how true that is.'

The woman batted her hand in front of her face. 'Don't

worry about it. Give yourself a break.' She looked Emmy right in the eye. 'And breathe.'

'Yes, yes, thank you.' Emmy repeated what she said back with a smile. 'And breathe.'

As Emmy wheeled her trolley towards the exit, she took the cashier's words literally. She forced herself to breathe, in out, in out. Life had been a whirlwind, and she'd started to do stupid things like leave her phone on show in the centre of her car. She thought about what the cashier had said. She had so much on her mind. Taking her spare packed work bag out of the car to make room and hanging it on the trolley hook, she loaded her shopping into the boot of her car; Emmy continued to take deep, pointed breaths. They did nothing to help with the guilt or the lies. They did make her a tiny bit less anxious, so that was a plus.

After pushing the trolley back to the trolley bay, she got in the car and sat there for a moment before starting the ignition. She needed to get home and regroup. Get the shopping put away, get the mince going, get a load of batch cooking sorted, and get a grip back on her life. With all the angst and stress of Katy's arrival back in her life, she was beginning to let things slide, and she didn't like how it felt at all. Emmy Bardot did not like feeling out of control.

∼

E mmy's heart sank as the ferry pulled away from the dock, and she immediately realised what she had done. **** *my life.*

She berated herself as she watched the water coming up around the ferry. How could she have been so careless twice in the space of what an hour? She mentally replayed walking from Waitrose out to her car, loading the shopping into the boot, and returning the trolley. She distinctly remembered temporarily hanging her work bag on the trolley hook while she loaded the bags towards the back of the boot so they didn't fall over. But in her distracted state of mind, she realised she'd forgotten to take the bag back off the trolley and put it back in the car.

She mentally kicked herself. The bag and its mate lived in her boot on rotation. It was always filled with a clean uniform, spare shoes, underwear, and anything else she might need for work. It also contained her spare work radio, spare employee badge, and a phone charger. She realised that her Love Emmy x notebook with important notes was also in there. She didn't quite need the bag for her next shift, but it was important. If she didn't have it, she might have to explain to Judy where the other radio was and all sorts. She weighed up her options. There was no way around it; she was going to have to turn right back around once she reached Darling and go back to the supermarket. The thought of more driving and another two ferry rides after the long day made Emmy want to cry in frustration. She did, in fact, start to cry. As the ferry engines rumbled beneath her feet, she watched the island get closer and closer with a sinking feeling in her stomach.

By the time she got to the other side, she'd decided that there was no way she was going back. She was grumpy, tired, and had a boot full of food. Pulling into the lane behind The Old Ticket Office, she Googled the supermarket and called.

A bored but friendly enough teenage-sounding voice answered. 'Hello. Customer service desk. How can I help you today?'

Emmy explained the situation, 'I think I left my bag in a trolley earlier on.'

'What, in the trolleys by the door?' the voice asked helpfully.

'No. In the car park. I think it might be in the trolley bay.'

There was an intake of breath and a whooshing sound. 'Hang on a minute. I haven't heard anything. Let me go out and check.'

'Thank you.'

What felt like an eternity passed. Emmy actually thought that the teenager had forgotten her. He came back on the phone. 'Sorry about that. Nothing yet. I've checked a few places and nothing has been handed in as far as I can see. I can get the trolleys double-checked later and call you if you like.'

Emmy sighed. 'Okay, yes. Thanks for your help.' She relayed her number and put her phone in her bag. She sat for a moment, gathering her energy before turning off the ignition and climbing out of the car. Popping the boot, she started gathering up the grocery bags.

'Need a hand?' Callum's voice made her look up. He was walking towards her down the lane.

'That would be great, thanks, Cal,' Emmy said with relief. She passed him a couple of the heavier bags. Together they lugged the shopping up to the flat. In the kitchen, Emmy began unpacking while Callum peered into the fridge.

'When's dinner? Or shall I make us pasta? My speciality.'

Emmy suppressed an ironic smile. Quite how Callum thought she'd cooked dinner while she wasn't even in the house was beyond her. 'I'm going to make a big batch of chilli in the multicooker. Should be ready in an hour or so.'

'Yes.' Callum pumped his fist. 'I love that. We haven't had it for ages. With tortilla chips?'

'Yeah. If you help chop the onions, it'll be done quicker,' Emmy said and slid a cutting board and knife towards him across the counter.

Callum chopped onions and peppers while Emmy multi-tasked by putting shopping away and browning the beef in the multicooker pot.

'How was your day?' Emmy asked as she scraped minced garlic into the pot. 'How was cricket?'

Callum nodded, sniffing loudly from the onion fumes. 'Yeah, it was good. Max says I'm improving a lot.'

'That's good to hear.'

They chatted about Callum's cricket team and school as the kitchen filled with the aroma of beef and garlic. Emmy dumped cans of tomatoes into the multicooker and gave it a stir. Callum put the chopping board and knife into the dishwasher and put a bag of tortilla chips on the worktop. 'Grandma called while you were out. She said she tried to call you, but you must have had your phone on silent. She invited us for lunch.'

Emmy's stomach twisted with guilt. 'Oh, lovely.' Inwardly, her mind spun with her secret meet-ups with Katy. She knew it was Katy's decision, but Emmy hated keeping her family in the dark. But it wasn't Emmy's place to tell them against Katy's wishes. She stirred the chilli absently, lost in thought.

Callum dipped a teaspoon into the mixture. 'I think this needs more spice,' Callum said, jolting her back to the room.

Emmy blinked. 'It's only browned. Chuck another bit in if you like.'

As she watched Callum sprinkle more chilli into the pot, she tutted as her mind flipped to the bag she'd left at the supermarket. There wasn't much she could do about it. She was going to pour herself a glass of wine, have a bath, sit with Callum, have a nice dinner, and not worry about anything else. For now, everything else could wait.

27

Emmy stood in the middle of the shop space downstairs in The Old Ticket Office and gazed around with a mix of pride and nervousness. Morning sunlight streamed in through the large front windows, glinting off the dark-stained hardwood floors. Everything for the opening of the shop was close to being finalised, and as she looked around, the vision that had been in her head for years had somehow come to life right in front of her eyes. Part of her couldn't quite believe it. The other part of her could see years of hard work and sacrifice staring back at her full-on in the face.

A lot had changed in the room in the time since Emmy had moved in. When she'd first arrived at the building, it was little more than a throwback from the 80s in the form of an insurance office without a lot going for it. Now it had loveliness going for it, alright. It had loveliness every which way she turned. She sighed at the vintage brass light fixtures now lining the wall. Her dad had actually found them in the basement. Amy had cleaned them until they shone, and now they were fixed happily in place as if they'd never been away.

The antique doors Tom and her dad had collected now

stood anchored to the walls, ready to display pretty sparkly things, and the mirrored dresser drawers she'd repurposed as display units ran along the right. On the far wall, the old fireplace had been given a new lease of life. Emmy remembered how everything was when she'd first viewed the place. When she'd first seen it, she'd been to Darling to collect a cake for Callum's birthday, and on the off chance, had seen Dan the estate agent outside. She'd walked in with him, put the cake on the side, and on spying things like the fireplace and the antique features had sealed the deal. The fireplace then had been painted in a horrible nicotine yellow cream and had worn discarded glass trophies from the insurance world. Now it was stripped back to its natural wood patina, a string of fairy lights ran back and forth underneath, and all along the top, little displays were ready for a bit of Love Emmy x bling. Ding dong.

Against the back wall stood the original ticket counter. When it had first been uncovered, Emmy had thought it was beautiful. Now it really took pride of place. The old brass bars had been polished, the wood panels repaired and treated, and the plaque on the bottom gleamed. Emmy thought about Darling-ites lined up long ago, buying tickets for ferries and trams. Now the counter would house different bits: her gorgeous lifelong dream of Love Emmy x things.

The shop had taken a lot longer than Emmy had thought to get ready. Part of it was generally that things had gone slowly, and manpower and budget were limited. The other part of it was that Emmy was apprehensive about failing, and putting the brakes on delayed the failure she thought might be somewhere lurking in the future. Now, though, push was coming to shove. Amy, her dad, Cherry and even Tom had spent a lot of time getting the place ready to go, and it was so close now she could feel it in the air. Months of renovating – stripping floors, painting walls, sanding, cleaning, polishing, sourcing, and restoring the beautiful old features like the ticket counter. Now it was time to set up shop.

Emmy dragged a huge cardboard moving box over the floor and started to unpack. She'd been gathering bits and bobs for her imaginary shop for years, and now she was unpacking them to fulfil the dream. She carefully pulled lamps from the box and began to unwrap the bubble wrap. Each lamp was a different style, with soft, pretty pastels and fabric lampshades. About ten minutes later, one lamp was on the fireplace, one on the vintage display unit, two on the mirrored dressers, and the rest dotted around the room. They did their job to soften the light, and everything just seemed to glow.

On a set of vintage mirrored drawers, little display parcels were ready for bracelets and necklaces, and an earring stand was ready to go. Emmy stepped back, envisioning how customers would browse the lovely, glowing space. This shop represented her dreams, independence from the rut of renting, and a fresh start on the island. She loved how that made her feel.

Emmy walked into the storeroom and ran her eyes down the large lidded plastic tubs that held her Love Emmy x dream stacked in order, so they could easily be accessed for her order packing. Even the boxes were now ready to be slid into their new home. She dragged two of them, which held her carefully selected display pieces, out from the back storeroom. Once in the shop, she snapped off the lids and unpacked her merchandise carefully. Each little packet seemed to make her happier as she went along. Beautiful bracelets, necklaces, and rings. She went around the room, fussing, checking, and setting things up.

She retrieved the payment dongle and the accompanying fancy new card reader the bank had sent. After a few tries, she got it paired with her phone, and Emmy beamed. Things were getting really real.

Glancing at the time, she realised her dad would be arriving soon to help hang up signage. Butterflies fluttered in her stomach. In not long at all, Love Emmy x would officially open its doors. Her little shop by the sea, on the most beautiful island and everything she'd worked towards and thought about for a very long time, was finally happening.

With most of the actual nuts and bolts of the shop done, she was now starting to plan the official grand opening. Taking a pew behind the old ticket counter, Emmy opened her laptop and methodically went down the list of things she still had to do for the shop opening. She nodded as she got to the heading noted as 'atmosphere' – in the vision that had been taking up space in her head for so long, she'd always thought about a harpist in the corner of the room. Part of her had thought it was a ridiculous, silly pipe dream; another part of her whispered, telling her to go for her life and that a harp was part of the Love Emmy x dream.

Opening a new browser tab, she Googled local harpists and started browsing listings. Before she knew what was happening, she'd been sucked into a vortex of beautiful harps and chords. What a very pretty world. She instantly knew that the harpist idea was right for her shop and what she wanted the place to feel like on opening day. She'd make it happen. The more she thought about it, the more she realised it was intrinsically part of a little scene that had been living in her head for a very long time.

After a few more searches where nothing looked quite right, she landed on the website of a woman named Louisa Seraphina, who specialised in background harp music for events and gatherings. Louisa's dreamy website had Emmy oohing and ahhing all over the show. Louisa Seraphina had her at flickering candles and harp playing in a woodland setting. The gallery showed Louisa at many a wedding, in a beautiful old library in Oxford at a book influencer's event, and at the Royal Albert Hall. How good could it get? Emmy scrolled through picture after picture, totally inspired. Louisa and her beautiful carved harp needed to be in Emmy's world for opening day.

Make your occasion magical with Louisa Seraphina. Immerse yourself in a symphony of beautiful melodies as Louisa Seraphina graces your special event with her transcendent harp artistry. With over two decades of experience enchanting audiences both nationally and internationally, Louisa Seraphina captures the essence of beauty and ethereal magic through her performance, offering a blend of classical and contemporary melodies that unfurl like a tapestry of sound. A master of her craft, Seraphina holds a plethora of qualifications from the prestigious Enchanté Conservatory of Music, and has been the recipient of multiple awards for her moving compositions and performances. Trained in various genres ranging from classical to Celtic to contemporary, her diverse repertoire allows her to customise her performance, creating a musical experience as unique as your event.
Graceful, captivating, and profoundly moving — Louisa Seraphina offers not merely a musical performance but a soulful journey wrapped in melodies as magical as they are unforgettable. Louisa guarantees you won't be disappointed.

Emmy listened to the audio samples on Louisa's site – covers of popular songs, pretty arrangements of classical pieces, and even a few whimsical tunes. She couldn't get enough and realised Louisa was exactly what she was looking for. She closed her eyes and listened to Louisa play. The music conjured up the soft, swirly feeling Emmy was hoping for in the shop – the same feeling that had been in her head for years. As she sat listening, she imagined lovely weddings, banquet halls, gardens in twilight, and secret forests. Louisa Seraphina was a done deal.

Copying Louisa's email address, Emmy sent an email enquiring about prices and availability and nodded to herself; things were getting real. Just as she was sitting with her chin in her hand, thinking about refreshments and whether the bakery where she'd got Callum's cake would be able to help out, her dad strolled in, toolbox in hand.

'Morning. How's it going in here?' he asked, peering around the door. 'Oh, wow! You've been busy. Look at the place. Fantastic! Nearly ready to go.'

Emmy quickly closed her laptop, gathering her thoughts. 'Just planning some finishing touches for opening day,' she explained. 'Still lots to figure out, but it's coming together!'

'We're getting so close,' Bob agreed. 'Well done, you.'

'Thanks, Dad.'

'I'm proud of you, Ems.'

'Aww, thank you.'

'You've worked your socks off for this, and it shows.'

'Yep, we all have. Right, best get on. We have to get that decal on the door. Then I've got the letters in lights that need to be put on the wall, and the garland needs the last few finishing touches. Then we really will be close.'

'So proud of you, Ems. You've done so well,' Bob repeated.

'Not without your help. Trust me, I appreciate it.'

'Always here for you, Ems. You know that.'

Emmy shuddered inside. Yes, Bob had always been there for her, and yes she was well aware of it, which made it all the more worse that she wasn't telling him the truth about what was going on in her life.

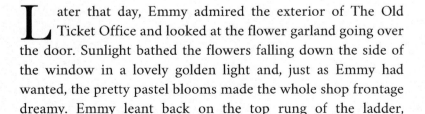

Later that day, Emmy admired the exterior of The Old Ticket Office and looked at the flower garland going over the door. Sunlight bathed the flowers falling down the side of the window in a lovely golden light and, just as Emmy had wanted, the pretty pastel blooms made the whole shop frontage dreamy. Emmy leant back on the top rung of the ladder, admiring the effect of the garlands. Pretty pink peonies and roses mingled with trailing ivy, little bursts of pale blue forget-me-knots were dotted here and there, and froths of white blossom punctuated in between the ivy. Emmy thought about the huge effort and work that had gone into the garland. She'd painstakingly chosen each set of imitation blooms whilst trying to keep to a budget, hoping that the combination would work to fulfil the vision in her head. As she peered at it all critically now, she could see that it had done just that. It really was more than lovely. It was so nice, she wanted to jump up and down in excitement as her dream came to life before her eyes.

'Looking stunning up there, Ems,' her dad called up from where he steadied the ladder on the pavement below. 'It's really coming together now. Not long until this place is open, eh? Last few bits and we're done.'

'Yep, it's looking great. I think just a few more touches, and we're finished with this. Let's hope it stays up through all weathers,' Emmy replied, shifting a wayward vine back into place.

Emmy was well pleased with herself. She'd envisioned the flower installation going around the imaginary door of her imaginary shop for so long; it was deeply gratifying to see it realised right in front of her eyes. The long hours late at night scrolling through flower websites, watching YouTube videos of flower installations, and sometimes wondering if she was very much barking up the wrong tree had been worth it. Dealing with the logistics of ordering had been a headache, installing the heavy garlands had required patience and gritted teeth, and she wasn't sure how weatherproof the blooms would be in real life, but overall it was a job very well done.

Emmy secured the last pieces and slowly descended the ladder, wary of slipping and ending up in a heap on the pavement. She stepped back beside Bob, and both of them stood there for a minute with their heads raised, looking up at their handiwork. The cascade of blooms and greenery softened the shopfront, just as Emmy'd hoped. Her pretty, English cottage garden look, tessellated front step and lovely cosy feel were happening – so far from the high street jewellers with their gaudy purple signs she'd abhorred for such a long time. As she stood looking up, a funny little part of her felt a little bit and very uncharacteristically *smug*.

'You've outdone yourself, Ems,' Bob said, shaking his head. 'This is something special. Have to say, when you first talked about it, I wasn't sure. Before I was initiated in all things floristry, that was.'

'I'm so glad it turned out how I imagined,' Emmy replied, adjusting a rose by the side of the door. 'It's actually better than I thought. It's just so pretty.'

As they continued to chat about how they were going to affix the decal to the front door, Xian, who owned the bakery down the road, came walking up from the direction of the ferry. Xian's voluminous fuchsia jumper was unmistakable; she held an iPad in front of her, and gigantic gold headphones on her head were nearly as big as she was.

Xian paused as she got to the shop and slipped the headphones to her neck. 'Hello. Wow. Stunning!' she exclaimed.

Emmy smiled. 'We just finished attaching the final bits. What do you think?'

'What do I think?' Xian puffed out a funny little sound. 'I think my daughter is going to be tapping you up to put one of those around the bakery. Delightful!' Xian declared. 'Like something out of a fairy tale. You've transformed this place. You really have done a good job.'

'That was the idea.' Emmy laughed. 'I wanted to create something pretty and sort of cottagey and magical at the same time.'

Xian nodded approvingly. 'Very smart marketing tactic.' Xian screwed up her nose and squinted. 'Nothing like those horrible jewellery stores. Darling peeps are going to love this.

Oh, and the visitors coming in from the ferry, they'll love this, too. Yeah, yep, well done you.'

Emmy flushed, really pleased Xian seemed to be genuinely enthusiastic. 'It's been a long time coming.'

Xian slipped a silver flask from a bum bag on her waist. In one super quick movement, she flipped the lid, put the flask to her lips, and swigged. 'Well, your hard work is certainly paying off,' Xian assured. 'With this installation, you'll have the prettiest little shop on all of Darling Island. You'll have Evie on your back if you're not careful.'

Emmy beamed. She'd worked so hard to create Love Emmy x, the shop; it felt nice for someone who wasn't just her family being nice to recognise it. 'Thank you.'

Xian smiled. 'See you later. I'll tell Holly to pop down and have a look when she's next here.'

'Thanks, Xian. See you soon.'

Emmy turned to Bob as they watched Xian pop her headphones back on her head and shuffle away. 'She's funny.'

Bob frowned and shook his head as if trying to compute what he'd just seen. 'Sorry, did she, errr, just swig from that flask, or was I seeing things? Those headphones are nearly as big as she is.'

'I know.' Emmy giggled. 'According to her daughter, the flask holds something disgusting. Some sort of homemade liquor.'

Bob peered down the pavement. 'It appears it's working for her.'

'I know, right?'

'I might have to have some of what she's having,' Bob joked.

Emmy laughed. 'Me too.'

'Maybe we'll have to get one of those flasks to celebrate all of this.'

Emmy smiled as she looked at the shop. 'Thank you again for your help, Dad. It's really all working out.'

'Don't be silly. I'd do anything for any of you three. You know that.'

Emmy shuddered inside at Bob mentioning all three of his daughters. She wondered how Katy would be with that statement. Katy would be of the opinion that Bob would do anything for her as long as it was met with Cherry's approval. Emmy tried to push it to the back of her mind as she started to gather the tools together. She changed the subject quickly. 'How about we get cleaned up, and I'll treat you to lunch?'

Bob chuckled. 'I never say no to that offer. Where do you fancy?'

'Darlings? Or the pub?'

'Up to you.'

Emmy didn't really mind. As long as the conversation stayed far away from the three sisters, she couldn't have cared less.

28

Emmy had spent the day working in the shop. She now had a Love Emmy x lit-up sign on the wall, and an Italian coffee machine was installed for her customers. All the pieces of the puzzle were finally slotting into place. By the end of the day, she was more than ready to put her feet up. She sank onto the sofa, wine glass in hand, pleased that the flat was quiet for a bit and Callum was at Kevin's for the night. She relished little snatches alone to decompress from the day. As she sat with her feet propped up on a pile of books on the coffee table, she sipped her wine and scrolled through her phone. Just as she was tapping through the Insta stories of an independent jewellery boutique in Aberdeen, a call lit up the screen. Katy. Emmy hesitated for a second, considering not answering. She'd just settled down for some peace and didn't really want it interrupted. Looking at the time, she thought it was an odd time of day to call, so she swiped to answer.

'Hey, Katy, everything okay?' she asked in a cheery tone.

'Hi.' Katy didn't sound cheery, far from it. Her voice sounded hurried and strained. 'Sorry to ring late. I just, I didn't know who else to call.'

Emmy sat up straighter, alarm rising. 'What's wrong? Are you alright?'

'It's nothing serious,' Katy hesitated. 'The childminder I had lined up for tomorrow has just cancelled on me. Elodie doesn't go to the childcare centre tomorrow, so she goes to a childminder, but her childminder's got a problem. Something about a family emergency, which leaves me in a right bind because I've got that big client meeting I was telling you about first thing that I can't reschedule. As I said the other day, Elodie's dad's on holiday. There's no one who I trust that much. I'm desperate here.'

'Oh no, that's a nightmare. What are you going to do?' Emmy asked.

'Well, that's why I'm calling.' Katy's tone turned. 'I know it's incredibly last-minute, but I was hoping, praying, that you might be able to help me out. Just for a couple of hours in the morning. Are you working tomorrow? If not, do you think you could come here?'

Emmy's first instinct was to say yes without hesitation, but doubt crept in just before she went to speak. This changed things and made the whole thing a *lot* more serious. It was no longer just her and Katy meeting up for a quick coffee here and there. She chewed her lip uncertainly. 'Err, sure.'

'I wouldn't ask, but my meeting is too important to cancel. I'll owe you hugely. It would only be a few hours at most.'

Emmy wavered. Katy had told her about the client when they'd had coffee a few weeks before. She hated to think of little Elodie being stuck in the middle of her mum's childcare crisis. She remembered being in the same boat many times herself. She thought about all the things she had to do to finalise the opening of the shop. 'Okay. I'll be there.'

Katy exhaled in relief. 'Oh, thank you, really, Ems, you're a lifesaver! This client could be make-or-break; their business is massive. I'll definitely make it up to you.'

'Don't be silly, it's fine,' Emmy assured her. 'What are sisters for, eh?'

They confirmed the arrangements and rang off. Emmy sat staring out the window at the trams going past the window below, exhaled slowly, mind racing. She pondered if she had done the right thing, but she could hardly turn Katy away in her hour of need. But this made her lies and secrets feel much worse. It was all getting calculated. She was digging herself deeper. She sat for ages, wondering how the whole thing was going to pan out. She considered calling Amy and blurting everything out to her, but hesitated. Keeping the reconciliation secret still didn't sit right with Emmy, but at the end of the day, she respected Katy's wishes.

Rubbing her temples, she carried her wine glass to the kitchen and topped it up. A generous pour was in order. As her head zoomed around with different thoughts, she hated the way the concealment made her feel as if something was hanging over her. She slugged back the wine guiltily. She hated not being upfront with her family about reconnecting with Katy. But the rift ran deep. Since their discussion, Emmy also understood Katy's caution, not that she wholeheartedly agreed with it, but she could see where Katy was coming from. Still, deceiving her family made her insides squirm. Sitting at the little table in the kitchen, she stared unseeing at the dark sky out the window, lost in thought. The sound of keys in the back door downstairs startled her.

'Evening!' Tom called, stepping into the flat. He halted when he saw Emmy's expression. 'Everything alright?'

'Hey! All good here,' Emmy replied brightly, sitting up straighter. 'How was work? How was the fast train?'

Tom eyed her shrewdly as he loosened his tie. Emmy cursed internally. He read her too well. 'It was fine – just the usual monthly reports to finalise. But you're dodging the question. Has something happened? You look stressed.'

Emmy got up and busied herself, rinsing her wine glass in the sink. 'No, nothing to worry about. Just the usual work and shop stuff playing on my mind.' She forced a smile over her shoulder. 'Beer?'

Tom sat down. 'I can tell something's bothering you.' His eyes searched hers worriedly. 'It's been going on for ages, too.'

Guilt flooded Emmy. She was tempted to confess everything about Katy at that moment. She grabbed a beer from the fridge and flipped off the lid. 'Honestly, I'm okay. Just overwhelmed trying to get the shop ready.' She kissed Tom's cheek. 'Why don't you go and change while I make some omelettes?'

Tom looked unconvinced but nodded, and Emmy's throat tightened with emotion. The secrecy was eating away at her. She wanted to confide in him about Katy – he was meant to be her partner – but Katy had insisted. As she got eggs out of the fridge, she thought about going to look after Elodie in the morning, how no one else knew and how she was lying. It didn't sit well. Katy didn't want her to tell a soul that they were back in contact. For the moment, she'd stay with that, but she could feel that it was all coming to a head.

Later in bed, Emmy felt as if she was never going to fall asleep. Doubt plagued her about agreeing to look after Elodie. But what else could she have done? She'd spent years resenting Katy's absence from her life, and now they were slowly rebuilding things. The other thing was that Emmy wanted to be there when Katy needed her, even if that meant keeping more secrets. She tossed and turned fretfully from one side to the other, every hour or so looking over at the luminous numbers on the clock. Finally, exhaustion claimed her not that long before dawn. It felt like she'd barely slept when the alarm blared at 6:30 a.m.

'What? Do you have to go in early?' Tom mumbled blearily, screwing up his eyes as Emmy slid out of bed. 'I thought you were here today.'

'Few things to collect before opening,' she fibbed, avoiding his eye as she pulled on her dressing gown. The knot of anxiety in her stomach tightened. She still had no idea how she was going to continue to lie.

After showering and gulping some tea and toast, she continued to weave the lies, making up a really pathetic excuse to Tom about going to pick up some packaging for the shop. Before he'd really had a chance to say much, she'd gone out to the lane, hopped in her car and headed to the ferry.

E mmy double-checked there were no messages on her phone after she'd pulled up and parked outside Katy's flat. Black wrought-iron railings lined the steps leading up to the pale blue front door. As Emmy gathered her bag and cardigan, she looked along the postcard-pretty street with its charming Victorian shoulder-to-shoulder houses. She turned and looked up at Katy's building, with its white exterior dotted with blue window boxes overflowing with pink flowers. Everything was pretty and calm and just nice, unlike what was going on in her head. Emmy Bardot's mind was a jumble. She almost felt as if she was living someone else's life.

After locking her car, Emmy put her huge tote bag on her shoulder and made her way up the steps. As she got to the front door, she suddenly remembered when she'd gone to the supermarket on the way home from seeing Katy and had left her work bag on the trolley. She'd now called twice to follow-up, but nothing had been found. She made a mental note to phone the supermarket again as she hesitated by the front door, smoothing her hair and straightening her top before pressing the buzzer. A faint chime echoed from inside, the main door buzzed and clicked, and moments later, the door to the flat was flung open by a frazzled-looking Katy.

'Ems, thank God you're here,' Katy exhaled in a rush. 'Come in, come in. Thanks so much for doing this. I'm *really* grateful. What a nightmare.'

Emmy stepped inside the hall as Katy closed the door behind them. As before in the flat, everything was tidy and lovely; the cushions on the enormous puffy sofa were perfectly arranged, Elodie's wellies were lined up on the dresser, and the shutters on the windows were pinned neatly back on the large bay. The cosy space really had been done very well.

'Sorry for the mad rush,' Katy apologised. 'Normally, I'd just cancel, but I've already done that once for this meeting. I didn't want to do an online meeting, you know?' She turned towards the sitting room. 'Elodie! Come, say hello to Emmy. Remember, I said she was going to look after you while Mummy goes to work for a bit.'

After a second, Elodie's little face peeked around the corner. Emmy felt her eyes go wide, the same as when she'd first seen Elodie; the resemblance to Katy was uncanny. Huge eyes considered Emmy solemnly, and fluffy white-blonde hair puffed around Elodie's head. Emmy's heart went in her mouth for a quick second. Her niece was even more adorable than the first time she'd met her.

'Can you say hello to Emmy?'

Elodie gave a shy little wave before tucking her head against Katy's leg. Katy stroked her curls soothingly, and she toddled off towards the sofa. Katy lowered her voice. 'She'll warm up once I'm gone.'

Consulting her watch again, Katy briefly outlined Elodie's routine, pointing to a list on the top of the hallway dresser. 'It's all on there. I'll only be gone for a couple of hours. To be honest, she can probably just watch Disney. Or pop around to the park if the weather holds.'

'All good. We'll be fine. You'll be back before we know it.'

'If you need anything at all, just ring me,' Katy said a bit anxiously. 'My meeting will go about an hour, max. Then I'll come straight back. I can work from home for the rest of the day.'

Emmy touched her arm reassuringly. 'We'll have a lovely time, don't worry.'

With reluctance, Katy grabbed her handbag. She lowered her voice. 'I might just slip out to save her from getting clingy. Make yourself a coffee and stuff.'

'Yeah, yeah, just go. We'll be fine.'

Alone with her niece, Emmy felt herself just standing in the sitting room, not sure what to do. Elodie was sitting in the corner of the sofa with her thumb in and an iPad on her lap.

'Right. What shall I do first?' Emmy said to herself. 'Coffee.'

As Emmy attempted to work out the intricacies of the fancy coffee machine in the kitchen, she paused to examine framed photos on the side showing a smiling baby Elodie with wispy white-blonde hair. The baby was the spitting image of Katy. Once she had made a coffee and the morning stretched away in front of her, she decided Katy's idea of the park was a good one.

'Let's get your wellies and coat on,' Emmy suggested and peered out the window up at the sky. 'It's a bit wet out, but we can still go to the park. How does that sound?'

Elodie's eyes lit up, and she wriggled down off the sofa so Emmy could slip on her pink spotty wellies and yellow waterproof jacket. Once Emmy had donned her own jacket, she held Elodie's hand, took the keys from the dresser and locked the door behind them.

Following Katy's brief directions, Emmy held tightly onto Elodie's hand, and they made their way to the end of the road and turned left. Emmy kept up a steady stream of chat as they strolled past charming homes. At the corner, a little cat sitting perfectly upright on a wall caught Elodie's attention. She pointed excitedly and chattered about the cat. Once they reached the park, Elodie let go of Emmy's hand, and they ambled along the

path towards the play area. Emmy watched her scamper immediately for the slide. Mindful of the metal and anything going
wrong, she hovered nearby, calling out warnings to be careful as
Elodie tried to climb up the slippery rungs in her pink wellies.
There was no way Emmy was going to risk Elodie falling, so she
scooped her up and plopped her at the top of the slide. As Elodie
zoomed down the slide, there was a peal of laughter.

After a few slides, they walked over to the pond, had a little
look at the ducks, bought a cookie from a kiosk, and sat on a
bench for a bit. Emmy looked up as clouds scudded across the
sky – miraculously, the rain continued to hold off, and Elodie
was being as good as gold. As they sat there, Emmy couldn't
quite believe where she was or what she was doing. Sitting on a
park bench with her secret niece, whom no one else in the
family knew about. Lying.

Eventually, Elodie's energy began flagging. Emmy checked
the time – nearly an hour had passed since they'd left the house.
Katy would be finishing her meeting soon.

'Shall we start walking back to see Mummy?' Emmy
suggested. Elodie took her hand obediently. Only the occasional
hop or twirl broke her concentration as she stepped carefully
over pavement cracks, and they retraced their steps through the
park. As they were about to leave the park, Elodie started to fuss
with the neck of her raincoat. Emmy bent down. 'Do you want
to take your coat off? It's definitely not as cold as it looks.'
Elodie nodded, and Emmy took the coat off, folded it neatly and
tucked it into her bag.

Once back at Katy's front steps, and just as they were
making their way inside, there was a text from Katy to say she
was on her way. After settling in, Emmy made a cup of tea, got
the snacks Katy had made out of the fridge, and settled Elodie
into the corner of the sofa with her blanket and a toy. Not long
after that, Emmy heard the key in the lock; Elodie was fast

asleep on the sofa. Emmy smiled as she got up and stood in the hallway and whispered. 'How did it go?'

'Really well, I think we're in with a good shot.' Katy's voice was hushed as she looked over towards the sitting room. 'How was she?'

'An angel. As good as gold. We went to the park, and when we got back, she sat down and promptly went to sleep.'

Impulsively, Katy hugged Emmy. 'Thank you again.' Pulling back, she added ruefully. 'Sorry, I called last minute.'

'Don't be silly. I didn't mind at all.'

Katy hung her handbag on the hooks by the dresser. 'I'm glad that's over.'

'How about I make us a cup of tea while you get settled?' Emmy offered and gesticulated over towards Elodie. 'Give you a chance to sit down for a bit, and you can debrief the meeting on me.'

'Sounds perfect, thanks.'

While Emmy busied herself making the tea, Katy sank onto a stool with a tired sigh. The meeting persona she'd been wearing slipped away as she stuck her feet out and rubbed her temples with her fingers.

'The meeting was intense,' Katy admitted as Emmy passed a mug of tea, and she cradled it in her hand. 'The company is massive, and getting this contract is a big deal. So the pressure to impress was on. Plus, the childcare thing. Working mums, eh? I don't need to tell you that.'

'It's not easy,' Emmy agreed.

'Honestly, I don't know if my presentation was enough to win them over. Their CEO was so reserved and gave little away. It could go either way at this point.'

Emmy touched her arm comfortingly. 'I'm sure you did brilliantly. And if it's meant to work out, it will. That's what I always think in the end.'

'I hope so. Anyway, sorry to unload all that on you. What did you get up to with Elodie? She's clearly worn out. Bless her.'

Emmy mimicked Elodie's giggle, sliding down the slide and her joyful little face. 'She's such a little darling.'

'I know. I lucked out with her.' Katy's expression softened. 'How can I repay you for that?'

'Just being here was nice.'

An awkward silence boomed, both of them keenly aware of the bittersweet undercurrent. Emmy's mind flicked to the lost years and memories that couldn't simply be glossed over. She also thought about what her mum and dad were missing out on.

Katy smoothed a hand over her hair and cut to the chase of what both of them were thinking. 'I know. You've every right to resent me for staying away so long. I just needed space to work through some things.'

'Yep. The past is done, though. It is what it is. All we can do is move forward from here. It's just good to see you.'

'Thanks,' Katy said briskly, clearly not wanting to dwell on the subject. 'Anyway, enough of me. What's happening with the shop? It sounds perfectly lovely from what you've described. It sounds right up my alley. I was looking at your socials the other day.'

Emmy wanted to say that if Katy could put things behind her, she could be part of the shop and the opening. She didn't and decided to steer clear of anything along those lines. 'Yeah, it's all quite surreal, in a way.'

As if reading Emmy's thoughts, Katy sighed. 'Elodie would love an adventure on the ferry.'

Emmy stopped herself from tutting. As much as she yearned to bang Katy on the head and tell her to get a grip, she couldn't force Katy to face their family before she was ready. 'Yeah, she probably would.'

Glancing at the clock, Emmy began gathering up her phone and things. Katy walked her to the door with a grateful look.

'Thanks again for everything today. It really helped get me out of a stitch. Sorry it was so last-minute.'

Emmy hugged her. 'Anytime. I mean it. Let me know how the meeting turns out, okay?'

'I will. Fingers crossed, it's good news.' Katy bit her lip. She chuckled. 'Maybe we can celebrate next time we see each other.'

As Emmy walked back to her car, she sent up a silent prayer that everything would work out in the wash once the truth came out. For now, she'd decided not to push it; baby steps were needed. Emmy, though, was very uneasy. All of it felt somehow as if it didn't bode well.

29

The evening sky was just beginning to turn to twilight as Emmy locked the door to the front of the shop. She turned to see Tom, hands in his pockets, coming through the storeroom at the back.

'Fancy dinner at the pub? Looks like rain later, but we've time if we stroll now,' Tom said as he stepped into the front room.

'Sounds perfect. Today was non-stop, I'm gasping and starving. I'll just pop up and get my jacket and bag.'

A few minutes later, just as they were walking along the back lane and heading to Darling Street, the wail of the foghorn sounded. Emmy shivered and hunched deeper into her jacket. When she'd started her day that morning, sunlight had filtered through the blinds. Now, as dusk came down on Darling, banks of rain clouds filled the air. The up-and-down weather most certainly mirrored what was going on inside Emmy's head.

As they strolled along hand in hand, Tom launched into an account of something that was going on at work. Emmy made vague noises of interest, her responses on autopilot, as inside she brooded about looking after Elodie and how Katy had been.

'...so I told him we'd have to redo that whole part of the report,' Tom said. 'Bit of a nightmare, really. What about you? Did you get that stuff you were after? Ems? Are you with us?'

Emmy jerked back to the conversation guiltily. In all honesty, she wasn't with him. Not even close. She was still sitting on the bench with Elodie, lost in a world of her own. She didn't really give a flying hoot about his report. In fact, she was so distracted that he was irritating her a little bit, which totally threw her. She wished he'd just shut up. She felt as if someone had rubbed at her edges with sandpaper. 'Sorry, miles away. Shop stuff on my mind,' she covered quickly. The excuse sounded unconvincing, even to her own ears.

Tom's brow furrowed. 'I asked how your morning went, finding those things you needed.'

Emmy's steps faltered briefly. The supposed errand had been yet another fabrication to explain her rushing off early in the morning. Lying to Tom did not fill her with joy. It was Katy's insistence on secrecy forcing her hand. She didn't like it in the slightest. Each bit of deceit seemed to pile on top of the last. She felt as if she was sitting at the bottom of the pile, waiting for the whole lot to topple and land on her head.

'Oh, right. Yes, I found everything I needed,' she said vaguely, avoiding Tom's gaze. 'How was your day?' she redirected lamely.

Her transparent change of subject deepened the crease between Tom's eyebrows. Emmy cursed internally. She definitely wasn't fooling him. Abruptly, Tom halted to the side of the pavement. 'Err, I've spent the last five minutes telling you about my day. I knew you weren't listening. Ems, what's going on? And don't say it's nothing. You've been on edge for weeks now. Has something happened with your family? Or I don't know, Kevin or something. You said he's useless with money and it affects Callum. Is he gambling?'

Emmy wavered. Tom looked so sincere, she felt even worse. She teetered on the brink of confessing. Emmy swallowed hard.

'It's nothing you need to worry about,' she insisted with fragile brightness. 'Come on, I'm desperate for a nice glass of wine.'

Before Tom could ask anything else, she squeezed his hand and quickened her pace a bit. Once at the pub, the warmth and chatter and pub smell enveloped them, and for a bit, the subject was hidden nicely under the table. After Tom went to the bar, Emmy sipped her wine and let out a gigantic sigh. 'Ahh, I needed this.'

'Wish you'd tell me what's bothering you, Em.'

Guilt roared in Emmy's ears. She traced the top of the glass with her finger, but Katy's words were in the back of her head. *Don't say anything to anyone, you have to promise.*

'No, all good. Everything's hunky-dory,' Emmy replied and quickly moved the subject to the shop opening. 'I just can't wait to actually get the shop open. It's been a long time coming. I can't wait to go and check out the harpist and everything. It's going to be fantastic.'

Emmy watched as Tom's mouth compressed, clearly not believing her. Just as he was about to respond, the server appeared with two plates of fish and chips. Emmy sighed with relief inside at the welcome interruption and made a big fuss about the food. 'Ooh, this looks and smells delicious. I love the food in here.'

Tom picked up his knife and fork. 'Got to love fish and chips Darling style.'

As they sat and ate, the foghorn went again, the windows started to rattle in the wind and spatters of rain splashed the window panes. Emmy jerked her thumb outside. 'What did you say the weather said?'

Tom followed her gaze outside. 'A quick downpour now that doesn't last long. We should be good to walk home.'

'Hope so. Otherwise, you're carrying me under your coat,' Emmy joked.

A couple of hours and a few drinks later, the rain had

stopped, though it was still wet outside as they emerged from the pub. Emmy slipped her hand into Tom's as the wet streets of Darling glistened, and the foghorn sounded just as it had when they'd left home. Just as they'd reached the point where it wasn't worth getting on a tram, Emmy felt a few raindrops on her cheek. She looked up at the sky and then to Tom. 'Looks like they were wrong. That was rain.'

'Too late now,' Tom said, nodding down Darling Street.

As they hurried along the pavement, rain started to hammer it down. Emmy blinked against the drops as it got harder, and sheets of water pounded down, and the gutters started to run with rain. She fumbled around in her bag for her umbrella, stopping for a second and opening the top of her bag wide. Tom shook his head and chuckled. 'Probs not worth it now. We might as well just get wet.'

Emmy giggled as she held her tote bag open further and peered in. 'I suppose so.'

Tom frowned at the yellow oilskin fabric of Elodie's coat. 'Oh, do you have a raincoat in there?'

Emmy went cold. She quickly pushed the raincoat down and then shut her bag. 'No, no.' She then made a huge show of pulling out her umbrella, struggling to get it to go up and battling with it, deciding not to bother.

When The Old Ticket Office shop awning finally loomed into view, Emmy nearly shrieked in relief. She fumbled numbly with the latch and keys at the door, cursing and laughing as her fingers trembled. Wordlessly, Tom took the keys, wiggled them in the lock, and ushered her inside out of the deluge of water now falling out of the sky.

Dripping rainwater on the mat, Emmy's bedraggled hair clung to her cheeks in sodden streaks. 'So much for your weather forecasting skills. That was nuts.'

Tom laughed. 'Too funny. We're soaked.'

'Bath is in order,' Emmy said as she peeled off the arms of her jacket. 'I'll get it running.'

'Yeah, and then maybe you can tell me what's wrong,' Tom said in a banter-ish way but with a serious tone to his voice.

Emmy hurried towards the stairs to the flat. If he thought she was going to tell him the truth about what was going on in her world, he had another thing coming.

30

A few days or so later, Emmy tapped her fingertips anxiously on the steering wheel as she drove to meet the harpist for the opening event. Amy chatted breezily in the passenger seat, admiring the sea views out the window as they whizzed along a coast road.

'Gorgeous day for a drive along the coast,' Amy remarked. 'I'm so excited to hear this harpist. The shop is going to be magical on the opening day with all the beautiful stuff you've got lined up. Can you even believe this is happening? So proud of you, Ems.'

Emmy managed a tight smile riddled with guilt that she was keeping secrets from Amy. 'Thanks. I'm so pleased you're here. Your eye for stuff like this is so much better than mine.'

Amy waved off the compliment. 'I'm just glad to help where I can. What are sisters for?'

Emmy winced and hoped it didn't show. 'No, I mean it. Thanks,' Emmy said and fiddled with her grandma Emily's diamond as she drove along. She dropped her hand as she felt Amy looking at her and the diamond.

'You sure you're okay? Did you want me to drive? I'm insured on this car, aren't I? You seem a bit distracted.'

'Me? Oh, I'm fine,' Emmy said hastily. 'Just thinking logistics for the big day. Making sure nothing falls through the cracks. There's so much to think about. Part of me sort of wishes I'd just quietly opened the door and got on with it. Less pressure that way, too.' Emmy forced herself to relax, though her white-knuckled grip on the steering wheel was saying the complete opposite. With everything on her plate, the last thing she needed was Amy picking up on anything amiss. It was bad enough that Tom had picked up on things.

As Amy chatted away, Emmy went cold when she suddenly realised that Elodie's coat was still in her bag and her bag was right next to Amy's feet. She cursed internally. She'd told herself as she'd walked up the stairs to the flat that she must remember to put the coat somewhere safe and unseen, but she'd forgotten all about it. It had totally slipped her mind. Now realising that the coat was about a foot away from Amy, her stomach lurched. It was as if the coat was burning a hole through her bag from the passenger footwell.

Amy pointed out the window as they pulled up at a set of lights. 'I could murder a coffee. There's a place over there. Do you fancy one?'

'Definitely, I'd love one.'

Luckily, there was a space right outside the little coffee shop. Emmy manoeuvred deftly into the spot and put the car into park. Amy unbuckled her seatbelt, grabbed her bag, and went to open the door. Emmy's heart was in her mouth as her bag fell open and the inside displayed for the world to see.

Amy certainly didn't look at the bag; she was more worried about her coffee. 'What do you want? I'm going to get a latte. Usual for you?'

Emmy gulped at the open bag in between them. 'Yep.'

'Back in a mo, then.'

The second Amy had closed the passenger door and disappeared into the shop, Emmy lunged over the centre console and snatched up her bag. Elodie's coat was tucked down in the bottom, so it probably would have been fine, but to Emmy it seemed to stick out like a sore thumb. Glancing frantically around the car interior, she wedged the coat on the floor under her seat. Amy emerged not long after, brandishing two cups of takeaway coffee. Emmy sighed in relief. Crisis narrowly averted.

As they drove along, Emmy pretended she was right into the chat about the shop. She kept up distracted small talk as Amy sipped on her coffee, and the conversation moved to Cherry's latest golf trip. All Emmy could think about was the yellow raincoat wedged under her seat, and her eyes kept drifting guiltily towards the back. She felt awful keeping her niece and Katy a secret, but she'd promised not to tell. The secrecy was taking a horrible toll, and lying by omission didn't come naturally to Emmy. She absolutely hated feeling so conflicted.

'You sure nothing's bothering you? You've checked the back a million times too,' Amy asked suddenly. 'Mum mentioned you are still distant. I know how much pressure you're under to get the shop ready. Dad said you were looking a bit under the weather when he came over the other day to get the last few bits fixed up. Maybe it's time to go on holiday, Ems.'

Emmy rolled her eyes. She loved Amy to bits, but sometimes she realised what different worlds they lived in. There was a fat chance of Emmy going on holiday right at the time she was starting the shop. That was even if she could afford a holiday, which she couldn't. Things like that weren't even on the radar of Amy's world. If Amy wanted a quick jaunt off to the sun, she did precisely that. Emmy's fingers tightened on the wheel. Amy always noticed when something was off. It had been Amy who had pushed so much that she'd found out Kevin was gambling. Emmy felt sick inside. She couldn't keep up the façade much longer without cracking. Releasing her grip on the steering wheel and plastering on a cheery face, she replied. 'Honestly, I'm fine, just overwhelmed like you said. Once the shop opening goes smoothly, I'll be back to normal. Yeah, a holiday would be good.'

'So, you *do* admit there's something wrong?' Amy fired back as quick as a flash.

'Nope. Just busy.'

Amy didn't look fully convinced, but thankfully she let the subject drop. The rest of the drive passed uneventfully, besides Emmy's hammering heart. About half an hour later, they were pulling up outside an old building with an outdoor fancy garden centre in an old house where Louisa, the harpist, had told her she was playing as a background musician.

Forcing herself not to check the coat under the driver's seat, Emmy grabbed her bag and jacket, and, walking in step next to Amy, they strolled into an opulent foyer. The click of Amy's heels on the marble floor echoed around them, and a huge round table filled with vases of flowers greeted them.

'Very fancy,' Amy whispered. 'When you said garden centre, I was envisioning something completely different. This is my kind of garden centre. Mum would love this!'

They walked towards the shop area where floor-to-ceiling windows overlooking manicured lawns, gilt-framed mirrors reflected the light, a black-and-white chequered floor looked up at them, and in the far corner in a large conservatory, they could see Louisa and a harp.

'Wow!' Amy breathed. 'This is incredible.'

A few minutes later, they were seated at a café table, and as they read the menu, they watched Louisa play. About half an hour after that, Louisa approached the table after Emmy had waved.

'Hi. You must be Emmy, I'm Louisa. I wondered if it was you when you sat down.'

Emmy got up, accepting Louisa's outstretched hand. 'Lovely to meet you finally, after all the emails. This venue is absolutely stunning.' She turned to Amy. 'This is my sister, Amy.'

'Hi,' Louisa said.

'Looks like you have a full house,' Amy noted.

Louisa laughed lightly. 'I know. These lunches are always a sell-out. I feel really lucky to play here.'

'Not quite the garden centre feel I was thinking.' Emmy laughed.

'No. Ha. I should have told you more,' Louisa said with a chuckle. 'Right, well, I'll get back to it. Let me know what you think. As I said, that day you're after is free at the moment, but I do get booked out really quickly.'

Emmy watched as Louisa walked away and then caught her breath as Louisa began to play.

Opposite her, Amy raised her eyebrows as the music swelled. She leant over and whispered. 'It's breathtaking. I take it this is the clincher.'

Emmy beamed. 'Yep, I'm so glad we came to have a listen.'

As Emmy gazed over towards the conservatory, she knew with certainty that the scene in front of her was the same as the one that had been in the back of her head in the Love Emmy x dream forever. It was just a shame that something had come along when her life had been going so well and decided it would like to throw a spanner in the works.

An hour or so later, Louisa had finished playing, Amy and Emmy had walked around the grounds of the house, and they met up with Louisa as she was packing up in the conservatory. 'That was absolutely incredible,' Emmy enthused. 'I got goosebumps.'

Louisa flushed. 'You're too kind. Thank you.'

'I'd love it if you could play at the shop,' Emmy gushed without wasting any time beating around the bush.

Louisa took out her phone and tapped on a bookings app. 'Lovely. Right, I'll pop you in. You should get an email right away for the deposit. Once that's cleared, we're good to go, and I'll send you all the details I need about clearance, space, insurance, etcetera.'

They chatted a bit about the logistics: what time Louisa would arrive, her preferred spot in the shop, what she would need, and then Emmy and Amy left, heading back to the car.

'Well, I'd say that was a resounding success,' Amy declared as they got back into the car. 'Louisa is going to make the opening absolutely magical. I can't wait to see it come together!'

'Neither can I. Thanks for coming.'

'Of course. I'm so pleased it's all come together so well, Ems. I was just thinking the other day about when we all came to see the place. Remember that?'

Emmy nodded. 'Yeah, it seems ages ago now at the same as seconds ago. It's funny how time goes like that.'

'Yep. Thank goodness for Mum and Dad, eh? They've been great with it all. Remember how Mum did that makeover on your kitchen?'

'I know.'

'I was only saying to Angie yesterday how supportive they are. You know how horrible Angie's mum is, and her dad left when she was tiny. She has no support in her life, well apart from me, that is, and sometimes it makes me realise how lucky we are, you know?'

Emmy swallowed. 'Yeah, we are.'

'They're just always there to help out. It's so nice to have that, isn't it?'

'It is.'

Amy looked out the window. 'When I think about how good they are and how much they do for us, it makes me even more sad about Katy. It must be so horrible for them not knowing where she is.'

Emmy felt sick as a dog. She nodded and gripped the steering wheel, the yellow coat right there beneath her seat burning into her brain. She wondered how long she could continue not telling the truth.

31

E mmy clicked send on the final email blast announcing the Love Emmy x opening event. Watching her carefully cultivated newsletter list receive the notification, her stomach fluttered with a mixture of excitement, fear, and nerves. Mostly fear and nerves. In not long at all, the Love Emmy x inside her head would finally come out to play to be scrutinised in the real world. Grandma Emily had started it all, and now here Emmy was years later, with a specialist boutique in a lovely little town on an island surrounded by hazy blue sea. For the most part, though, Emmy was actually *terrified*.

'That's the digital invites sorted,' she announced, swivelling in her chair behind the ticket counter to face Amy, who was perched on the other side. 'Now for the tricky part – the physical invitation list.'

Amy glanced up, surrounded by Emmy's neat list of names and piles of creamy card stock. 'Don't worry, this is the easy bit. We know this lot are coming, anyway. Just a formality,' Amy assured, waving a hand at the piles and the spreadsheet open on her laptop. Meticulous as always, she had taken over managing the guest list and had everything under control.

'I don't know what I'd do without you,' Emmy said gratefully. She leaned over, reviewing the columns of names and categories. A pang caught in her chest seeing 'Family' listed prominently at the top, followed by subsets like 'Mum & Dad' and 'Callum.' She winced at the thought of Katy, hoping she wouldn't come up in conversation.

Trying not to constantly churn it over and overthink it, she refocused on Amy's sorted piles of invitation envelopes, calligraphy pen at the ready. She had to keep reminding herself that it was Katy's choice to remain hidden, not hers. No use dwelling on what couldn't be changed. 'So I've got all the local shop owners here, plus your friends from work,' Amy remarked. 'Did you want to invite anyone else? Kevin?'

Emmy chewed her lip, staring down at the invitations without really seeing them. Her mind kept straying to Katy, imagining her being part of it all, helping address envelopes, chatting and laughing. How lovely it would be to be back together. No such luck.

'Em? You still with me?' Amy interrupted, waving a hand. 'I asked if there was anyone else you wanted to add to the guest list. I know you're not keen on Kev but for Callum's sake, possibly? What do you think?'

Emmy jerked back to the present, plastering on a smile. 'Oh, umm, yeah, no. That would mean going through the whole Kev meets Tom thing.'

'Oh god, yes, of course.' Amy inhaled and nodded at the same time.

'I'm so not up for that. Not on top of everything else.'

Amy's eyes narrowed. 'On top of everything else? Like what?'

'Just all this!' Emmy said brightly, avoiding Amy's gaze.

'So, it's a straight no for Kevin?'

'Yep, it's a no. Definitely.'

'Right. No doubt he'll have something to say about that.'

'No doubt, and also not my problem.'

'Yup. Just blame Kevin,' Amy joked.

'Just trying to remember if I've forgotten anyone important; you know how my brain gets.' Emmy forced out a laugh, hoping it sounded natural. The last thing she needed was Amy picking up on her conflicted mood. Keeping Katy concealed felt like a constant stomach ache, exacerbated as the shop opening loomed.

'Well, there's not a lot of time now.'

'I should have done the invitations ages ago.'

'You didn't have a date.'

Emmy nodded. She knew she'd not made a date concrete because she'd been stalling. She didn't really want the possibility or the reality of the shop failing and so, despite what she'd told herself, she'd put it off. The shop dream had always sat nicely in the back of her head as just that – a dream. Opening it was a whole different ball game altogether. She looked at the pile of cream envelopes sitting on the counter and wished it was as simple as just adding Katy's name to the top of one of them. Choosing to brush it nicely under the carpet, she got up. 'Right. Let's have a cup of tea.'

Ten minutes later, she and Amy were sitting with mugs of tea, and a packet of fancy shortbread biscuits was in between them on the counter. Emmy went down the list of things still to do and the plan for the decorations.

Amy nodded as she went down the list and then looked around the room. 'Yep. It's going to be magical. It already looks lovely. You really are very good at this, you know.'

'I've been thinking about it for long enough,' Emmy joked. 'Plus, when you're standing looking at lines of people who ask the same questions all day long, there's lots of room in your brain for dreaming.'

'Too funny. Seriously, though, everyone is so proud of you, Ems. Creating this shop is an accomplishment, and you've been working part-time through it all. Plus wining and dining a new man.' Amy chuckled. 'Go Ems. Life goals.'

Unexpected tears pricked Emmy's eyes; she blinked them away and fired back the banter. 'You must wish you were me.'

'All joking aside, you've done so well. The opening will go beautifully, I can just tell.'

'Hope so. It wouldn't have been possible without you – you've all helped with the shop so much. Remember when I was so down in the dumps when I first moved in? You all rallied around me.'

'That's what family is for,' Amy tutted. 'It's always been the same with us. Thick as thieves, right?'

The family word seemed to pierce Emmy in the side. Thick as thieves who didn't tell each other everything. Ouch. Emmy took a biscuit, dipped it in her tea, and tried not to think about it.

After finishing their tea, Amy left to head back home. As Emmy pondered their conversation, she felt absolutely terrible. Shutting Amy out felt wrong on a primal level. It just made Emmy feel icky and uncomfortable. Going up to the flat to go to the loo, when she was back in her bedroom by the bedside putting on some hand cream, she caught sight of a framed photo of her, Amy and Katy in their teens. Happy and sun-kissed, arms slung care-lessly around each other. She picked it up with a sad smile. Nobody could have predicted the rift that happened, and now here Emmy was slap bang in the middle of it. A bit of Emmy was monumentally irritated by Katy for everything she had done both in the past and now. Could she not just put up and get on with it? It appeared not. Emmy supposed that that wasn't her call to make.

She replaced the photo with a sigh, stood rubbing the hand cream in, and stared out the window for a minute or two. She watched a tram trundle up to the stop and then go on its way again, a few seagulls wheeled overhead, and a thick set of clouds gathered ominously on the horizon. Emmy gazed at the clouds for ages, just staring and pondering them in silence, watching them float from right to left and swirl in front of her eyes. She felt similar to the clouds, unsettled inside, her thoughts choppy and all over the show.

The worst thing about it all was that Emmy just deep down felt as if the secrets were all wrong, and her conscience needled her. She was actively deceiving not just Amy and the rest of their family, but Tom and Callum too. Emmy shuddered at how often Amy had been over to the shop to help, how Amy had always supported her dreams tirelessly from the start. How Amy deserved to know the truth.

Mind churning, Emmy wandered back down to the flat, made herself another cup of tea, and went back downstairs to the shop. So much had gone into transforming it, and now it was almost ready for its doors to open. Everything was going well except for the bitter taste in her mouth about Katy, but there was nothing really she could do about that. That problem was way out of her control.

32

'A little to the left. Yeah, I mean, no. Right a bit. Yep. Hmm. Yes. Perfect!' Emmy called out as Tom adjusted a string of fairy lights above the surprise antique display cabinet he'd bought her. She stepped back, head tilted appraisingly. The tiny twinkling bulbs perfectly outlined the detailing along the top of the cabinet.

'How's that look?' Tom asked, stepping back and squinting.

Emmy smiled. 'Good. Yeah, we're getting there. How many times have I said that now?'

'Too many.'

Emmy did a slow spin, taking in the shop's interior. Multiple strings of fairy lights were now draped along the tops of the walls and criss-crossed across the ceiling. It had not been an easy job to get them into place, but now as they twinkled, the effort of getting them there was more than worth it. The whole of The Old Ticket Office was sparkling. The effect was exactly as she had envisioned for Love Emmy x's opening day. The images in her head were coming to life, as if they'd been dormant for years and were now waking up.

'Good job. The place looks great,' Tom remarked appreciatively, slipping an arm around Emmy's shoulders. 'Your vision is shaping up in front of our eyes. Now I get what you were trying to tell me.'

Emmy felt herself go nuclear inside. Here she was, standing in her own shop with a lovely man by her side. It all felt so nice. She gazed around the shop and wondered what the people coming to the opening would think. Would they be oohing and ahing over the flowers, lights and jewellery as much as she was? Of that, she'd have to wait and see. Then there was Louisa, who would hopefully be in the corner to top it all off. She felt as if that really was going to seal the deal of making the whole thing fabulous.

'Do you think we have enough lights on that side?' Emmy worried and pointed up to the far side of the ceiling, flicking her eyes over to the few remaining unopened boxes of lights piled up on the counter.

Tom squeezed her shoulder. 'Plenty up there. We'll use the rest to line the doorway there, I reckon.

'I don't even know why I'm asking.' Emmy chuckled. 'No such thing as too many fairy lights, if you ask me. They make everything look and feel better.' *Apart from estranged secret sisters, they don't do a lot for those,* Emmy said in her head.

'Well, you're the boss.'

Emmy loved being with Tom. He just had a sort of calm bordering on arrogant confidence about him. It had been there right from the word go when she'd bumped into him in the street. Just having him around felt nice. Safe. She started to gather boxes whilst panicking a bit inside. There was loads to do, and her list seemed to be getting longer by the minute, but most of the finishing touches were nearly complete. She allowed herself a little glow of happiness mixed with anticipation topped with a splodge of fear. After all the years of working hard, all the months of planning and all the thinking, her dream was nearly about to arrive. She wasn't quite sure what to think at the end of the day.

'Thank you for all your help. I couldn't have done this without you.'

Tom's eyes crinkled. 'That's what I'm here for. What's next on the list?'

Emmy looked down at her expansive to-do list and set Tom to stringing lights around the door while she focused on the setting up of a drink station. There were all sorts of drinks lined up to be served, but she wanted a water station with gigantic glass pitchers of lemon and elderflower water. It had been one of the pictures in her head for a long time; now she was making it happen. She had a freezer full of ball ice cubes filled with elderflower and gooseberries and a vintage table ready for the jugs and glasses.

Humming under her breath, Emmy pottered around, putting a white linen tablecloth in place when Callum emerged from the back room. 'How are the windows out there coming up, Cal?' she asked as Callum retrieved a spray bottle of glass cleaner and a roll of paper towels from a cleaning bucket wedged by the front door.

'Good, nearly done the ones over the sink.'

Emmy grimaced inside, wondering how good a job Callum had done. She didn't let her concern about his teenage window cleaning skills show from the outside. 'Right. Great. Would you start on the inside of the front here next? I want everything sparkling.'

Callum nodded, tucking the spray bottle under one arm. 'Will do. Place is looking good, Mum.'

Emmy stopped what she was doing and put her hands on her hips. 'Thanks. Tom just said the same.' Emmy ruffled his hair affectionately in passing. She watched as he walked away.

She couldn't quite believe how tall he was, and that he was the same being as the tiny little baby she'd once had. She did know she was grateful not only for his willing help but also for the fact that he appeared to be interested. She'd heard horror stories about teenage boys, and though he was far from perfect, overall he was turning out not too bad at all. She crossed her fingers that it would stay that way.

Once she'd done as much as she could with preparing the water station, she ticked 'iced water' off the seemingly endless list with a flourish. Getting there.

'Right. All the lights on the doorway are up,' Tom announced, wandering over. 'How about I turn the big lights off and we get the full effect?'

He walked over to the corner of the room and hit the switch. Emmy gasped. With the lights off, the twinkling bulbs and hundreds of tealights looked amazing. Her hands flew to her mouth. 'Wow. Yes! I love it!' she exclaimed, impulsively throwing her arms around Tom's neck.

'It really looks brilliant,' Callum concurred with raised eyebrows.

'How good a job have we done?' Laughing, Tom fished another decoration box off the pile Emmy had stacked up by the door. 'Now, what's next on the agenda?'

Emmy stared at her phone for a bit, consulting her list again and nibbling her lower lip. 'Just the flower garlands, I think. Yeah, then all the rest of it is more last-minute stuff.'

Callum wrinkled up his nose. 'What? More flowers? How can there be more?'

'Like fairy lights, one can never have enough.' Emmy laughed. She rummaged in a box and held up a garland of pink and white roses. 'These are going to be draped in and out of the lights.'

Half an hour or so later, the garlands were strung all over the place. Emmy stood back to scrutinise the result. Simple garlands massed together had an amazing effect. After what felt like hours on the ladder securing garlands, she finished the last length and hopped down gratefully. She rubbed the back of her neck as she looked upwards, and Tom stood by her side. Fairy lights flickered overhead, the garlands draped just so, and the tealights dotted on every available surface made the whole place feel magical. She could almost see the space filled with people, mingling and laughing over flutes of champagne, the harp in the background, the jewellery displayed beautifully.

Emmy just stood staring for a bit, imagining the opening day and being surrounded by people she loved. She thought about Tom and Cherry and Bob, and her mind flicked to the fact that she knew where Katy was and they didn't. It ruined the dream. She was brought back to the room with Callum interrupting her thoughts.

'You still with us, Mum?' Callum asked.

Emmy blinked. 'Sorry, miles away, imagining having this place open.'

'Not much to do now,' Callum noted.

'Pah! Just all the last-minute stuff. The real hard work is yet to come. It's going to be stressful.'

'It's all coming together beautifully. Try not to stress, you've done everything you can,' Tom said.

Emmy shivered. There it was again, the sort of strong confidence that had been sorely missing from Emmy's life for as long as she could remember. Sensing her thoughts, Tom wrapped an arm around her shoulders and squeezed. All the stressful months of renovation now felt worth it, seeing it all take shape in front of her eyes. She clapped her hands together. 'Yes. All going well; it's perfect. Thank you both, truly,' she said thickly.

'What you've achieved here is no small feat,' Tom acknowledged. 'Don't keep thanking everyone else. You're the driver on this.'

Emmy's cheeks warmed, and she stopped herself from thanking him again. 'Hmm.'

'You had a vision, and you stuck with it,' Tom noted. 'That's half the battle. That and turning up and putting in the graft. You've already succeeded just by doing that.'

The nuclear reactor in Emmy's stomach fizzed away. Having Tom in her life really was very nice. Long may it last.

33

Emmy leaned back, admiring their handiwork. It was amazing how what was once an old insurance office had been transformed for the opening. The fairy lights overhead, the mass of flower garlands draping from the ceiling, the antique dresser Tom had surprised her with, and the hundreds of candles all looked fabulous. On top of that, there were hidden diffusers pumping geranium and vetiver scent into the air. Emmy was feeling quite chuffed with herself. The space was finally coming to life after so many months of hard work, which had been preceded by years of dreaming.

Watching Tom up on the ladder stringing the final lights, Emmy felt she might burst with happiness. Despite her under-lying worry that the retail side of Love Emmy x was something that was really completely out of her hands, she was pleased with how it had so far turned out. Emmy felt something in her stomach flutter; little butterflies of nervousness and anxiety rolled into one. She smiled at Callum's lanky frame as he sprayed and cleaned the side of the windows. As if he felt her thoughts in his back, he turned around.

'The place looks really good, Mum. So different to when we

moved in,' Callum remarked. 'Hard to believe it's nearly ready after all this time.'

'You're telling me,' Emmy agreed. 'I can't wait for the event now.'

Tom hopped down from the ladder and slipped an arm around Emmy's shoulders. 'All your vision and hard work is about to pay off. Although the real reward will be when your first customer steps through the door.'

Emmy's cheeks grew warm. She wasn't really that used to praise. It felt more than nice. 'As long as it all goes well and Louisa wows everyone, I'll be happy,' she quipped.

Truthfully, though, she was *very* nervous. Petrified. It was all very well opening a shop, but the actual bottom line of it was whether or not it was going to make her money. The whole Love Emmy x thing wasn't just a little whim for fun; it was about her *future*. She knew, though, deep in her soul, that The Old Ticket Office as it was now had been worth every sacrificed hour and penny. She'd spent many hours of her life thinking about and scheming it.

'Right, that should just about do it,' Tom announced, coiling the last bit of spare lights. 'There can't be much more left to do on the list.'

Emmy pondered. 'Let me have a look.'

She scrolled through her phone notes, trying to recall if any final details needed addressing. The shop practically gleamed. There wasn't a single nook or cranny she hadn't thought about. She nodded to herself, satisfied.

'I think we're actually all set,' she realised aloud. 'Just need to give it another quick tidy on the day and all the stuff that we can't do now. I need to get the storeroom sorted, too.'

Tom chuckled and addressed Callum. 'Your mum says we're allowed to knock off for the night.'

Callum nodded. 'Sweet. Feels like I've been cleaning for ages. Plus, I'm starving.'

Emmy laughed. 'You're always starving!' Some things never changed. 'Right, yeah, let's call it a day. I'll just finish the last bits here, and why don't we order in?'

'Couldn't have said it better myself,' Tom joked.

'You go up, and I'll lock the front up while I close down my computer. Use the app on the iPad. I'm logged in on that,' Emmy instructed. 'It's upstairs in my bag. I'll be up in a sec.'

While Callum collected the cleaning supplies and finished putting the lights in a box, Emmy started to close down tabs on her computer. After sliding the bolts across on the front door and switching the lights off, she made her way up the steep stairs in the middle of the building, went to the loo, and then strolled into the kitchen where Tom was standing by the kettle waiting for it to boil. Callum was by the table where Emmy's large tote bag was sitting on the chair.

'Tea?' Tom asked.

'Yep, love one. It's been a long day.'

'Err, Mum. What's this?' Callum asked.

Emmy turned to see Callum with a quizzical look on his face. He held her handbag unzipped in one hand, brow creased. In the other hand was the yellow raincoat. It had yellow bumblebees embroidered around the hood and, in Callum's hand, looked impossibly small.

Emmy panicked big time. She'd again completely forgotten about Elodie's jacket that she'd hastily stuffed in her bag from underneath the seat in the car after the trip with Amy. She'd intended once inside to hide it. It had totally gone out of her mind. Now here it was, impossibly tiny and childlike and looking completely out of place. Emmy's pulse roared in her ears. She tried to think quickly, grasping for plausible explanations. How could she possibly explain the presence of a toddler's raincoat in her handbag?

Oblivious to her spiralling panic, Callum joked, 'Where did you get this from? Not quite your size, is it? It's absolutely tiny.'

At that moment, Tom turned around with two mugs of tea. 'Get what from?' His gaze landed on the incriminating raincoat. 'What do we have here?'

Ice flooded Emmy's veins. She stared helplessly between Callum and Tom with absolutely no idea what to say about the coat. To her, it had Elodie's name all over it. To them, they were wondering where it had come from. She didn't say anything for a second. She couldn't seem to get her brain to work quickly enough.

'Well, it can't be yours, Cal.' Tom chuckled. 'Unless you're keeping secrets about a whole other life we don't know about.'

Callum looked baffled, laughed and held the coat up, dancing it in front of him. Tom redirected his gaze to Emmy. 'Why do you have a toddler's coat in your bag?' He was still joking around. 'What aren't you telling us?'

Emmy's mind whirled uselessly, and she seemed unable to form words. She willed a coherent sentence to come out of her mouth, but she just shook her head.

Callum shifted his weight between feet, Elodie's rain jacket still dangling from his fingers. 'Mum?'

Swallowing hard, Emmy forced herself to laugh and be jovial. She rolled her eyes. 'Long story. It was at work. I picked it up and then promptly forgot to take it to lost property.'

Callum frowned and she willed him to shut up. He didn't. All she could see was Elodie's face in the little yellow jacket as she zoomed down the slide. 'What, and you put it in your bag? At work?'

Tom wrinkled up his nose. 'Why didn't you just take it to lost property or put it in your locker?'

Emmy stumbled over her words. 'No, no. It wasn't *in* work, *at* work. The car park. Yes. It was in the car park on the ground, and I stuffed it in my bag and then forgot about it.'

As Emmy looked at both of their expectant faces, she felt terrible. The deception overwhelmed her. She *hated* the lies. She seemed to be making so many excuses and spinning half-truths all the time. The worst thing was that Tom was frowning, and Callum was shaking his head. It was totally clear to all three of them that neither Tom nor Callum believed Emmy in the slightest. This really wasn't good.

34

It was a couple of days or so after Callum had pulled the coat from Emmy's bag. Emmy realised that her teeth were so tightly gritted together that the little muscles at the side of her cheeks were standing to attention. She sighed loudly as she drove onto the floating bridge and pulled her bottom jaw away from the top and wiggled it back and forth. The early morning light glinted off the calm waters of the Darling estuary, and there was a bite in the fresh air coming in her open car window. Most of Emmy, though, was oblivious to the delightful Darling view going on around her as cars and foot passengers loaded onto the ferry, and she certainly was not as calm as the water. Her mind was far too preoccupied with going over the heated words she'd had with Tom the night before. At least her brain wasn't totally consumed with Katy; there was that.

She took a long sip of coffee from her travel mug that she'd wedged into the cupholder in the centre console of her car and waited for the clang and bang of the ferry gate behind her. As she heard the now familiar sounds of the chains underneath, she picked up the cream cheese bagel she'd made the night before and pulled off the beeswax wrap. The bagel bought from the bakery just along from The Old Ticket Office was delicious, as was the cream cheese from the Italian deli on the other side of Darling Street, but it sort of stuck in a sludge in her mouth as her mind replayed her and Tom's first fight. She was still churning with anger and resentment over how things had gone down with Tom. He had not been happy at all, and neither had she.

The day before, she'd been out in the afternoon to see Katy. It had all been arranged via text message, and as far as she was concerned, no one was any the wiser. What she hadn't figured was that just as she'd been walking down the path at the back of the building with the yellow coat over her arm, Tom came the other way. He'd frowned because she'd told him she was spending all afternoon packing Love Emmy x orders. When she'd cobbled together a quick excuse, he'd clearly not believed her. He'd pointed to the coat and asked if she was going to pick up a cricket thing for Callum why she was carrying the coat. She'd replied that she was just putting it in her car, ready to take it to the lost property office the next day. Both of them had been aware that she wasn't telling the whole truth. Neither of them were happy.

After returning from her secret visit with Katy, she'd gone to pick Callum up from the ferry, they'd had dinner together, and then she'd left Callum supposedly studying in his room and gone to Tom's. What had started as a nice evening had escalated into tense words when Tom had asked her about her trip, his face clouded with suspicion. He'd come right out and asked her where she'd been because he didn't believe that she'd been to collect something for cricket. Caught off guard, Emmy had stammered some weak excuse about running errands. But Tom had pushed back, saying he could tell she was lying. Emmy had not liked that *at all*. In fact, she'd baulked inside. Her hackles had risen and then some. She hadn't liked the accusatory tone in his voice one little bit. It had immediately put Emmy on the defensive.

'Why do you need to know every little thing I do?' she'd snapped at him.

Tom's eyes had flashed with hurt and disbelief. 'You've been acting cagey and distant. Sneaking around, keeping secrets. I'm worried about you. To be quite frank, I don't like it one little bit.'

Emmy'd crossed her arms defensively across her chest. 'I don't have to report my every move to you, Tom. I'm allowed to have parts of my life that are private. You need to trust me.'

'Trust goes both ways!' Tom had argued, his voice rising in frustration. 'How can I trust you when there is clearly something you're not telling me? Plus, a mystery yellow jacket. Do you think I was born yesterday or something?'

The accusation had stung, and Emmy had been absolutely *incensed*. Her face had gone bright red, and she'd felt as if steam was pouring out of her ears. The nuclear feeling that had accompanied her ever since she'd first started going out with Tom was there, but not in a good way. How dare he question her? She'd tried to convince herself that this was the reason she was so angry. Deep down, though, she knew Tom had a point. She knew she was lying. She knew she was distant. She didn't want to tell him the reason why when she wasn't able to tell her family. All around, it was easier to keep the whole thing hidden.

Emmy took another sip of coffee and felt it slip down through her chest and throat. She felt trapped and angry and at a loss as to what to do. Tom had *really* annoyed her. Who did he even think he was, asking her if she was telling the truth? She didn't owe him or anyone a full disclosure of her activities and whereabouts every second of the day. She was an independent person who could do exactly what she liked, thank you very much.

It had not ended well. She'd been furious that Tom had called her out and in the heat of the moment, she'd lashed out, telling Tom he could take a running jump if he thought he could question her. She'd hissed that she wasn't going to have anyone checking up on her and trying to control her. Tom had also been incensed. He'd shot back as quick as a flash that he didn't give a hoot about controlling her, but he wasn't going to be taken for an idiot.

Their voices had risen, not quite to shouts, but they definitely weren't having a friendly little chat, and the argument had snowballed. Emmy had ended up storming out of the house, slamming the door to punctuate her exit. She'd walked back up to her flat fuming with rage, and after banging and slamming around the kitchen getting her work stuff and Callum's lunch ready for the next morning, she'd promptly had a shower and gone to bed.

Now, the morning after, Emmy's throat clenched as she replayed the scene in her head. She stared straight ahead through the windscreen as the floating bridge travelled across to the other side. Internally, her emotions churned – mostly because she knew she was *completely* in the wrong. Mostly because she was well aware that she'd been evasive, distant, and lying for quite a while. Mostly because Tom was right, and didn't she know it. She sighed a big, long, dramatic exhale and made a strange little growling sound. This was precisely why she hadn't wanted to keep the secret in the first place. Lying didn't sit well with her, and everything always ended up in a mess.

Tom's attitude had been no different than usual. He'd been the same confident, bordering on arrogant person she'd first fallen in love with. And he was right. The whole thing filled Emmy with despair. At the same time as knowing he was right, she was irritated by his attitude. Who was he to ask her where she'd really been? He had no right to demand she account for her activities or whereabouts. The thing with Katy had nothing to do with him or anyone else until Katy decided what she wanted to do. Emmy couldn't risk any interference, even from someone who loved her and wanted to understand what was going on.

As she exited the bridge and Emmy merged onto the main road, she took a deep breath. There was nothing she could do about it. Tom would just have to wait. There was no way she was going to tell him about the secret. She clicked a button on the steering wheel to turn the radio on, listened to the news and then the weather forecast, flicked through a few stations, and settled onto one playing Queen. Repeatedly pushing the button to turn up the volume, she sped up and belted out a few lyrics as she drove along. Tom P Carter was just going to have to hang on. She would let the argument recede into the background and spend the day concentrating on work. By the end of the day, she'd probably have a bit of perspective. There would be time later to process it all and figure out how to reconcile.

Once she got to the car park, she went through her usual routine. She slid her makeup bag out from under the front seat, unzipped it, pulled down the mirror, and layered on her work face. Fixing her hair with her smoothing brush into a neat high pleat, she sprayed the sides, checked for strays, flicked the mirror back into position, put the brushes and makeup back in their correct compartment, and slipped the whole lot back under the front seat.

By the time she'd got into her morning, Tom, Katy, the yellow jacket, and the guilt about keeping secrets had all faded. She'd spent the morning authorising all sorts, liaising with someone in customs about a strange package, and dealing with a passenger who'd left her suitcase on a train. The busy morning had been a most welcome distraction, forcing her not to dwell on the argument.

When lunchtime rolled around, Emmy wandered through the bustling port, stretching her legs, trying to clear her head, and made her way to the staff canteen. As she walked, she reflected on the clashing perspectives during the fight. She could understand Tom's suspicion. Her secrecy *did* make it seem like she had something to hide. She could also see now, with time giving some clarity, that Tom's concern came from a place of care. He'd still annoyed her, though. She wasn't ready for someone to be asking what she was and wasn't doing and questioning if she was telling the truth.

Emmy felt entitled to privacy. Tom was just going to have to put up with it. She needed him to respect the little piece of her life she was currently keeping separate. She told herself relationships were complicated – no couple went through life without some conflict. She mulled it over as she stood in the queue in the canteen. As she got her lunch and took it over to her usual table, she felt the knot in her chest loosen slightly as one of her colleagues, Jessie, looked up from her table.

'Hey. How are you?'

'Good, thanks.'

'How was your morning? I heard it's busy down there in the madhouse today.'

'Yeah, good busy though.'

'Makes the time fly, eh?'

'Yep, and takes your mind off other things.'

'Oh, like what?'

Emmy sighed. 'Ah, nothing important.'

'Trouble in paradise?' Jessie joked.

'You could say that.'

'Have we had our first lover's tiff?'

'I think we might have,' Emmy said, glad that Jessie's tone was lightening the air.

'Oh, really? What about?'

Emmy wasn't going to start explaining the whole thing about Katy to Jessie. She hadn't told a single soul about Katy, and she wasn't about to start now. 'He just got a little bit too nosy about where I'm going.'

'Really? From what you've told me about him, that doesn't sound right.'

The truth of Jessie's words slapped Emmy in the face. Jessie had never even met Tom, but she was reading the situation correctly right from the word go. It didn't make Emmy feel any better. 'Hmm.'

'Sounds like he's a bit concerned. Have to say you haven't been yourself lately,' Jessie noted.

Emmy paused, Jessie's observation landing heavily. She picked at her salad. 'I suppose you're right,' she admitted. 'I have been a bit distracted.'

Jessie leant forward, her expression open and non-judgemental. 'Want to talk about it? Might help to get an outside perspective.'

Emmy hesitated. She couldn't talk about the real reason behind her strange behaviour and secrecy. If she started talking about Katy to anyone, the secret would start to unravel somehow and she'd end up confused. Jessie, though, had known her for a long time through their lunchtime exchanges. It was a strange but nice relationship. It had never strayed outside of work, but it had always covered a multitude of life's topics and ups and downs.

'It's just...' Emmy searched for the right words. 'I've got this thing going on. It's sort of from the past. Nothing bad, but it's occupied a lot of my time and headspace. I didn't tell Tom about it because, well, it's complicated.' She sighed. 'Really, *really* complicated.' She stared down at her salad, pushing a tomato around with her fork.

'Right, I see. Not something to do with Kevin, is it? He's not gambling again and asking you to secretly get him out of debt?'

Emmy shook her head. Half of her wished it was that because she'd be able to tell Kevin to take a running jump. 'No, not this time. For once. I can't blame Kevin for this.'

'You clearly have a lot on your mind.'

'I do, and Tom's noticed me being distant and preoccupied. Started questioning me about where I was going, what I was doing. It didn't feel good.'

'Too much?' Jessie offered.

Emmy nodded. 'Yeah, exactly. I got angry and defensive. Refused to answer his questions and stormed off. I pretty much *totally* overreacted, now I think about it.' She sighed, shoulders slumping.

'Ouch. Right.'

'You know what I realised while I was thinking about it this morning? I know he's just worried about me. My secrecy probably seems shady from his perspective.'

Jessie gave her a sympathetic look. 'I can understand both sides of the coin, to be quite honest. You deserve privacy, but he also cares about you. Tricky one.'

Stirring a little bowl of fruit, Emmy said, 'I want to protect this thing that's just mine right now. But not at the cost of pushing Tom away. God, I really ripped into him when he questioned where I was.'

'Have you tried explaining that to him? Not the details, just that you need some space?'

Emmy shook her head, poking morosely at a melon cube. 'I was too angry. I sort of yelled and left. He must be wondering what in the name of goodness is going on.'

Jessie lightened the air. 'You've had your first fight. Relationship goals.'

Emmy chuckled. 'I suppose we have.'

'It's a good thing. The honeymoon period is *officially* over. That doesn't mean the relationship is doomed. It's all in how you recover.'

'Listen to you sounding like a relationship counsellor.' Emmy laughed.

'Ask me how I know. I have this knowledge through bitter experience.'

Emmy nodded slowly. She knew Jessie was right – a single argument didn't negate how she felt about Tom, even though she was still cross with him. She just needed to make things right again. She sighed. 'Now I have to apologise and do all that. Ahh.'

'Just soften him up.'

'I was too defensive right away.'

Jessie took a sip of her tea. 'It's okay to tell him you're not ready to share this thing that's going on. But avoid making it seem like you're hiding stuff from him.'

'I'd hate that if he said that to me.'

'Yeah. True.'

'Frame it as protecting your privacy? I don't know.'

Emmy turned what Jessie had said over in her mind. The Katy secret had been making her act completely out of character. No wonder Tom was worried. 'You're so right,' she told Jessie gratefully. 'I need to own it. Just say it's private but not a threat to "us."'

'Well, at least you can try that avenue.'

'I will.'

'You're experiencing your first little bit of relationship turbulence.'

'I am indeed. Ahh, thank goodness for being here, eh? Giving me a bit of perspective on things. Gets me out of my own head. Always works.'

Jessie gathered her stuff. 'I'll hold you to that next time you're moaning about the place.'

Emmy chuckled. 'Which is all too often.'

'Anyway, see you later. I'll be waiting for the next episode. We've had the romance of the century, now we've got the first argument.' Jessie rubbed her hands together. 'Love it.'

'I'm glad to be your entertainment.' Emmy chuckled. 'Thanks for the listening ear. You really helped me get perspective.'

'Anytime. You're welcome,' Jessie replied. 'Let me know how

it goes with Tom. But from what you've told me about you two, I'm sure you'll work it out.'

Emmy fiddled with the corner of her fruit salad bowl as she went through what Jessie had said. She realised that she'd been way over the top with Tom. She needed to wind her neck in and apologise.

Back on the concourse, Emmy adjusted her neck scarf, tapped the back of her hair to make sure it was still neatly in place and tried focusing on work despite the lingering feelings about what she was going to do about Tom. She checked on her watch to see if there was a message from him. Radio silence, and she didn't blame him either. She could see now that she'd acted way out of line.

As she went about helping behind the check-in desk, she told herself that all couples experienced rocky patches and life was full of storms, and weathering them was what made you stronger. None of her self-talk made her feel any better.

By the time she'd got to the end of her day, she was both sick of thinking about it at the same time as worrying about what to do. Walking to her car, Emmy took deep breaths and played out the coming conversation in her mind. She would apologise and remain calm and not get irritated that he was pushing all her buttons by not believing her lies.

Pulling into the lane, she sat for a moment and decided that before she even went home to sort out the dinner, she'd go straight to Tom's. She went up to his flat, and he looked up as she entered. He wasn't looking too chuffed.

'Hey. How are you?'

Tom's expression was definitely guarded. 'Not too happy about last night, to be quite honest.'

Tom P Carter did not beat around the bush. She didn't blame him for being annoyed. 'First, I want to say I'm sorry. I shouldn't have got so angry and stormed off last night.'

She saw Tom's eyebrows lift slightly in surprise. 'Right. Okay.'

'I know you thought something was up, and it worried you. I get that.'

Tom's expression softened a fraction. 'Good. You've been really odd.'

'There is something I have been thinking about a lot. I should've been more upfront about needing some space to process it alone. It's nothing to do with anyone else.'

'Why didn't you just tell me that, then?' Tom still didn't sound either convinced or happy.

Emmy sighed. 'Honestly? I felt defensive right away when you interrogated me about where I'd been. I got tunnel vision. It's been years since I've, well, you know, been in a relationship where I have to tell anyone anything. You know?'

'That's no excuse. It's called common manners. Or decency. Either one will do.'

Emmy gulped. Tom P Carter took no prisoners. 'I'm really sorry.'

'I could've approached it better, too,' he admitted. 'Coming on so strongly made you feel attacked, I guess. I'm worried about you, Ems. I don't need every little detail of your life, but just need to know you're okay.'

'I am,' she assured him. 'Let's just put it behind us, yeah? Deal?'

'Deal.'

35

On her way home from work the next day, Emmy had stopped in to see Amy. She was sitting in Amy's kitchen at the table. A plate of cinnamon buns, which had just been warmed in the oven, was on the table, rain poured down the windows, and Amy chatted as she finished making the tea.

Amy put the mugs down on the table with a bit of clink and sat down. 'So, how are things with you? We're getting very close to D-Day at the shop now.'

'Yeah, it's all very real.'

'What else has been happening?'

'Oh, nothing, you know,' Emmy replied breezily. 'Same old. Getting ready for the opening, Callum's cricket has been busy, and work yesterday and today has been crazy. No rest for the wicked,' Emmy replied, purposely leaving out the argument with Tom. There was no way she wanted to mention anything to Amy in case it swayed off course and went anywhere near the Katy subject. She'd rather just keep well away.

'And everything's good with Tom?' Amy probed.

Emmy knew right away by the look on Amy's face that she knew about the argument. She maintained an air of nonchalance. 'Yeah, we're great. Just trucking along happily.' She forced an easy chuckle.

Amy raised an eyebrow. 'Really?' she said, taking another sip of tea.

Emmy felt uneasy. Amy didn't miss a trick, and something about her sister's tone suggested she knew more than she was letting on. Trying not to show any reaction, Emmy smiled and nodded. 'Yep, can't complain at all. Tom's great.'

'Hmm, interesting,' Amy said slowly. She set her mug down again and leaned back, folding her arms across her chest casually. 'Because that's not exactly what I heard.'

Emmy's stomach plummeted. Attempting to seem unfazed, she rolled her eyes. 'Oh really? What have you heard then?'

Amy raised her eyebrows. 'That the two of you had quite the ding-dong.'

Emmy pressed her lips together. The only way Amy would have known about the words with Tom was via Callum. 'How do you know? Callum, I guess.'

'Yup.'

'Just a little tiff. Our first one. Not even worth mentioning, so I didn't. You know how it goes.'

Looking sceptical, Amy turned her mouth upside down. 'Callum seemed to think it was pretty serious by the way you were slamming and banging. That's what he told Dad, apparently.'

'You know Cal. He probably embellished the whole thing for effect,' Emmy said, making light of it at the same time as groaning inside. 'Tom and I disagreed about something, and he irritated me. End of story. It had to come sooner or later.'

Amy pursed her lips. 'What was it about, then?'

Emmy didn't want to get into it. She didn't want Amy getting even the slightest whiff that there was a secret involved, that she was lying about a lot of things and that she was keeping secrets. 'It was just a little spat. We talked it through after, and we're completely fine now.'

'So there's nothing going on? Nothing bothering you lately that could've caused friction between you two?'

Emmy's chest constricted. As much as she hated lying, she'd told Katy she would keep quiet, and she would. That had to come first. 'Nope, nothing at all. I've just been stressed and overtired about the opening. You know how it goes. Once it's over and done with, I'll be much happier, to be quite honest.'

'Right. So everything is fine with Tom?'

'Yep. Tom is wonderful. I'm lucky to have him – nothing to worry about. Callum just got the wrong end of the stick. Honestly, most of the slamming was because I came back, and as per usual, Callum hadn't managed to put his stuff in the dishwasher. He thinks there are fairies to do that for him. That's why I was banging around in the kitchen.'

Amy searched her face a moment longer. 'If you say so.'

Emmy chuckled and sighed inside. Crisis averted. Again. Lying was getting very old. She was so over it.

'You have been *weird* lately, though. You're sure there is nothing really wrong?'

Masses and masses of guilt flooded through Emmy at the concern in her sister's eyes. 'Yep, absolutely positive.'

'Good. Trust me. Tom seems like a keeper. Don't let him get away,' Amy joked.

Emmy smiled. 'Believe me, I won't. He's the best thing that's happened to me in a long time. Wait. Let me correct that. I'm the best thing that ever happened to him, ha.' She smiled at the same time, thinking how true it actually was. Since she'd been with Tom, she'd been really happy. She didn't want to lose it by silly arguments or tying herself up with secrets and lies.

Taking one of the cinnamon buns and cutting it in half with a knife, she popped a bit into her mouth and then moved the subject swiftly onto something else. She sighed in relief as the conversation moved onto safer and more cheerful subjects. By the time they'd finished their tea, she was happy to have smoothed over another problem. Overall, though, she wasn't quite the ticket at all. She wondered how much longer she could lie and pretend. It wasn't much fun, as far as she was concerned. She tried to reassure herself, as she had done countless times since she'd been keeping the Katy secret, that with time everything would come out in the wash. As far as she was concerned, the wash needed to get a wriggle on.

36

It was a week or so later, and Emmy was counting down until the shop opening. Most of the invitations were back, the event she'd created on Facebook was sold out, and she'd been over her lists and to-dos so many times she was sick of the sight of them. Everything she could do, apart from the things that had to be completed on the day, had been done. She was going through her lists on her iPad as she sat at the kitchen table with a plate of toast and jam and a cup of tea. Along with checking off tasks, she was mentally checking her work things were ready when she remembered the bag she'd left in the Waitrose trolley. She'd called again and asked for an update on the off chance that someone had handed it in. Although the woman on the other end of the phone had been really helpful, the bag hadn't come to light. The woman had said not to give up hope, because if someone had taken it home with the intention of bringing it back, it could take ages. Emmy, though, had more or less written the bag off and had added putting a new one together to her list of jobs to do once the shop was opened.

She'd had a long week and sighed about leaving the bag, irritated that she'd both been careless and that it had given her another job to do. She was tired and it was beginning to show – she'd been up since dawn sending emails and wrapping Love Emmy x parcels, had a mid-morning walk planned with Tom, and loads of things she wanted to get done. She squinted at her phone as it buzzed with an incoming text. Picking it up from the kitchen table, she smiled when she saw it was from Katy. She swiped up to unlock the screen.

Katy: *Hey, so sorry, but I desperately need a favour. My child-minder just cancelled at the last minute again and I have to work. Is there any way you can watch Elodie for a few hours? I'm completely stuck again!!!*

**** *me dead.* Emmy shook her head and her stomach dropped. She'd been looking forward to her morning and the walk around near the sailing club with Tom. What with all the work involved with the shop, her double shifts, and the tension after their words, the walk was long overdue. She grimaced, knowing full well that if she said yes to Katy, Tom was not going to be impressed with another one of her half-hearted excuses, but Katy clearly needed her help.

Thumbs flying over the keyboard, she typed back:

Emmy: *Of course. Don't worry about anything. Give that girl of yours a big kiss from me!*

Katy: *You're a lifesaver!! I owe you huge.*

Emmy was in a two and eight. She'd drop everything to help Katy out after what she'd been through, but now it really was Katy coming before Tom. They'd been planning the long walk all week. Chewing her lip, she chickened out of calling him and pulled up her text thread with him.

Emmy: *Really sorry. Something's come up, I've got to pop out this morning now. I'm really sorry! I'll see you later. xxx*

She watched the three dots instantly pulse as Tom typed out his reply.

Tom: *What? We've been looking forward to this all week. What came up that could be more important?*

Emmy's nerves jittered. Tom was nothing if not direct. She shook her head and sighed. She should have known Tom wouldn't accept a vague excuse. He wasn't that sort of bloke. She needed a concrete reason that seemed plausible.

Emmy: *It's Judy at work. She's in a bind. I really can't say no, I owe her big time. I feel terrible cancelling our plans. I'll make it up to you later, I promise. xx*

The typing dots appeared again right away:

Tom: *I don't understand, Ems. Is it some kind of emergency or something? This all sounds very sudden.*

Emmy exhaled sharply through her nose. Of course Tom was going to react. She was being evasive again. She didn't blame him one iota. She really felt as if she had little choice in the matter.

Emmy: *All good. I feel awful cancelling, but I just can't leave her in the lurch. I'll explain it properly later. Please don't be mad. Love you xx*

Tom: *Is this some kind of a joke? Call me and explain what's going on.*

Emmy's anxiety spiked. She didn't have time for a lengthy discussion and interrogation from Tom about where she was going and why. She knew she was not only being completely unreasonable but also quite nasty, but his questioning her again irritated her. There was no way she wanted to talk to him, but she'd have to. Deciding to just take the bull by the horns, she pressed his contact.

Tom picked up on the second ring. 'Hey. So, what's going on?' His tone was clipped. He did not sound happy. At all.

Emmy jumped right in, aiming for a casual air. 'I'm so sorry about cancelling the walk. One of the girls from work called in sick, meaning Judy needs me to watch her daughter for a bit. She's really stuck, so I couldn't say no.'

'Who do you mean? Judy? Why can't her husband handle it?' Tom asked shortly. 'I thought she was miles away.'

'He's away on business,' Emmy lied, cringing at how easily the lies were now rolling off her tongue one after the other. She was becoming quite the expert at not telling the truth. 'I would have said I had plans, but she was really begging. I won't be long, I promise.'

'So, you're leaving right now to go and babysit for someone at work?' Tom did not sound like he believed her or that he was happy.

'I know it seems sudden,' Emmy interjected hastily. 'She just texted, and I said I wouldn't mind helping out. I've been there when Callum was that age. Judy's been so good to me over the years, as you know. We'll talk later, okay? Love you.'

Before Tom could argue further, Emmy ended the call. Her mind mingled with guilt and frustration. She hated deceiving Tom, but she didn't have a whole lot of choice. This was about helping Katy. She couldn't turn her back on Katy. She almost felt as if Katy had some kind of a hold on her, and if she said no to Katy, that would be the end of that.

Grabbing her bag and keys, Emmy hurried out to her car. As she drove, she tried putting Tom and her nagging conscience out of her mind. She'd have to seriously creep around him when she got back. Once she'd arrived at Katy's road, she pushed Tom out of her mind, found a spot to park in, and hurried out of her car. Emmy made her way up the front steps, heels clicking on the wet slabs. Katy opened the main pale blue front door before Emmy could press the buzzer on the intercom. Elodie was in her arms, and Katy looked frazzled but grateful.

'Morning, Elodie. How are you? I thought we might have a little walk today. What do you reckon?' Emmy said with a bright smile and turned to look back out onto the street. 'I brought my wellies too,' she said, fishing them out of her bag. 'We can have a little walk in the rain as long as it just stays as this drizzle.'

Elodie smiled and nodded shyly as all three of them went up to the flat and chatted. Emmy felt flooded with emotion on so many levels. She still couldn't believe how much Elodie looked like Katy, couldn't believe she was part of the secret, and couldn't believe she was mingled up in a load of lies. Some of the stress of deceiving Tom melted away as she realised how much she wanted to make things better with Katy.

'Thank you, thank you,' Katy gushed, juggling her handbag and iPad once they'd got in the flat. 'I'm so sorry to call you like this. I know last time I said it was very unusual to happen, and now it's gone and happened twice! You're a godsend. Thank you.'

'Don't worry about a thing,' Emmy assured her. 'We're going to have fun, aren't we, Elodie?'

Elodie was fussing with her wellies. Katy smiled tiredly, batting her hand towards the kitchen. 'There are snacks and toys and everything. Call me if you need anything! I won't be too long.'

Emmy lowered her voice. 'Is she allowed a hot chocolate if we walk down to the coffee shop?'

Katy nodded. 'Sure. Not sure if she'll actually drink it, but she always likes the idea of one. A babycino is what she really likes.'

'Don't you worry, we'll have fun,' Emmy assured her. 'Say bye-bye to Mummy.'

Katy dropped a quick kiss on Elodie's head and hugged her close for a moment. 'Be good for Emmy.'

After Katy had rushed out the door, Emmy carried Elodie into the living room. She set her down near the toy box, lifted the lid, and pulled out a doll. 'What should we do first, Miss Elodie? Puzzles? Dolls?'

Elodie contemplated seriously before pointing to a shelf of books. 'A story, please.'

Emmy smiled and settled into the sofa with Elodie as drizzle tapped on the windows, and she read aloud. Elodie snuggled back against the sofa and stroked a little threadbare brown stuffed toy. As Emmy heard herself reading a book she remembered from Callum being little, the guilt that had been needling her dissipated a little bit. She did a silly voice for one of the characters and laughed as Elodie dissolved into giggles and the complicated outside world receded a touch.

After a few books, Elodie wiggled down from the sofa and began to lose herself in Lego. Soon she was fully engrossed in building a tower, tongue poking through her teeth in concentration. Emmy watched her, remembering Callum at the same age and marvelling at the activity of being a toddler. After assisting in the tower building, more stories, then apple slices on the sitting room rug, Elodie seemed keen when Emmy suggested going out for a walk. Emmy helped Elodie put on bright pink wellie boots and coat, and grabbed a tiny clear umbrella covered in pastel polka dots. 'Okay. Let's go and get ourselves a hot chocolate and a babycino.'

Outside, the sky was chock-full of white-grey clouds, and it was very lightly drizzling, but it wasn't too cold or wet. Emmy chatted away to Elodie as they walked along, gripping Elodie's hand tightly. Elodie jumped and splashed in the puddles on the glistening pavement.

After fumbling to get their umbrellas down, Emmy bundled Elodie into the coffee shop. It was busy with prams parked by the door out of the rain and a short queue at the counter. Emmy took Elodie's coat off and helped her onto a chair.

'Alright, are we thinking marshmallows in our babycino today?'

'Yes, please,' Elodie agreed, wiggling excitedly in her seat.

When two steaming mugs arrived, topped with piles of marshmallows that had Elodie's eyes widening to saucers, Emmy laughed. 'That's a lot of marshmallows!'

Elodie smiled as Emmy spooned a couple of the marshmallows out and gave them to Elodie. She slurped and came away with a marshmallow moustache that made Emmy grin. As they sat there in the busy café, Emmy felt herself relax a little bit, but the guilt still lingered at the back of her mind. Stirring her hot chocolate absently, Emmy mulled over the situation. The bottom line of it was that until Katy decided what she wanted to do to move forward, she was pretty much trapped in secrecy.

Emmy wondered if she was being selfish, maintaining this double life. She felt conflicted and pulled in so many different ways. As Elodie babbled happily through her marshmallow foam moustache, Emmy wished that things could be simple. But it never really worked like that, not in her case, at least. Real life was always so complicated and full. She just had to hope that when the truth finally emerged, everyone would understand the position she was in.

By the time they returned to the flat, pink-cheeked from the drizzly air, just as she had last time, Elodie had climbed up onto the sofa and promptly fallen asleep.

When Katy returned, she found Emmy in the kitchen tidying up. 'How was she?' she asked, hanging up her coat.

'An angel. Good as gold,' Emmy said.

'Thanks, Ems,' Katy said earnestly.

'It's fine. Honestly, not a problem at all.' She hesitated, then added, 'Have you thought any more about what we said before?'

'I have. The main thing is Elodie's happiness and well-being. I still feel the same.'

Emmy nodded. 'One step at a time.'

After a few more minutes of chatting, Emmy gathered her things. 'Right, well, I need to shoot off.'

Katy walked her to the door. 'Give Elodie a kiss for me.'

Katy smiled. 'I will. See you soon. We'll go for a coffee again, yeah?'

'Yep.'

'Let me know what shifts you're on, and I'll work around you.'

'Great.'

Stepping outside into the grey drizzle, Emmy felt as if the dreary weather matched her mood. When she arrived home, she sat motionless in the car for a few moments, dread creeping over her as she thought about lying again to Tom. She had a feeling that none of it was going to end well. She wasn't wrong.

37

Later that day, after chatting to her mum on the phone and again lying about her whereabouts, Emmy put her earphones in, loaded a podcast, and started to clear up the storeroom. The shop was ready, but the spillover of various bits and bobs had meant the back room had become a dumping ground for all sorts. Not only did the room need a serious tidy-up, but she needed to channel her energy into something mind-numbing. As she tidied and sorted, her mind went to Tom. She was not surprised he was fed up with her, but she tried not to think about it. After she'd listened to three podcasts and the room was spick and span, she was spraying the sink in the toilet, unable to put him out of her mind. There was no doubt that her secret-keeping was driving a wedge between them. It was no wonder he felt shut out; Amy did too. In fact, everyone, even Judy at work, had noticed Emmy's out-of-character behaviour. Her constant evasiveness was wearing thin on herself, let alone everyone else. The secrecy had taken on a life of its own, with Emmy feeling like she was digging herself in deeper and deeper, more or less every time words came out of her mouth. She found herself too often weaving more and more elaborate lies to avoid telling Tom or anyone else the full truth. None of it was good. All of it was stressful.

The light rain that had been falling all day was showing no signs of letting up, and not only that, a thick Darling fog had rolled in. Emmy went out to collect something from the car in the lane. Lost in her own thoughts, she was yanking open the door of her little car when the crunch of tyres on the gravel made her turn. Tom's black car was pulling up alongside her. She smiled and waved as she peered in. What with the fog and drizzle, his face was obscured, and she couldn't see how she was going to be received. He pulled directly in front of her car and climbed out, shoulders hunched against the drizzle.

'Hi,' Emmy said with forced brightness, hoping to head off any tense conversation. As any good Englishwoman would, she focused on the weather. 'I was just running out to grab something from the car. Wow, the fog has really come in. I don't remember hearing the foghorn.'

Tom's expression was unreadable as he came around to her side of the car; his tone held an edge. 'Yeah, it has. How was your day?'

Unease trickled down Emmy's spine. He didn't sound too friendly. She continued to be breezy. 'Good. I managed to get the storeroom sorted out this afternoon, thank goodness.'

'And how was this morning?'

Emmy's stomach plummeted. He'd cut straight to the chase. She feigned cheeriness. 'Good. Judy was grateful.' Inside, Emmy cringed at the ease at which her lies were coming.

Tom lifted his chin a bit, his jaw was taut. 'Cut the act, Ems.'

'What? What do you mean?' she stammered, grimacing at how unconvincing she sounded.

Tom's eyes flashed. 'I got a call.'

'A call? Who from?'

'About your bag.'

Emmy frowned. 'Sorry? What?'

'Your work bag,' Tom stated flatly.

'Oh, yes, yes.' Emmy remembered the bag, surprised that it had come to light. She'd written it off as lost. 'Oh, what, really? I left it on a shopping trolley. Wow, that's so good of them. What? Wait. Hang on. They phoned your number, did they? How did they get that?' She frowned. 'I've phoned like three times and there was no sign of it.'

Tom shook his head. 'The supermarket didn't call me, no. My business card was in the front pocket. Someone had put the bag in their car and completely forgotten about it. *They* called me.'

Emmy remembered when she'd first met Tom and she'd seen one of his business cards. They'd both laughed at how he'd not used them for years. She'd taken a couple, one had ended up in her car somehow, and one morning, when she'd been in the car park at work, she'd picked it up from the centre console and tidied it away into her work bag. It all zoomed through her head and reiterated why she hated lying. You always got found out. 'I see.'

'Thing is, Ems. You were in a Waitrose completely in the opposite direction of where we live and where you work. Plus, it's *miles* away.' He screwed his nose up. 'Bit odd if you ask me.'

Emmy swallowed. 'I had to go there for a cricket thing.' It was sort of the truth.

Tom continued with a face like thunder. 'Anyway, so I didn't tell you because I thought, you know what, I'll wait and see.'

'Right.'

'And then this morning, when you cancelled, I decided that enough was enough. So I followed you to see which way you went.'

Emmy shook her head. How dare he! She now felt as angry as he looked. 'What? You're kidding me! You followed me!'

He stepped closer, peering down at her intently. 'I really think you should have just called it off between us.'

'What? What are you talking about?'

'Don't worry because I'm doing that for you.'

Panic roared in Emmy's ears. She couldn't admit she'd been with Katy and Elodie. 'I just...' she faltered, hating herself even at the thought of more lies spilling out.

Tom cut her off. 'I'm tired of the lies and secrecy. I want the truth about what you are up to.'

The look on Tom's face jolted through her. He looked *really* hurt.

'Tom, please...' she implored, eyes welling up. 'I never meant to.'

'I don't get it. Why would you want to be with me if you're going off to see someone else at the same time? I mean, really? Why bother?'

'I'm not seeing someone else! I can't believe you would think that! It's not like that. There are things I can't explain yet.'

Tom sucked in a breath. 'You're not wrong there. Because you're not going to have to explain this to me. You won't be getting that opportunity anytime soon. We're toast. I'm calling it. I don't have time for this sort of crap in my life. Been there, got the T-shirt, and it won't be happening again.' Tom's eyes were shiny with emotion. He looked *furious*.

Emmy crumbled inside. She also went quite nuclear at angry Tom. Hot. 'I know it seems bad.' She reached for his hand, but he flinched away.

'Don't ask me to understand when you refuse to tell me why you've been acting so odd.'

'Tom, listen.'

Tom turned away. His whole body looked angry. 'Let me know when you're ready to tell me precisely *what* is going on. Actually, no, don't. I won't be waiting around.'

With a flash, he was gone, and Emmy was left standing rooted to the spot in the fog and drizzle, wondering what had happened to her life. His words rang in her ears. She'd *monu-*

mentally stuffed up. For a couple of minutes, she just stood in the rain, shaking her head. Right as she was slamming the gate open with her shoulder to go back in, someone came rushing up behind her.

'Mum. Where's your phone? You said you were picking me up from the ferry!'

'Oh, Cal, I'm so sorry. I completely lost track of time.'

Callum frowned. 'What? You never do that.'

'Yes, I do.'

Callum smiled. 'No, you don't! It's fine anyway. You never forget things, though.'

Both of them knew he was right. Since Emmy'd had Callum and had left Kevin, she'd never had the luxury to forget things. That was for other people. 'Just busy, Cal.'

Callum touched her on the arm. 'Are you okay? You look awful.'

No, no. I'm not okay. I am so very much not okay. 'Yep, fine. How was your day?'

'Bit boring.'

'How about I make you a nice cup of tea and a sandwich?' *Whilst I try to forget that it looks like I've just been dropped from a height by a very good thing that was happening in my life.*

'Love one.'

Emmy nodded. At least she had Cal. There was that.

38

Emmy had not had a fun night. She'd even scrubbed the bath and made a load of sandwiches to put in the freezer for Callum's lunch to try and quieten her racing, sad mind. It was that bad. Things were dire. Neither of her jobs worked. She felt rotten to her core. She had no idea in the slightest what to do about Tom. Part of her was a bit taken aback at his behaviour. He clearly took no prisoners. It reminded her a bit of the feeling she'd had when she'd been to a Chamber of Commerce event, where he'd seemed to flick her off like a fly. Is that what he was doing now?

The other part of her knew darn well that she was lying through her teeth a lot of the time. He'd picked right up on that. She didn't blame him really for telling her to take a running jump.

She'd wondered whether or not to text him and gone back and forth on a message what felt like a hundred times. She'd also walked out into the lane with the intention of knocking on his door and talking it through, but she only got as far as his gate. The only real way to move forward, as far as she could see it, was to come clean and tell the truth. She wasn't sure whether she was ready to do that and risk the whole Katy situation going bang.

It was the next morning, and Emmy was alone in the house with her thoughts. She'd had cup of tea after cup of tea interspersed with cups of coffee in between, none of which had helped. Just as she was standing at the storage tubs collating orders for Love Emmy x, her phone buzzed with a call from her mum. She looked down and sighed. There was no way she wanted to talk to her mum, either, but she couldn't ignore yet another of her mum's calls.

'Hi, Mum. How are you? How was your golf?'

'Hi, darling. It was lovely despite the weather. What are you up to?'

'Currently standing in the storeroom, knee-deep in orders and packaging.'

'Oh, right. Off to the post office later, are you?'

'Yep. I'm going to go on my bike and then have a bit of a cycle around down by the front there.'

'Nice. All set for the opening. I was going to come over and give you a hand.'

Emmy shook her head. There was nothing really left to do except for the stuff on the day. She also felt racked with guilt around Cherry. She really didn't want her mum around. She pretended to consider. 'Err, hmm, actually, I think I'm all sorted.'

'Oh, right, okay.'

'Yep, Dad and Amy here the other day means there's not much left to do.'

'How about I just pop over then? We could go for a coffee at Darlings. I love that place.'

Emmy scrambled for an excuse. If Cherry came over, she'd have to skirt around the Tom issue, which might lead to the Katy issue. 'Ahh, I have loads of work reports to catch up on later. I'd earmarked some time for that.'

'Oh, okay.' Cherry paused for a second. 'Are you sure you're okay, darling? You don't sound right.'

'I'm fine.'

'It's just like the Kevin thing. Your voice sounds like that.'

'No, no.'

'Callum said the same, too.'

'Did he?'

'Yeah.'

Emmy tensed, cursing Callum. She tried to keep her tone light. 'Really, I'm okay, Mum. Just the usual stress of work and getting the shop ready. You know how I get.'

Cherry didn't sound convinced. 'If you say so, darling. I know my daughter, though. Something's off. Remember, Mum knows best.'

Emmy cringed. Katy certainly didn't think Cherry knew best. Guilt pricked at her. She hated shutting Cherry out, but if she started telling Cherry about Tom, it would lead to questions. She didn't need her mum to start with her questions. Her mum liked to know every single detail about every single thing,

'I promise I'm fine. Once the shop opening is behind me, things will calm down.'

'And everything's fine with Tom?'

Emmy gritted her teeth. 'We're great, honestly,' she lied. *We are so not great.* She forced an easy chuckle.

Cherry also sounded cheery. 'Rightio. Time will tell, darling. I know *everything*, remember.'

Emmy rubbed her forehead wearily, wishing the conversation was over. She just needed everyone to stop reading into things and leave her be. 'Mum, I've got a million things to do. I must get on. Love you.'

As she continued with her orders, Emmy was tied up in knots inside. The secrecy felt as if it was suffocating her. It had done a very good job of alienating Tom too. Deciding that she needed to at least clear the air, she typed out a message to Tom.

Emmy: *Can we talk?*

The reply came within moments:

Tom: *Thing is, Ems, you'll just breezily say everything's fine. So what's the point?*

With a sinking feeling in her stomach, Emmy decided it was time for push to come to shove. As she stood by her storage tubs, surrounded by packets and envelopes, she decided she'd tell Tom about Katy. She'd spent too long telling lies, and she was sick to the back teeth of it. Katy was a big girl. It was time for Emmy to put herself and her relationship first.

Emmy: *I know. I promise I will explain everything. I miss you already. Xxx Are you free to meet up later?*

The ball was firmly in Tom's court. She waited as the little dots flashed.

Tom: *I am.*

Emmy: *I'll be round later. Thx. xx*

Emmy picked up her parcels and shoved them in her post office bag. The time had come to come clean.

39

Emmy stood outside the back door of Tom's building with her pulse racing. She clutched her phone tightly, rehearsing what she needed to say. A small part of her was thinking that she would only tell half the story to try and somehow still keep the secret. That wouldn't be too sketchy, would it? Her mind flitted back and forth. It totally would. It didn't take a lot of deliberation to realise there was no way that was going to work. It wasn't the time to continue with any further lies. That was how she'd found herself dumped in the first place. She realised she wouldn't be able to tell Tom where she'd been going without telling him why.

There were a couple of main reasons why she had to go down the honesty road; firstly, Tom actually deserved to know the truth and secondly, the secrecy really was eating away at her. At the end of the day, it had jeopardised them and their relationship. More deception would only cause more damage. As she'd known all along, honesty was the best policy. She'd just decided not to heed it and that she knew better. How wrong could one be?

Tom had more or less told her it was over, but she'd sort of taken that as a heat-of-the-moment thing, but maybe this was it. A thought in the back of her head was whispering to her that it hadn't taken a lot for him to jump ship. A little part of her winced at that. Was she not worth standing by? It hadn't taken a lot for him to run. Then again, she'd been lying, dropping him, and had been distant for ages. She thought about what it might have been like if the boot had been on the other foot. She didn't like that feeling one little bit. Not at all.

Taking a big breath, Emmy decided to knock on the back door rather than let herself in. That in itself was huge in the status of their relationship. She could hear muffled footsteps coming down the stairs, across the back, and then the door swung open. Tom just about managed a smile, but he looked guarded and dark. It had to be said that he also took Emmy's breath away. A nuclear reaction occurred. Tom P Carter was, in fact, on fire.

'How are you?' Tom asked gruffly.

'Good. Actually, I'm not good,' Emmy faltered. 'I really need to talk to you. I know you said we're done, but I need to explain what's been going on. You must be so over it. I can see that now.'

Tom studied her face intently, stepped back, and ushered her silently inside. Emmy followed him up the stairs and then hovered awkwardly in the sitting room, arms wrapped around her middle defensively.

'Drink? Glass of wine? Tea?'

Emmy's stomach felt as if it was turning over and over. She nodded her head, sat down and then perched gingerly on the edge of the sofa. 'Yep. Wine, please.' Emmy didn't want wine, but she said yes anyway. All she wanted to do was vomit out the huge pile of deception that had suffocated her for too long. 'I need to clear the air and tell you what's been going on.'

Tom still didn't speak. She quite liked this Tom. The eyes. He did not look at all happy. He came back in with two glasses of red wine without a smile on his face. His whole demeanour was cloudy, and to Emmy, the gulf between them felt cavernous. She took the wine and then twisted her fingers around the stem of the glass, unsure how to start unravelling the Katy story. She wasn't quite sure what to think about it herself, let alone telling someone else. She gulped. 'First of all, I want to say sorry for all the secrecy.'

'Right. So you *have* been secretive, and I'm not going mad. That's a start, I guess. At least you're admitting it now.'

'Yep, I have been secretive.' Emmy decided to lay it on thick. In for a penny, in for a pound. 'Plus, there has been a lot of lying on my part lately. I'm so very sorry for that.'

Tom's eyes softened slightly, though his body remained tense as he took a sip of his wine.

Emmy pressed on. 'You were right that I've been hiding things from you. I want to explain why.'

'Go on.'

Emmy steeled herself. She was still unsure about telling Tom, but it had to be done. 'Remember I told you about my other sister?'

Tom frowned and squinted his eyes. 'Yes.'

'I've been in contact with her.'

Tom's frown deepened. 'Sorry, what? When?'

Emmy took a hasty gulp of wine for courage before continuing. 'It started a while back.'

Tom frowned. 'What did?'

'I've been meeting up with her and such.'

'Where? When?'

'Remember I went to pick up that cricket helmet for Callum ages ago?'

'Yep.'

'If you remember, I went on the train because I thought the parking and traffic would be terrible.'

'Sorry, what has this got to do with your sister?'

'I saw her from the train window. None of us have been in

contact with her for years. It was like seeing a ghost in a way. Yeah, it pretty much knocked me for six.'

'Right.'

'Before I'd really known what I was doing, I'd jumped off the train and followed her.'

'Wow.'

Emmy twisted the stem of her wine glass. Her palms were clammy. 'I couldn't believe it. I didn't know what I was doing, but anyway, I followed her home. It sort of sounds creepy saying it like that. I didn't know whether to approach her or what to do.'

'Why wouldn't you just go up to her? She's your sister, for goodness sake!'

'I know. It's complicated and Katy is, well, she's very head-strong. Knows what she wants. I was totally unprepared and wrong-footed, so I didn't really know what I was doing. None of it seemed to make any sense.'

'Hmm.'

'Long story short, she has a little girl. She went to collect her from childcare, and I saw them go into their flat.' Emmy shook her head. 'She looks so much like Katy it took my breath away. That's when the secrets began.'

Tom shook his head and squinted his eyes. 'Hang on. So, you haven't told Amy about this? Or Cherry? This is all weird. How could you do that?'

'No. I haven't told anyone at all.'

Tom let out a whoosh of breath. 'Wow.'

'It's complicated. Katy made me swear I wouldn't say anything.'

'I'm surprised you've kept secrets, seeing how close the lot of you are, supposedly are,' Tom noted. 'Why would you not just tell them?'

'I didn't have a lot of choice, and I felt like I owed it to Katy to do what *she* wanted.'

'I didn't see this coming. Right, okay, some of it makes sense now.'

'I swear my intention was never to hide things from you deliberately. But the more Katy and I talked, the more I learned about everything she's been through. I was just so unsure what to do. She asked me not to talk about it.'

'What, so you approached her that day? The day of the cricket helmet.'

'No.' Emmy sighed, remembering yet another occasion when she'd lied. 'I went back and sat outside her house in the car. Long story short, I approached her in the street, and she asked me in.'

'I see.'

'She has a little girl. She's been co-parenting but doesn't really have a support system.'

Tom's eyes widened in surprise. 'You have a niece you didn't know about!'

'Exactly.'

'I can't believe you haven't told your mum and dad. They're going to be devastated.' Tom frowned. 'You really think it's a good idea to keep this a secret and not tell them?'

Emmy squeezed her eyes tightly shut for a second. 'I know. I just didn't know what to do for the best. Which is why I didn't tell you or anyone.'

'Okay.'

Emmy's shoulders slumped. 'You were right to be upset. I created this whole separate part of my life and didn't let you in. The worst part was that the lies just kept piling on. The more I told, the worse it got.'

Tom sat silently for a long moment, processing her words. 'I appreciate you telling me the full truth.'

Relief coursed through Emmy, and she further gulped her wine. 'I just kept getting myself deeper and deeper in it. I knew if I told anyone at all, it would make it worse, which is why I didn't tell you or Callum or anyone.' She clasped her hands, willing them to stop shaking. 'I want to be fully open with you from now on. No more secrecy between us.'

Tom nodded slowly. 'I can understand, but the lying feels hard to move past.' He exhaled heavily. 'I've been constantly thinking I'm going crazy.'

Emmy's heart cracked at the hurt in his eyes. 'I know. I made a mess of things.'

'Thing is, I've been down this road before. Once a liar, always a liar.'

'No way! That's harsh!'

Tom raised his eyebrows. 'You know the story with Sarah.'

'Not all of it.'

'You know the gist of it and what happened there.' He turned his mouth upside down. 'I don't like liars.'

Emmy felt a little bit of indignation and a lot of irritation. 'Sorry, are you comparing me to her?'

'What would you do?'

Emmy pressed her lips together. 'You have a point.'

Tom shook his head and grimaced. 'Your mum and dad aren't going to be happy. Ditto Amy. I'm very surprised you haven't told them after everything they do for you!'

Emmy shook her head. 'I know. That's *if* they find out.'

Tom frowned. 'You really think it's a good idea not to tell them?'

'It's not *my* choice.' Emmy felt tears prick at the side of her eyes. She willed herself not to start crying. 'It's Katy's choice.'

'I suppose not.'

'I feel guilty on all sides.'

'Why would you feel guilty?'

'Guilty for lying and then guilty about Katy. There's loads more. She was pregnant when she left all that time ago.' Emmy let out a huge sigh. 'But she lost the baby.'

'Right.'

'So yeah, there's a lot to it.' She looked right into Tom's eyes. 'So what about us?'

'I don't know. At least it makes sense now,' Tom said simply. 'I've been constantly on edge worrying what in the name of goodness was going on.'

Emmy's heart lifted slightly, hearing Tom say her explanation made sense. She took a shaky sip of wine for liquid courage. 'I know it doesn't justify the secrecy and lying, but now you understand why I felt compelled to keep Katy's confidence, misguided as that was. I never for a second meant to push you away.'

Tom set his wine down and reached for her hands. 'I get it now.'

'Thank you. So what does this mean?'

Tom joked. 'You get one chance only.'

'Ha.'

'Let's focus on moving forward. I understand.'

Emmy nodded, attempting a watery smile. 'Right. No wallowing allowed.'

'Definitely not. Just don't lie, Ems. It never gets anyone anywhere.'

'Easier said than done on this occasion.'

'Have you eaten?'

'God, no. I've felt sick all day. For weeks, in fact.'

'Why don't I make us something to eat?'

'That would be really nice, actually. Thank you.'

'Stay there. Don't move a muscle.'

Emmy rested her head on the back of the sofa and took Tom at his word. She felt like a balloon that had been popped. All the secrecy and lying did not now feel quite as bad. Even though she still had her mum and dad and Amy to deal with, now Tom knew what was going on in her life, she felt better. She sort of sat deflated and zapped on the sofa with her wine resting in her lap. With her eyes closed, she just sat there sipping on the glass and thinking with the sounds of pots clanging and the fridge opening and closing. She felt strange, just like the first time Tom had told her he loved her, safe. She resolved she'd never even get close to letting the feeling go again. She'd never shut him out again.

What felt like seconds later, but in actual fact, half an hour or so had gone by, Emmy realised she'd been sitting in the spot where Tom had left her for ages. The smell of garlic drifted in from the kitchen, and he appeared bearing two heaping plates of pasta and a bottle of wine under his arm.

'Comfort food looked like it was in order. Pasta with loads of butter, loads of parmesan, and loads of pancetta,' Tom said as he put the plates on the coffee table and pulled it closer to the sofa.

As they ate, Emmy felt relief flood through her. It looked like she'd rescued herself from being dumped by Tom P Carter. She told Tom more about Katy, what had happened with their mum and dad, the drug situation, and Elodie. He listened and didn't say much at all. She felt as if she had emotionally purged herself. She hadn't realised how much she'd been bottling everything up about Katy inside.

'You seem exhausted.' Tom noted.

Emmy considered what he'd said. 'I'm just so pleased you know now.'

'That makes two of us.'

'I feel wrung out from it. But so relieved we're back on solid ground.'

'Same.'

Emmy went to say something about the fact that it hadn't taken much for Tom to tell her to shove off. She thought better of it. 'Thank goodness.'

'So what are you going to do?' Tom asked.

'I just don't know,' Emmy replied and bit her lip. 'Katy is very set in what she thinks. I'd hate to pressure her if she's not ready. It's like the whole thing is very precarious, which is why I've been so stressed.'

Nodding contemplatively, Tom replied, 'Is that fair, though?'

'I don't know.'

'What about Amy and your parents? I'll say it again - I can't believe you haven't told them. Your mum is going to be so upset!'

'As far as they're concerned, Katy is still estranged. I don't know how to tell them. No, I can't tell them.' Emmy twisted her hands together anxiously. 'I hate keeping them in the dark. But I don't feel it's my secret to share unless Katy wants me to.'

'It's a big call to make. It's like you're backed into a corner.'

Emmy sighed heavily. 'I know I *should* come clean. I just can't stand the thought of everyone's disappointment and disapproval. I never should have got myself into this in the first place.'

'No.'

'Everything feels so fragile.'

'Half-truths have a way of unravelling. That's the problem.'

'Thank you for understanding,' Emmy said. 'I am so pleased you know.'

'I thought I'd seen the back of you,' Tom joked.

'Not funny.'

'Ems, just don't do it again.'

40

It was a few days later, and Emmy had been walking on a cloud of relief since her heart-to-heart with Tom. The heavy burden of her secret reconciliation with Katy was finally off her shoulders. She felt so much lighter, like a weight she'd carried for too long had been lifted. She'd spent the morning at work walking around with a beam on her face and a much clearer head.

As she made her way to the canteen during her break, she bumped into Jessie, who was chatting with a few other colleagues by the entrance. Jessie immediately noticed the difference in Emmy as soon as she appeared.

'Hello. Ooh. Look at you.' Jessie called out, waving her over. 'You look so much better. What's got you glowing like that? Thank goodness. I was actually a bit worried about you.'

Emmy smiled. 'Hey, do I?'

'You really do. I take it the lovers' tiff has been sorted,' Jessie joked. 'Thank goodness for that.'

'It's a long story, but I'll tell you over lunch.'

'I knew this would be good,' Jessie said as she took a tray

from the pile by the counter and handed another one to Emmy. 'Can't wait to hear all the details.'

'I'm glad to be your entertainment,' Emmy said wryly.

'Well, there's certainly nothing else going on in my life. I can live vicariously through your dramas.'

A few minutes later, they were sitting in their respective seats. As Emmy settled into her chair, she smiled. 'Phew. I'm shattered.'

'So, spill the beans. What happened?'

'I finally opened up to him.'

Jessie leaned in. 'Right. Good. Well done.'

'You said to me to own it. I took your advice... eventually.' Emmy hesitated for a moment, then decided to share the truth. 'I've been secretly reconnecting with my sister, Katy. You know, the one we haven't seen for years. I hadn't told anyone about it, not even my family or Tom. Anyway, I finally told Tom everything.'

'Wow, gosh, you *have* had a lot going on. No wonder you were looking stressed!'

'I know.'

'Never tell lies, that's what my nan used to say.'

'Yup. She was right.'

'I'm so glad you confided in Tom. How did he react?'

'He was fine. He listened to my side of the story and tried to understand why I kept it a secret. We had a long conversation, and it felt like a huge weight was lifted off my shoulders.'

Jessie smiled. 'I'm really glad to hear that. Sounds like a keeper, as we said before.'

Emmy nodded. 'Yes, exactly. I feel like we're on the same page now, and it's such a relief not to have this secret hanging over us anymore.'

'It's wonderful to see you looking so much happier. Good for you. Easier said than done to be honest.'

The conversation continued, with Emmy sharing more

details about seeing Katy on the train and following her. As they wrapped up their lunch, Emmy reflected on how much had changed since she'd opened up to Tom. The weight of her secret was gone. She still had her family to deal with if and when that happened, but for now, she was going to sit tight.

E mmy had deliberated for ages about what to do about Katy. Katy had asked her not to tell anyone that they were back in contact, and Emmy had bought into that for a long time. Now that she'd told Tom, she wanted Katy to know. She'd thought about it a lot, and she'd also chatted it through with Tom. In the end, she'd decided that she wanted the least amount of secrets in her life as possible. It was true that her mum and Amy didn't know about Katy yet, but she'd sort of made peace with that. She wanted to be frank with Katy, though, and let Katy know that Tom was in on the act. She wasn't quite sure how it was going to be received.

Mulling it over and over in her head, she'd walked to her car during her afternoon break to phone Katy. She'd already messaged Katy earlier that day to set up the call and wondered how Katy was going to react. Emmy walked across the packed car park, slid into her car, and pulled the door shut. She sat motionless for a moment, phone in hand, gathering her thoughts. Telling Katy that Tom now knew the truth about their secret reconciliation concerned her. It was a conversation she could no longer avoid. Things were fragile with Katy, and telling her Tom knew might make the whole thing hang precariously in the balance, but she was determined not to get as tangled up in lies. It was time to lay her the cards on the table, at least about this.

Before she could overthink any further, Emmy decisively

tapped Katy's name to video call. After a couple of rings, Katy's face filled the phone screen.

'Hey Ems!' Katy greeted brightly. 'Thanks for calling on your lunch break. We needed a catch-up.'

Despite her nerves, Emmy smiled. 'No worries. Yes, loads going on my end!'

'Like what? The shop?'

Emmy steeled herself. Time to bite the bullet. 'Well, yeah, but listen. There's something important I need to tell you.'

Katy's sunny expression clouded over immediately. She knew Emmy's serious tone meant something significant. 'That doesn't sound good. Is everything okay?'

Emmy reassured her. 'Everything's fine.' She cut to the chase. 'Tom knows that you and I reconnected. I told him everything. It came to a head between the two of us. I didn't really have any choice.'

Katy looked stunned, mouth half-open. 'Oh, okay. You told Tom? About us, about Elodie? Everything?'

Emmy nodded, holding Katy's surprised gaze through the phone. She wasn't going to apologise. She held her nerve. 'Yup.'

'Blimey, okay.' Katy fiddled with her hair.

'I agonised over it. But I couldn't keep lying to him about where I was disappearing to. It was causing too many issues with our relationship.'

Katy looked a bit dazed. 'Right. Just, umm, processing.' She fiddled with her ear. 'He must have been well shocked.'

'He was a bit at first,' Emmy acknowledged. 'But it felt like this huge weight lifted after finally being honest. And Tom was very understanding once I explained.'

'Hmm.'

'I know you value your privacy, Katy, and the last thing I want is to violate your trust,' Emmy said gently. 'But deceiving Tom long-term just wasn't an option for me.'

Katy's posture relaxed slightly. 'No, I mean yes, I get it. I appreciate you being honest with me now.'

Relief washed over Emmy. She'd been so anxious about Katy's reaction. This was the absolute best she could have hoped for. 'Thanks, Kates.'

Katy waved her hand, blinking rapidly. 'It's fine. Too late now, by the sounds of it, anyway.'

They both laughed, the temporary tension broken. It was just like Katy to deflect with humour.

'So Tom's really on board with everything then?' Katy asked after a pause. 'You've told him all of it?'

'I think he just feels glad I'm no longer telling lies left, right, and centre.'

Katy nodded slowly. 'I guess I hadn't realised how challenging it was for you. Sorry.'

'It was difficult at times,' Emmy acknowledged.

'Well, thanks. I still don't want you to tell the others.'

'No.'

'You're okay with that?'

Emmy shook her head and screwed up her face. 'No, not at all.' There was no way she was going to say she was fine with it when she felt the opposite. 'I'm not okay with that.'

'Right.'

'In fact, I hate it.'

'Sorry. I just need time.'

Emmy sighed. 'I'll keep quiet for now. Yeah, we both need some time. I want to get the shop over and done with anyway. I'm going to have to tell Mum and Amy at some point.'

'Right.'

Glancing at the clock, Emmy sighed. 'I'd better run, but I'm glad we talked.'

'Me too,' Katy agreed.

'Thanks for understanding.'

Katy made a funny face. 'So, now that Tom's in on it, reckon we should let him babysit Elodie next time? Joking.'

Emmy burst out laughing. 'And imagine Mum finding out about that. I shouldn't be laughing. It's not actually funny.'

'It is in a way. See you later, then.'

'Yep, I'll call you. We'll go for a coffee.'

'Yep, Bye Ems.'

Emmy sat holding the phone and sighed in relief. Another hurdle over. She hoped there weren't too many more to come.

41

It was the day of the shop opening, and Emmy was standing downstairs in her dressing gown. Pale dawn light filtered through the turquoise windows of The Old Ticket Office and glinted off the antique display unit Tom had surprised her with. Emmy stood cradling a steaming mug of tea, surveying the space she had poured just about everything in her life into and wondering what on earth she was doing. She was so stressed she felt as if liquid adrenaline was gushing out of her pores. Here was the dream she'd been having for a long time, really real and raring to go.

As she stood with a cup of tea in her hands, surveying everything, she was jittery. Everything was as done as it could be, so she wasn't quite sure why she was so stressed. She had transformed the neglected space into a gorgeous little shop where her jewellery collections took pride of place. In terms of the opening, every box was ticked, but she was so nervous it was untrue. There was one reason for this which she wasn't quite admitting to herself; as had been often in her life since she'd divorced, when things were going well, she felt as if they wouldn't last long, and she would somehow mess up. Things just didn't go smoothly for Emmy Bardot. Long smooth runs of that thing they called life were for other people.

In particular, with The Old Ticket Office and Love Emmy x, there was just so much that could go wrong – not just on the day of the opening but with the long-term efficacy of her business. What if the whole thing was one big gigantic flop? What if no one came to the shop? What if her idea was a dud? What if she'd put all her eggs in one basket and not a nice, pretty Darling basket at that?

Emmy shook her head, trying to dislodge the negative thoughts, but all she could envision were all her dreams going down the pan. Wandering around the shop, she trailed her fingers over the vintage doors and moved the top of an antique leather suitcase showcasing delicate earrings an inch. She flicked a speck of dust from one of the mirrored dressers and turned to look out the window as a tram trundled past. She reminded herself how every item had been lovingly selected, how her online shop did well enough, and how in her heart of hearts, she just *knew* jewellery and that that was half the battle.

In the little nook by the front window, she adjusted a massive vase of flowers and counted the water glasses by the water station for the umpteenth time. Everything that could be done had been done. All that was needed was to go and collect the cinnamon buns from the bakery, for Louisa, the harpist, to set up, and for people to actually start to arrive.

Her phone pinged with a message from Amy.

Amy: *Morning. How are you?*

Emmy: *Good.*

Amy: *Nervous????*

Emmy: *Very. I'm shaking.*

Amy: *Don't worry, the best sister in the world will be arriving soon to take charge. X*

At the word 'sister' Emmy felt a rush of guilt about Katy. She shoved it under the carpet. There was no way she was going to let the secret ruin her day.

Amy: *I'll be there soon.*

Emmy: *OK. I'm heading up for a shower and then we'll go to the bakery.*

Amy sent a thumbs-up emoji, and Emmy slipped her phone back into her dressing gown pocket. She made her way up the shop stairs and then up the next stairs to what was known as the Top Room, her bedroom. After showering, she stood by the window near her bed for a bit, just staring at the view and musing how her life had changed. She now had so many good things in her life: a lovely flat, a business, a partner, a healthy son and a lovely family. Even Kevin had been on his best behaviour in recent months. That in itself was worth celebrating. She felt so fortunate she hardly wanted to let herself believe it. The only blip on the landscape was the fact that she knew where Katy was and that she was keeping it a secret.

She'd decided though that she would cross that bridge when she came to it. Since she'd told Tom, it was like a weight had been lifted off her shoulders. She didn't feel good about the fact that her mum and dad didn't know, but having him on her side was a whole different ball game altogether. She smiled as she heard a car in the lane, went to the back window and saw Amy's car bumping up onto the verge down by the back gate. A few minutes later, she was standing by the back door.

'Hi!' Amy called out and then stopped in the middle of the path. 'Wow! What's happened?'

'What?'

'You look about a million times better than the last time I saw you.'

'Do I?'

'Err, yeah! Just a bit! You looked awful before.'

Emmy shuddered inside. She knew why she was looking better. It was just a shame Amy didn't. She'd deal with that issue if and when it arose. 'I think I must have had a virus or something.'

'Pah! Yeah, right. It was a very long virus. One day you'll tell me what it was about.'

Not any day soon, Emmy said to herself. 'Don't know what you're talking about.'

'Right. What's on the agenda?'

'Not much apart from going to the bakery to pick up the buns.'

'Sounds easy.'

'I know. I feel too organised.'

'I'll just put my bag upstairs.'

About ten minutes later, they were walking down Darling Street. The blue and white bunting fluttered above, a tram dinged its bell as it went past, and Darling was going about its business. Amy let out a huge sigh. 'Ahh, I love it here on the coast.'

'Yeah, me too.'

'Since you moved here, I'm really thinking about moving.'

'What? First I've heard of it! To Darling? Wow!'

Amy shook her head. 'Not quite, but to the coast. We're thinking about it. I'd be nearer to you, and I don't know, it's just nice to have the sea air around all the time, not just for the day. Know what I mean?'

'Oh, absolutely. I love it. Have you told Mum?'

'No way! I won't tell her until I've thought about it more. You know what she's like. Likes to be in control.'

Emmy nodded. She knew that only too well. Katy certainly did too. Emmy was very tempted to tell Amy. It wasn't the time or the place. 'So, when are you going to start looking?'

Amy flicked her hand dismissively. 'Not sure yet. Just a thought.'

'Exciting. I do love me a bit of online house hunting.'

'Gosh, we did enough of it when we were looking for a flat for you. Years of it, in fact.'

'Yeah, we did.'

They got to the door of the bakery and as they walked in, a bell tinkled overhead. The bakery was bustling, and Emmy was reminded of the day she'd been in there to collect Callum's birthday cake. As if sensing that they'd arrived, Holly, the owner, zipped out from a side door. She clapped her hands together, and a sparkly butterfly diamond around her neck caught the light. 'Morning! You two are here bright and early.'

'Yep. Never can be too early on a day like this.'

'I walked past last night. That flower arch around the shop is amazing. It truly looks beautiful.'

'Thank you.'

'My mum said I'd like it. She wasn't wrong.'

'Ha, yes, she said that.'

'I'll have to get you to do me one.' Holly laughed as she pulled four huge paper bags out from behind a counter. 'Okay. All present and correct for you here.'

'Thank you.'

'Now. I've packaged them so that if you don't need them all, you can just shove a box in the freezer. The vanilla whirls are in separate boxes.'

'Ooh, yes, good idea.'

Holly lowered her voice. 'And you have a special icing. We only use it for some orders.'

Emmy was surprised at how serious Holly sounded. 'Thanks.'

'Don't tell anyone.'

'Your secret is safe with us,' Emmy said and grimaced at even the mere mention of keeping secrets. She'd had enough of those already.

'What did you decide on in the end for the refreshments?'

'We went with what you said and kept it simple,' Emmy

replied. 'Tea, coffee, bubbles, mini cinnamon buns, and vanilla whirls.'

'So all you have to do is put these out and serve a few drinks,' Holly said, holding up the bags. 'Trust me, you made the right call on that. I've opened a few shops in my time. People won't be coming for the food, and it will make life a whole lot easier for you.'

'Good advice,' Amy said.

'Right, well, I'll see you later,' Holly said. 'I can't wait to see the harpist. Mum said the same.'

'I know. Let's just hope she turns up.'

~

Louisa had most definitely turned up. She was sitting in the corner of The Old Ticket Office playing her beautiful harp. It was about half an hour before the shop was officially open. Emmy, in a floaty black wrap maxi dress with billowing full sleeves and her hair in an elaborate updo at the nape of her neck, stood outside the shop with Amy, Callum, Cherry, and Bob. The flower arch going over the door and window looked nothing short of magnificent. The faux blooms, cascading swaths of peonies in shades of blush and pale pink, were intertwined with sprays of baby's breath. White hydrangeas peeked out from ivy and greenery. Emmy sighed; it was precisely what she'd envisioned in her head for so long - cottagey, English-y, and mostly just lovely. The sun shone down on Darling Street, just as Emmy had prayed for, and a breeze coming in from the estuary was fresh in their hair.

'It's so beautiful,' Amy breathed. 'I can't believe this is really happening! How exciting, Ems.'

'I know. It's been a long road getting here. It all started with Emily and the jewellery boxes.'

The ding of a tram bell sounded behind them as Cherry and Bob pointed at the flower arch.

'Absolutely gorgeous!' Cherry noted and looked down towards the ferry and then up at the sky. 'We're lucky with the weather.'

Bob wrapped Emmy in a hug. 'Knew you could do it. I'm so proud of you.'

Emmy hugged him back, feeling a lump form in her throat. Her family meant the world to her. She so wished Katy could be there too. It wasn't the time or place to be dwelling on stuff she couldn't control. She wasn't going to go down that avenue again.

'Right, well, we'd better get on,' Emmy said as she glanced at the time on her phone. 'Twenty minutes and counting.'

Just then, Holly and Xian came bustling up. 'Morning, everyone! Don't you all scrub up well? Oh, and the shop looks fabulous,' Xian said.

'Mum, Dad, this is Holly and Xian from the bakery down the road. Dad, you remember Xian from the other day.'

'Lovely to meet you both,' Holly said warmly. 'You must be so proud of Emmy. This shop is going to be the talk of the town.'

'That it is!' Bob declared. 'Our girl always had a good eye and a creative spark. Glad she finally chased this dream. Yes, we're very proud.'

'Won't be long now until the doors open,' Amy said. 'I'll just pop inside and check on everything.'

'It's days like this that make you count your blessings,' Cherry remarked.

Emmy slipped an arm around her mum's shoulders. 'Too right, Mum. I'm so grateful for all your help.'

'Hard to believe you started out playing make-believe shops with your costume jewellery as little girls,' Cherry mused. 'Now look at you – living the dream.'

'We had some good times,' Emmy said nostalgically, trying not to think about Katy and hoping Cherry wouldn't mention her. 'I'm so glad you're here. Means the world to share this with you, Mum.'

Just then, Tom came into view, weaving his way up the road toward them. Emmy's face lit up when she saw him.

'Sorry I'm a bit late!' he called out a bit breathlessly.

Emmy hurried to give him a kiss. 'You're right on time. I'm just happy you're here.'

Tom produced a gigantic hand-tied bouquet of white flowers. 'Congratulations.'

'Oh, thank you!' Emmy's insides went nuclear.

'Ooh, what lovely flowers.' Cherry sighed and joked. 'Got yourself a keeper here, Ems. Told you that the first time I set eyes on him, didn't I?'

Emmy felt her cheeks flush, but she fired back in a flash, 'Yep, he's lucky to have me more like.'

Tom laughed. 'I am indeed.'

Just then, Amy emerged from the shop. 'Not long till go time! You ready for this, Emmy?'

Emmy turned to take one last long look at the shopfront. It really was a vision, flowers cascading gracefully, window displays lit to perfection. 'Ready as I'll ever be.'

She felt Tom squeeze her hand as everyone moved inside, and Amy and Cherry set out a red velvet ribbon across the doors. Amy then adjusted the 'Open' sign and gave a thumbs up.

'You go ahead and cut the ribbon, darling,' Bob said, patting Emmy's shoulder. 'This is all you.'

Clutching a pair of oversized scissors, Emmy moved to stand before the doors. She glanced over her shoulder and saw her family beaming. This was it. The moment she'd worked so hard for. With a decisive snip, the ribbon split and fluttered to the ground; everyone gave a little cheer as she held the door open wide.

'The Old Ticket Office is open for business!' Amy said with a chuckle.

Twenty minutes later, the sounds from the harp were in the corner, the shop was busy with people, and Emmy's insides felt as if they were on fire. A few guests began making their way inside and Emmy stood proudly, hardly believing what was happening was real. She caught glimpses of the harp, her dad zigzagging through the displays with drinks, and Tom greeting people at the door. It was everything she could've imagined but just so much better. The time flew by in a blur of chatting, explaining the origins and vision behind the shop, and the history of the building.

Before she knew it, Amy popped open another bottle of bubbly and began pouring glasses to pass around. She then tapped on the side of her glass with a spoon, and the whole room fell silent. After a few words, which brought a prick of tears to Emmy's eyes, Amy finished. 'To my beautiful sister, Emmy, on the official opening of Love Emmy x and The Old Ticket Office!' she toasted. 'May it see nothing but success.'

'Hear, hear!' Everyone chorused, clinking their flutes together.

'So? How's it feel seeing your dream taking flight?' Tom asked.

'It's indescribable,' Emmy said, shaking her head. 'I can hardly believe I'm standing here in my own shop, on opening day no less! Everyone's been so lovely and enthusiastic too.'

Tom chuckled. 'How could they not be? It's amazing in here.'

Emmy felt her eyes unexpectedly well up at his words. Her vision was real. It had been so long in the making that it made her feel overwhelmed with emotion.

'Thank you,' she said earnestly to Tom. 'You've helped make the dream possible.' *You are part of the dream.*

'Don't be silly. That's what I'm here for.'

Emmy sighed as the chatter of customers was punctuated by

the harp music, and she spied Callum chatting to Xian. Nearly everything was right in Emmy Bardot's world.

'There you two are!' Cherry bustled over. 'How lovely is everything?'

'Yep.' Tom nodded. 'I was just saying the same thing.'

'I'm just so glad people seem to like it. Makes all the work worthwhile.'

'Quite right, darling!' Cherry patted her daughter's shoulder.

The next couple of hours passed in a blur. Before long, it was just family and a few stragglers left amidst the twinkling lights. Emmy blinked, hardly able to believe the big day had come and gone already. It seemed like she'd been visualising it forever, and now it was a memory.

'Congratulations again on a successful first day!' Holly effused, stopping to give Emmy a hug on her way out the door. 'I'll be back soon to do some Christmas shopping.'

Emmy laughed and saw Holly to the door. 'Hopefully I'll make it to Christmas.'

Amy locked the front door and flipped the sign to 'Closed.'

'You did it. I'm so ridiculously proud of you! Today was absolute perfection.'

Emmy hugged Amy tightly. 'It went better than I ever could've imagined. But it wouldn't have been complete without you all here.'

'Too right!' Bob gave a deep chuckle.

Cherry chimed in. 'Always here for you, Ems. Anything you need, you just say the word.'

'The Old Ticket Office is going to thrive. This is only the beginning,' Bob stated.

Gazing around, Emmy soaked it all in. 'You're right, today is just the first step,' she said slowly. 'I hope I can make this little shop really shine.'

'It already does, darling,' Bob said.

'Right, I think this calls for more champagne!' Amy declared, producing another bottle seemingly out of nowhere. Laughing, they gathered around the front counter as Amy popped the cork.

'To The Old Ticket Office,' Cherry toasted, raising her glass. 'And to our beautiful Emmy, who made it all possible.'

'Cheers!'

Emmy sighed contentedly. It really did seem as if she had finally done well. She was still keeping a secret and wasn't sure what to do about it, but she had to stop worrying about that. She'd taken her dream by the scruff of the neck and made it happen. No one was going to take that away from her. She nodded to herself, inhaled and flicked her eyes upwards for a second and silently said a silent thank you to Emily for twiddling the knobs on Emmy's world. It seemed Emily had been the instigator of a job well done.

42

E mmy pedalled her bike along the coastal path with the brisk sea air whipping through her hair. Despite the chill of a strong wind, the sun shone brightly overhead, warming her face. She glanced over at Tom riding beside her and smiled. Living the dream, baby, living the dream. It had been a few weeks or so since the shop opened, and Emmy's life had settled into a happy routine. She'd stuck to her plan of opening the shop doors a couple of days a week while she worked on the digital side of Love Emmy x at the same time. It had been slow, but every time the tinkle of the shop doorbell sounded, she'd felt a strange flutter of anxious butterflies in her stomach. Mostly being in the shop filled her heart and reminded her of her grandma Emily. So good.

She mulled it over as she cycled along. Love Emmy x was finally a thing, and despite whether or not the shop itself was a success in the long run, it was an achievement she was proud of. Whatever happened, she could say that she'd had a go.

Ringing her bell as she whizzed along, she felt buoyed by lots of good things, but especially her bike. Tom had bought it for her as a surprise, and she hadn't looked back. Riding it along the coast after long days helped clear her mind and made her feel alive. Pedalling hard against the wind reminded her of her care-free childhood days racing Amy and Katy to the beach. As they rounded a bend, the expanse of the sea came into view, shimmering in the light. Emmy coasted to a stop, taking in the sight. No matter how often she saw it, the vast sea always took her breath away.

Tom pulled up alongside her. 'Good view, eh?'

'The best.' She gazed out at the horizon. 'I'll never get tired of this. Thank goodness you bumped into me that day.'

Tom smiled, leaning his bike on its stand and then perched on the sea wall, looking out over the water. Emmy unzipped her jacket slightly, warmed from the ride.

'Hard to believe it's been a few weeks since the grand opening,' Tom remarked. 'Seems like yesterday.'

'I know, it's flown by.' Emmy smiled, thinking back to the day surrounded by loved ones. 'I'll never forget everyone raising their glasses and toasting the shop. Lovely memories to have.'

'Your dad was having the time of his life.'

'Wasn't he just! I don't think he could believe we'd finally pulled it off. He did loads of the work. It really meant so much. Funny how life turns out.'

Tom joked, 'Just blame Kevin as your sister would say.'

'Ha. Good old Kevin. He doesn't get the blame for this one.'

'Nah. I do.'

Emmy smiled, feeling happy. She knew how lucky she was to have such a lot of support. The shop wouldn't have happened without it. Most of her family were supportive, she thought ruefully. Her mind drifted to Katy, as it often did. She wondered what would happen in the continuing saga that was playing out in the wings of her life. Would Katy be part of the family again? Since she'd told Tom she and Katy continued their meet-ups and she had looked after Elodie again, but there had been no more mention of anything further. The difference now, though, was that Emmy was so much less stressed. After telling Tom, she'd decided to leave it be and that time would tell. She still felt very uneasy about not telling her family but she'd decided for the time being to let it lie.

Pushing those conflicted thoughts aside, she focused on the dazzling Darling view. The sun made little water diamonds dance, and further out, white-capped waves rolled. It was Emmy's favourite time of day when the angle of the light cast everything in what she and those around her referred to as the Darling glow.

'We'd better head back before it gets dark,' Tom eventually suggested, standing and stretching his legs.

Emmy hopped on her bike and took off down the path, Tom close behind. The air stung her cheeks as she pedalled hard. She felt giddy, like a child again. Up ahead, the Darling ferry came into view. Emmy spared a quick glance over her shoulder. 'So happy you bought me this bike. Best present ever.'

'Just let me catch my breath. For those of us without the aid of a battery.' Tom fake wheezed jokingly.

Emmy smiled, leaning her bike against the ferry railing. Fading light softened the landscape, strings of lights strung around the top of the ferry tower sparkled, and the water glinted. They stood in contented silence for a few moments, watching seagulls wheel overhead, echoes of the ferry clanged and a couple of foot passengers by the gate chatted.

Emmy smiled, drinking it all in. She'd been fairly concerned about the ferry before she'd moved to Darling. Now she simply adored leaving and arriving on it over the little stretch of water. It was calming before and after the day.

As if reading her thoughts, Tom slid an arm around her shoulders. 'Happy to be here?'

'How could I not be?'

Emmy marvelled at the first time she'd been out with Tom

and how now here they were an item. 'Thank you for everything. I honestly couldn't have done this without you.'

Tom hugged her. 'You could have, Ems. You're a trooper,' he joked. 'I'm just the icing on the cake.'

Emmy pulled back to look up at him, eyes suddenly misty. Overcome with emotion, she rose on tiptoes and kissed him. Tom chuckled.

'What brought that on?'

'Just feeling very grateful. For you, for the shop, for this life here.' She squeezed his hand.

'Nowhere I'd rather be than right here with you, Ems. Home sweet home.'

Emmy smiled. 'Hard to believe I actually live here now.'

'You made it happen.'

'I guess I did.'

'Tired?' Tom asked, noticing her silence.

'Mmm, a bit. In a good way, though.'

'We'll have to make these evening rides a regular thing before it gets too cold.'

'Deal.'

They stood quietly for a bit, lost in their own thoughts. Glancing sidelong at Tom, Emmy felt a rush of gratitude for his support since undertaking the purchase of The Old Ticket Office and completely uprooting her life. 'Thank you again. For the bike ride and the shop and you know just… everything.'

'You don't need to keep saying that. Here's to many more adventures together. We'll be riding our bikes down here when we're pensioners. I love you, Ems. So much.'

Emmy Bardot smiled, and her insides went nuclear. She was intrigued to see what dreams might unfold next. But for now, she didn't really need adventures or dreams or excitement because, bottom line, she was content. Standing looking at the ferry with Tom, Emmy Bardot felt happy and safe. That in itself was worth the world to her, and she was determined that she'd never ever let it go.

Buy the next part in Emmy's story.
Surprises at The Old Ticket Office Darling Island

MY NEW SERIES IS HERE.
COME ON IN AND DISCOVER THE DELIGHTS OF LOVELY BAY!
THE SUMMER HOTEL LOVELY BAY

SURPRISES AT THE OLD TICKET OFFICE DARLING ISLAND

A lovely old shop, a beautiful island and perhaps one big happily ever after…

Since Emmy Bardot moved to Darling Island to open The Old Ticket Office she has finally ended up in her happy place. In the utterly gorgeous old shop by the sea, her new life is panning out really rather well indeed, thank you very much.

Living the shopkeeper dream she settles into life on the island quite nicely as the weather cools down and her business hots up. Despite the secret she's still keeping she's over the moon with how her decision to take a chance is turning out. It just so happens though that there are a few more surprises in store for our girl Emmy. None of them any of us had seen coming. You'll so enjoy the ride.

SURPRISES
AT THE OLD TICKET OFFICE DARLING ISLAND

♥

'Polly Babbington is the new voice in **romance**. If you haven't dropped into her world yet, be warned it's highly addictive and will have you under the covers with a torch reading into the night.'

READ MORE BY POLLY BABBINGTON

(Reading Order available AT Pollybabbington.com)

The Summer Hotel Lovely Bay

The Old Ticket Office Darling Island
    Secrets at The Old Ticket Office
    Surprises at The Old Ticket Office

Spring in the Pretty Beach Hills
    Summer in the Pretty Beach Hills

The Pretty Beach Thing
    The Pretty Beach Way
    The Pretty Beach Life

Something About Darling Island
    Just About Darling Island
    All About Christmas on Darling Island

The Coastguard's House Darling Island

Summer on Darling Island
Bliss on Darling Island

The Boat House Pretty Beach
Summer Weddings at Pretty Beach
Winter at Pretty Beach

A Pretty Beach Christmas
A Pretty Beach Dream
A Pretty Beach Wish

Secret Evenings in Pretty Beach
Secret Places in Pretty Beach
Secret Days in Pretty Beach

Lovely Little Things in Pretty Beach
Beautiful Little Things in Pretty Beach
Darling Little Things

The Old Sugar Wharf Pretty Beach
Love at the Old Sugar Wharf Pretty Beach
Snow Days at the Old Sugar Wharf Pretty Beach

Pretty Beach Posies
Pretty Beach Blooms
Pretty Beach Petals

OH SO POLLY

Words, quilts, tea and old houses…

My words began many moons ago in a corner of England, in a tiny bedroom in an even tinier little house. There was a very distinct lack of scribbling, but rather beautifully formed writing and many, many lists recorded in pretty fabric-covered notebooks stacked up under a bed.

A few years went by, babies were born, university joined, white dresses worn, a lovely fluffy little dog, tears rolled down cheeks, house moves were made, big fat smiles up to ears, a trillion cups of tea, a decanter or six full of pink gin, many a long walk. All those little things called life neatly logged in those beautiful little books tucked up neatly under the bed.

And then, as the babies toddled off to school, as if by magic, along came an opportunity and the little stories flew out of the books, found themselves a home online, where they've been growing sweetly ever since.

I write all my books from start to finish tucked up in our lovely old Edwardian house by the sea. Surrounded by pretty bits and bobs, whimsical fabrics, umpteen stacks of books, a plethora of lovely old things, gingham linen, great big fat white sofas, and a big old helping of nostalgia. There I spend my days spinning stories and drinking rather a lot of tea.

From the days of the floral notebooks, and an old cottage locked away from my small children in a minuscule study logging onto the world wide web, I've now moved house and those stories have evolved and also found a new home.

There is now an itty-bitty team of gorgeous gals who help me with my graphics and editing. They scheme and plan from their laptops, in far-flung corners of the land, to get those words from those notebooks onto the page, creating the magic of a Polly Bee book.

I really hope you enjoy getting lost in my world.

Love

Polly x

AUTHOR

Polly Babbington

In a little white Summer House at the back of the garden, under the shade of a huge old tree, Polly Babbington creates romantic feel-good stories, including The PRETTY BEACH series.

Polly went to college in the Garden of England and her writing career began by creating articles for magazines and publishing books online.

Polly loves to read in the cool of lazing in a hammock under an old fruit tree on a summertime morning or cosying up in the winter under a quilt by the fire.

She lives in delightful countryside near the sea, in a sweet little village complete with a gorgeous old cricket pitch, village green with a few lovely old pubs and writes cosy romance books about women whose life you sometimes wished was yours.

Follow Polly on Instagram, Facebook and TikTok
@PollyBabbingtonWrites

PollyBabbington.com

Want more on Polly's world? Subscribe to Babbington Letters

Printed in Great Britain
by Amazon

39735275R00165